DARKNIGHT

BOOK 2 OF THE WITCHES OF CLEOPATRA HILL

CHRISTINE POPE

DARK VALENTINE PRESS

This is a work of fiction. Names, characters, places, and incidents are either the product of the author's imagination or are used fictitiously. Any resemblance to actual events, places, organizations, or persons, whether living or dead, is entirely coincidental.

DARKNIGHT

ISBN: 978-0692217504
Copyright © 2014 by Christine Pope
Published by Dark Valentine Press

Cover design and book layout by Indie Author Services.

To learn more about this author, go to
www.christinepope.com.

To Allie, Arynn, and Kat, my intrepid beta readers.
I couldn't do this without you!

DARKNIGHT

CHAPTER ONE

———◦◦◦———

Barriers

THE CEILING ABOVE ME WAS UNFAMILIAR, COOL WHITE crossed by dark wood beams. I blinked up at it, but this wasn't like one of those books or movies where the heroine wakes up in a strange place and has no idea of where she is.

Unfortunately, I knew exactly where I was.

I sat up in the narrow bed and glanced over at the clock sitting on the table a few feet away. Nine-twenty. Usually I was up long before that, but since I hadn't managed to fall asleep until nearly five, I knew I shouldn't be all that surprised by the hour.

The door to my room was still closed and locked, the way I had left it the night before. Obviously, Connor Wilcox hadn't done anything to disturb me as I slept. Was he even up yet? I had no idea whether he was the type to wake up early, or whether he slept the morning away.

So much I didn't know…so much I wasn't sure I *wanted* to know.

After pushing back the covers, I got out of bed and tiptoed to the door. In the duffle bag Connor had given me the night before, I'd found flannel pajama bottoms and a thermal top to match, so I was mostly covered up. Whoever had done the shopping for me hadn't bothered with providing any frilly babydoll nighties or lacy teddies, the sort of thing I imagined Damon Wilcox might have preferred for his captive *prima*. Maybe he'd envisioned me not wearing anything at all.

I shivered then, pushing back the dark memory of his mouth on mine. Things were bad, yes, but they could have been so much worse.

Barely daring to breathe, I cracked open the door and peered out into the hallway. The window I'd noticed the night before was uncovered, letting in a flood of brilliant white-gold morning light. It felt somehow incongruous to me, as if the weather should be dark and stormy so it would be a better match for my current situation.

I went to the window and looked down onto a street already clotted with vehicles, most of them splattered with mud. The road was clear enough, although snow was piled high on the curbs. Plows must have come through sometime during the night. People bundled in hats and scarves and heavy jackets moved along the sidewalks. All the buildings looked fairly old, possibly as old as those in Jerome, which told me my guess of the night before had been correct—Connor's apartment was in the historic downtown section of Flagstaff.

From downstairs I caught the rich loamy scent of fresh-brewed coffee and a faint drift of music, a steel-string guitar playing a complex melody that was somehow wild, compelling, as if evoking the dark forests and high snowy mountains of the landscape just beyond the city's borders. The tune also sounded strangely familiar, like I'd heard it somewhere before. Maybe I had; lots of local bands played small clubs everywhere from Flagstaff to Jerome to Prescott. They weren't bound by the same constraints I'd suffered my whole life. After all, normal people could go where they pleased without worrying about which clan ruled which particular territory.

The smell of the coffee and the sound of the music told me one thing—Connor was definitely up and about. Looking down at my flannel pajama bottoms and thermal top, I wondered if I should hurry back to my room before he realized I was awake. Did I really want him to see me like this?

Why should you care? I scolded myself. *It's not like you're trying to impress him....*

True enough. I was doing my best to forget the sweet fire of his lips against mine, the heat that traveled through every limb and vein as we made the *prima* and consort bond. I *couldn't* want him, no matter what my body might be telling me. No, I had to get out of here, even though escape didn't seem very likely at the moment, not with the wards that had been set on the windows and doors.

I had just turned to go back to my room when I stopped, freezing like a deer in a hunter's sights. Connor stood at the end of the hall, a dark-glazed mug of coffee in his hand.

Unlike me, he was already dressed, hair combed, although a faint dusting of dark stubble along his cheeks and chin indicated that he hadn't bothered to shave. "I thought you could use this," he said, extending the hand with the mug toward me.

The coffee did smell divine. Without meeting his eyes, and careful not to touch his fingers, I took it from him. "Thanks."

He was being careful, too, I could tell. After all, it would have been easy enough for him to slip his fingers over mine, to wake that unwelcome heat in my core. But he held his hand still, letting me extract the mug from his grasp without making any movement until it was safely cradled in my own hands.

Maybe I should have been worried that he'd doctored it or drugged it somehow. But I had a feeling he hadn't. It would have been all too easy for him to come to me as I slept, to touch me before I even knew what was happening. Instead, he had let me sleep unmolested. Whatever was going on here, I had begun to get the feeling that Connor was no more a willing participant than I.

The coffee was good, strong and hot, with just enough cream and sugar to take the edge off. Goddess knows I needed it, after getting only about four and a half hours of sleep.

Connor waited until I had taken my first sip before saying, "I have to leave you here for a little while. There are some fresh towels in the bathroom, and I think there should be a bag with a toothbrush and that sort of thing in the duffle I gave you last night."

Only one word seemed to register fully. "Leave?"

For the first time, he smiled. Just a little, but it reminded me of how he'd smiled at me when I'd believed him to be Chris Wilson, just a cute guy I'd met at a dance. No agendas, no lies. He gave a sort of apologetic lift of his shoulders and said, "I own the gallery on the first floor. I need to open up and get things going. When I have a break, I'll come back up."

He seemed awfully confident that I wouldn't try to bust myself out of here the second he left me alone. Then again, he'd pretty much proved last night that the spells locking me in were more than effective at making me stay put…at least for the moment.

"You don't have anyone to help with your business?"

The smile faded. "I do have someone who works in the gallery, but she just helps with sales. I'm the only one with keys."

"You Wilcoxes aren't exactly the trusting sort, I suppose," I remarked, then swallowed some more coffee.

He didn't rise to the bait. "Some of the pieces I have for sale are very valuable. It's easier this way. So I'll be back in a while. There are some bagels in the fridge, if you're hungry."

So casual, still behaving as if I were merely a friend who'd come over to crash at his place for a day or two. I wanted to snap at him to stop acting so normal, that there was absolutely nothing ordinary about our situation, but I realized there wasn't much point to that. The situation was bizarre all around. If this was how he wanted to handle it, fine.

Besides, it would be a lot easier to take a shower if he was safely downstairs handling business in his gallery.

"Okay," I said, affecting an air of supreme unconcern, and began to turn back toward the guest room where I'd slept.

He hesitated, as if he wanted to say something else, but then shook his head and headed downstairs. I waited in the doorway of my borrowed room, listening as his footsteps sounded on the wooden floor in the living room. That wild, strangely melodic guitar music stopped abruptly, and a minute after that I heard the front door shut with a soft, heavy *thud*.

I was alone.

For some reason, that realization was not as reassuring as I'd thought it would be. I waited for another minute, just in case he came back for something, but it seemed as if he was truly gone, at least for now.

Yes, I needed a shower, but first things first. After taking a large swallow of coffee, I set the mug down on the table. Then I moved over to the window in the guest room and pulled the wooden blinds up and out of the way, pressing my hands against the freezing glass, even as I took in a breath to try one of my unlocking spells. At once an excruciating jolt of energy shot through me, and I backed away immediately, hands stinging and body shaking from the aftermath of my contact with the glass.

All right, so the usual methods weren't going to work. That didn't mean I couldn't try a little brute force. After flexing my fingers to get the worst of the tingles out, I picked up the heavy wooden chair next to the table and went back to the window, then swung with all my might.

The chair bounced off the glass as if the window were made from rubber, the rebound feeling like it was about to pull my arms out of their sockets. Immediately I dropped the chair onto the rug, and reached up to rub my aching biceps. So much for that idea. I had no way of knowing who had cast the containment spell—Damon Wilcox or Connor or someone else in their clan—but whoever it was, they'd done too good a job of it.

On to Plan B. Or Plan C, I supposed.

I went back out to the hall and peered into Connor's room. It was a good deal larger than the guest room, and had a king-size bed with a dark brick-colored comforter on it. More paintings hung here, but they looked different from the ones I'd seen in the rooms downstairs. These pictures still depicted local landscapes, as far as I could tell, but the style was more delicate, more feminine.

But I wasn't concerned with Connor's choices in art. I spied what I'd been looking for—a MacBook Pro sitting closed on the round table beneath the large picture window. Well, all right, I'd been hoping for a phone, but his laptop would do just as nicely.

Luckily, he didn't have it protected with a password, so when I opened the lid, the screen came alive right away, showing a scene of Mt. Humphreys still topped with snow, but with meadows of yellow flowers beneath it.

Very pretty, Connor, I thought. Then again, what was I expecting? Naked women, or maybe a nice picture of a ritual sacrifice?

The urge to snoop through his email or his browsing history was almost overwhelming, but I had a more important goal in mind. I opened a new tab in his browser, then went to Google and the Gmail web interface. My aunt had an email account, of course, but she maybe looked at it once a week, since she didn't really interact with much of anyone outside Jerome. Sydney, on the other hand, was religious about checking her email, even if she preferred to text.

I logged in, then hit the "compose" button and typed "Cottonwood_Syd@gmail.com" in the "to" field. No point in lengthy explanations; I just wanted to let her—and by extension, my family—know that I was okay.

For the moment, anyway.

I threw a quick glance over my shoulder, as if to reassure myself that Connor hadn't suddenly reappeared and wasn't standing in the door, watching me use his laptop. But I appeared to be alone still, so I typed quickly, *Syd, please let Aunt Rachel know that I'm all right. Tell her I'm in Flagstaff. She'll know what to do. Thanks, Angela.*

Then I pressed "send" and let the message wing its way through the ether. I closed the tab and made sure to clear the browser cache so Connor couldn't immediately figure out what I'd been up to.

My fingers reached up to close the laptop…and then I paused. Would I get another chance to peek, to give myself the opportunity to learn something more of Connor Wilcox?

One minute, I told myself. *That's it.*

His bookmarked sites weren't all that salacious—a blog about hiking trails in northern Arizona, Amazon, Overstock.com, Facebook, DeviantArt, which I knew about because some of the artists back in Jerome had accounts on the site. He wasn't logged in to Facebook or any other social media sites, so I couldn't do any snooping there. And when I allowed myself a brief scan of his email, that all seemed pretty innocuous, too. The usual advertisements from places where he'd bought things online, a few exchanges with people about planning a skiing get-together, fundraising solicitations from ASU. So that part of his story had been true at least, although he'd admitted that it had been a few years since he attended college. What did that make him… twenty-five, maybe twenty-six?

I didn't have time for any more speculation—or snooping. Connor had said he'd be back in "a while," which could've meant anything from fifteen minutes to an hour or more. I really didn't want to find out what his reaction would be if he caught me poking around in his room.

Just to be safe, I took the hem of my shirt and wiped down the laptop's lid in case I'd left any fingerprints behind. Then I hurried back to the guest room, and knelt down and rummaged through the duffle bag. Sure enough, there was the underwear I had picked out at Nordstrom Rack in Phoenix, and the bras, although the tags had been removed, and they felt as if they'd been washed. Someone was being conscientious, that's for sure.

I took the underwear and a pair of jeans and a lace-trimmed silver-gray tank with me to the bathroom. The room was larger than I'd expected, and the shower far more up-to-date than the claw-footed monstrosities I'd used in both my aunt's apartment and the house I inherited from Great-Aunt Ruby. Here was warm rustic tile and a huge square shower head in an equally huge glassed-in enclosure.

Big enough for two, part of my mind whispered at me, and I shut that notion down as soon as it popped up. Goddess, was I going to have to fight these thoughts even when Connor wasn't in the immediate vicinity?

Scowling, I locked the door behind me, then wiggled the knob just to make sure the mechanism had caught. Not, of course, that a locked door was much good in keeping out a witch or warlock determined on getting in, but it gave me a spurious sense of security.

The hot water came on fast, strong and steady. I quickly climbed out of my night clothes and got into the shower enclosure, letting the water from that amazing shower head run all over me, rinsing away some of the dregs of last night's terrors. Not all, but it's hard to feel completely depressed in a hot shower.

Connor had some kind of natural-brand shampoo and conditioner for dark hair, and a big bar of a creamy soap that smelled of cloves and mint. Obviously he wasn't getting his toiletries at Walmart. Wherever he'd bought it, it all felt wonderful, and I soaped myself up well, then let the water wash away the richly scented suds.

I didn't lose myself so much that I allowed myself to linger, however, and it was probably only about ten minutes later that I shut off the water and reached out to the rack for a towel. The one closest to me felt damp, which meant that Connor must have used it earlier that morning. I lifted my hand quickly and grabbed the other towel, which was big and brown and fluffy. A fast dry-off, and then I wrapped it around my hair and got out, and just as hastily put on the underwear and the tank top and the jeans. At least now if Connor decided to burst in on me, I was covered up.

But there was no sign of him as I blotted my hair, and then refolded the towel and put it back on the rack. A quick glance of the toiletries under the sink showed nothing that I could really use. Then I remembered the small bag of odds and ends in the duffle, the one Connor had mentioned.

So I went back to the guest room and rummaged around, locating a nice little care packet with a toothbrush still in its package, some deodorant, a comb and brush, and a minimal amount of makeup: blush, mascara, rose-colored lip gloss. There was also some kind of leave-in spray for my hair that promised "beachy waves," the sort of thing Sydney had always urged me to try, although I couldn't really be bothered to spend money on something that I was pretty sure wouldn't do much to tame my unruly locks.

Still, what the hell.

I took the care package with me back to the bathroom, brushed my teeth, applied deodorant, and then put on some makeup, mostly because I was annoyed that Connor had seen me this morning with bedhead and the smudged remains of the cosmetics I'd worn out the night before. Might as well put on a good front.

The spray I scrunched into my hair and then left it to air-dry. Normally I wouldn't have gone around with wet hair, not in the depths of December, but Connor's apartment seemed fairly snug and warm for a building so old. It definitely wasn't as drafty as the big Victorian I'd left behind in Jerome.

Feeling a little more human—actually, I was surprised I wasn't hung over, considering how much I'd had to drink the night before, but maybe all the shocks had knocked the alcohol right out of my system—I returned to the guest room and placed my supplies back in the duffle bag. There was a zippered pocket at one end, and I shoved yesterday's underwear in there. No way was I going to allow that to mingle with Connor's dirty clothes in the wicker laundry hamper I'd spied in the bathroom.

One of the sweaters I'd picked out at Nordstrom Rack was folded neatly in the bag, so I pulled it out and put it on, glad of the soft cashmere against my skin. After that it was just socks and boots, and the turquoise jewelry I'd worn the night before when I'd gone out with Adam.

Adam.

Connor had said he was all right. I had to believe that. I had no faith in Damon Wilcox's inherent humanity, but I did believe that even he wouldn't do something that might risk intervention by the "civilian" authorities. But just because Adam was alive didn't mean he might not still have been hurt in some way. How long had he lain there in my bedroom—the bedroom we'd planned to share—before help had come?

I didn't want to think about that. If I did, then I'd start thinking about Aunt Rachel and Tobias and everyone else realizing I was gone, realizing that the Wilcoxes had finally succeeded in stealing the McAllister *prima*.

My throat tightened, and I blinked. Crying wasn't going to solve a damn thing. I was trapped here for now, and I'd have to figure out how to deal with that. Yes, I'd sent an email to Sydney to let Aunt Rachel know what was going on, and I'd said she'd know what to do, but would she? No one in our clan had ever faced a situation like this before.

As far as I knew, no one in *any* clan had ever faced a situation like this before.

I made the bed, and folded my pajamas and put them back in the duffle bag. Still there was no sign of Connor. I glanced at the clock, noted that it was now almost eleven, and shook my head. Then I wanted to shake it again, only this time at myself. What, was I *disappointed* that he'd left me alone for so long?

Well, he'd said there was food downstairs, so I figured I might as well go and check it out. Now that I was clean and reasonably put together, my stomach was telling me it really needed a little bit more put in it than just a cup of coffee.

Besides, it couldn't hurt to do a bit more exploring while Connor was still out of the apartment.

As soon as I stepped out of the room and shut the door behind me, I froze. Standing in front of me was a woman maybe ten years or so older than I. A frightened little squeak formed in my throat, then disappeared as I took in her clothes and hair. Plain drop-waisted dress, Mary Jane–style shoes with chunky heels. Auburn hair carefully finger-waved around her head.

This was no girlfriend left behind, or a stray relative.

This was a ghost.

She looked me up and down, then remarked, "You're new."

I found my voice. "I am?"

"Yes. I haven't seen you here before."

My brain started to add things up. "Um…does Connor have a lot of girls here?"

Her head tilted to one side as she appeared to consider my question. "He did. That is, I suppose I haven't seen anyone here lately. That's why I was surprised to see you."

All right, so maybe Connor wasn't a total man-whore. That knowledge shouldn't be enough to justify the wave of relief that went over me. To cover my irritation at myself, I asked, "How long has it been since someone else…another girl, I mean…was here?"

"I'm not sure." Her brow puckered. She was very pretty, in a sort of porcelain-doll way, with her thin penciled brows and Cupid's bow of a mouth covered in dark red lipstick. "I don't pay much attention to time, I'm afraid."

I'd heard that sort of thing before, from Maisie. Just because ghosts hung around in our world didn't mean they were tuned into the ebb and flow of days, weeks, months. Judging by her dress, the woman before me must have been haunting this building for at least eighty years, maybe more. Differences in a few months or even a few years might not have registered much with her.

"What's your name?" I asked. Generally, I liked to be more personal with ghosts, if they allowed it.

"Mary Mullen," she replied. "I lived here once… such a lovely apartment. My husband made it real nice for me, with furniture shipped all the way from Chicago. But then the girls caught diphtheria, and so did I. They went first, and when it was my turn, I thought I should stay here, to make sure my husband was all right." She frowned again. "But then he went, too, and I was still here. Have you seen any of them?"

I shook my head. I wanted to tell her that they must have moved on, that there was no reason for her to remain here, but I wasn't sure she was ready to hear that…even after eighty years. Maybe later, if I had a chance to speak with her again. Not that I really wanted to have the opportunity, since that would mean I'd be stuck here for a lot longer than I wanted to be.

She didn't appear upset, only resigned. "I thought I should ask, since you're the first person I've been able to talk to since...well, *since*. And you have a kind face."

That was the first time anyone had ever said anything like that to me. "Um...thank you. I'm sorry I couldn't help you more."

"It's all right. You take care...and take care of that boy, too. He's lost, that one." And she disappeared then, just as Maisie always did. Here one second, gone the next.

I waited for a moment, just in case she decided to come back, but she seemed to have left this plane for the time being.

A frown of my own etched my brow as I continued downstairs.

What did she mean, Connor was lost?

CHAPTER TWO

An Unexpected Visitor

I DIDN'T KNOW ABOUT "LOST," BUT CONNOR DEFINITELY seemed to be MIA. After I wandered into the kitchen, I found a bag of bagels in the refrigerator as promised, then extracted one and cut it in half using a knife and a cutting board I found sitting on the counter. A few crumbs indicated that Connor had apparently used it for this same purpose earlier that morning.

That kitchen was the sort of room I'd dreamed about while poring over catalogues in preparation for updating Great-Aunt Ruby's house. Stainless-steel appliances, warm-toned granite countertops, floor of red Spanish tile. Someone had poured a lot of money into this place, and recently, judging by the style of the fixtures.

The toaster oven *ding*ed, indicating my bagel was ready. I pulled it out and buttered it. Luckily, the butter had also been sitting out, so it was soft and spread-able. I'd just taken a bite when the front door opened and Connor came in, carrying a white paper bag and wearing an exasperated expression on his face.

Looking at him, at the clean lines of his jaw only partly obscured by stubble, at the glint of those green eyes from between the heavy dark lashes, I could feel another of those unwelcome waves of heat pass over my body. I tensed, then forced myself to glance away, to stare down at the bagel in my hand as if it were the most important thing in the world.

Maybe it was, if it could keep me from launching myself directly at him and tearing his clothes off.

"How was work, dear?" I asked, and his eyes narrowed.

"I got tied up," he said shortly.

"Sounds like fun," I replied. Okay, where the hell had *that* come from? I wasn't supposed to be banter-ing with him—I was supposed to be demanding that he let me go.

"Looks as if you've gotten settled all right," he said, ignoring my remark and moving past me to deposit the bag he held on the counter. "I brought us some sandwiches—if you'll still have room after eating that bagel."

"Oh, I will. You'll probably go broke feeding me. I eat like a horse."

"I somehow doubt that."

"What, that you'll go broke, or that I eat like a horse?"

"Both." He opened the refrigerator and pulled out some bottled water. Just watching him do something so simple, seeing the width of his shoulders and the way his biceps strained against the dark sweater he wore, was enough to set my body throbbing. Goddess, if I couldn't handle standing a few feet away from him, I was doomed.

I cleared my throat and forced my mind toward something that had nothing to do with having him take me right there on the kitchen floor. "Did you know this place was haunted?"

At that question he shut the refrigerator door abruptly and turned back toward me, eyebrows raised. "What?"

"It's haunted by a ghost named Mary Mullen. Died of diphtheria, sounds like. She's been hanging around here, trying to find her husband and her children. You've never seen her?"

Connor was staring at me as if he'd never seen me before. Maybe he hadn't. Not really. "How do you know that?"

"It's my talent. I'm surprised your spies didn't tell you that."

"He didn't—I mean, no one ever mentioned it."

I was sure the "he" in that sentence had to be his brother Damon, but I let it slide. At least Connor hadn't bothered to deny that the Wilcoxes had been collecting information on me.

"So you talk to dead people?" he asked.

"Yes, I communicate with earthbound spirits, if that's what you mean by ghosts," I said primly.

Once again, he didn't rise to the bait. "That's interesting. And no, to answer your previous question, I've never seen her. No cold spots, no personal items moved around, no nothing. Not that my talent is conversing with the spirit world."

"And what *is* your talent, Connor?"

A cloud seemed to pass over his face, but then he replied, his tone casual, "Nothing so spectacular, I assure you."

"Well, it has to be pretty good, to be able to hide the fact that you're a warlock." It was something that had been troubling me ever since I realized he'd managed to hide his true identity from me so well. Normally, I should have sensed that he was a member of a witch clan from the very moment I met him, even if I couldn't have known he was a Wilcox. But I'd felt nothing. He'd seemed like a civilian to me... up until the moment he bent down to give me the consort's kiss.

Voice even, he replied, "That wasn't me. That was Damon's spell."

"Damon's quite the multi-tasker, isn't he? Any other little tricks I should know about?"

He gave a humorless laugh. "A few. But I don't think we need to talk about that now."

"Fine," I said. I could tell from his expression, the tight set to his jaw, that he wouldn't appreciate any prodding on that subject from me. "But we do need to talk, don't you think? I mean, last night you said we would 'hash this over in the morning.' Well, it's almost noon, and you haven't said much of anything except to tell me where the bagels are."

Surprisingly, he said, "You're right. Take these"— and he handed the white paper bag holding the sandwiches to me—"and I'll get some plates and water and stuff."

The first floor of the apartment was pretty much open-plan in style, except a few closed doors that might be a guest bath and a coat closet. The dining area sat just on the other side of the bar of granite that acted as a sort of separator from the kitchen, so I went there and settled myself in one of the heavy wooden chairs. Like the table, they were simple, almost rustic in appearance, but that didn't fool me. I'd spent too much time shopping for furniture recently not to know that they, like almost everything else in the apartment, had not been cheap.

Connor came out of the kitchen carrying a couple of glasses and a bottle of Evian water, along with some brown earthenware plates. He set everything down at the table, then seated himself across from me. Probably just as well that he didn't sit directly beside me; one brush of his knee against mine under the table, and I would've been in serious trouble.

After he sat, he busied himself with pulling the paper napkins and the sandwiches out of the bag, not really looking at me as he set a sandwich wrapped in white paper down on my plate. "I didn't know what you'd eat, so I got you smoked turkey with provolone. Hope that's okay."

"It's fine," I said. The bagel notwithstanding, I was ravenous. Probably my body trying to make up for all the energy it had lost last night through stress and sleep deprivation.

He poured some water into my glass, then did the same with his. After that there wasn't much left for him to do except eat. He began to unwrap his sandwich.

"Eat first, then talk?" I asked. It was pretty obvious that he really didn't want to have this conversation.

Something that was almost but not quite a sigh escaped his lips before he set the sandwich back down on his plate. "I just want you to know that none of this was my idea."

"I had a feeling," I said wryly, "considering you can barely even make yourself look at me."

This time he did glance up, and I had to hold myself steady as the eyes I had dreamed of so often met mine, and held. The muscles in his jaw visibly tightened. "I *want* to look at you," he said. "It's just... dangerous."

So he was feeling it, too. I'd begun to wonder. "It's all right. We're both adults. We can control ourselves, right?"

His hesitation was obvious. At length he said, "Right. Anyway, I know how bad all this looks. Believe me. And you have every right to think the worst of me. Only..."

"Only what?"

"Did you ever stop to think that all those times you dreamed of me, I might have been dreaming of you?"

His tone wasn't exactly pleading. Not quite. But I could sense something in him was begging me to listen to what he had to say.

"No, I didn't," I replied. "So...why do your brother's dirty work for him? Why not tell him the truth?"

"I think he knew it, deep down, but didn't want to acknowledge it. My dreams became...distorted...these past few months. I think he was trying to interfere."

"Doing a pretty good job of it, too."

Connor frowned then, the straight dark brows pulling together. "He was in your dreams?"

"Yes," I said shortly. I didn't want to go into any more detail than that.

"Well...." He reached out and drank some water, then set his glass back down. "I didn't interfere, because I knew he wouldn't be successful in trying to bind you to him. And then once you were here, he'd be so desperate to make sure you were at least bound to a Wilcox that he'd have me try to make the binding."

Maybe that made some sense, but I still didn't like it very much. I unwrapped my sandwich and forced myself to take a bite, although my appetite seemed to have deserted me. After I had sipped at my own water, I said, "But you knew I...liked...you. Why not kiss me at the Halloween dance, or down in Sedona when we met at the Day of the Dead festival?"

"We weren't in Wilcox territory."

Anger flared then, hot as the desire I still felt for him. Another tradition, another ritual. One might think that a *prima* should travel to meet her prospective consorts, rather than make so many men come to her, but I'd always been told the binding must happen on her clan's land, so that her powers might remain within her domain. By sealing me to Connor here, in the heart of Wilcox territory, it meant that my loyalties were now supposed to lie with them, rather than with the family I had left behind.

So Connor might profess distaste for his brother's methods, for the way I'd been brought here by force, but in the end he'd still gone along with Damon's plan, compelling me to join myself with the Wilcox clan. Well, almost. Connor and I had made the consort bond, but it wouldn't be complete until we slept together, and as far as I was concerned, it would be a cold day in hell before that happened.

"You're just as bad as your brother," I snapped, and pushed my chair back and stood. There was no place for me to go except that cramped little guest room, but I'd rather stay in there for the next ten years than spend another minute in Connor's company.

"Angela, please—" He reached out, his fingers wrapping around my wrist.

Warmth surged through me. *Yes, let him touch you...let him take you....*

"No!" I cried out loud, and wrenched my arm away.

He let go at once, wide-eyed, as if shocked himself by the reaction he must have felt within his own body. "I'm sorry—I didn't mean to—"

I didn't want to hear his excuses. Ignoring his pleading look and the barely eaten food on my plate, I turned and hurried up the stairs, running for the guest room and then locking the door behind me. A whispered spell put an extra binding on the lock, but I had no idea whether it would be effective. I didn't know what to think, here in the heart of enemy territory.

A long silence, and then I heard slow, heavy steps outside in the hallway. Connor said, sounding close enough that he must be right on the other side of the door, "I'll leave your sandwich and water here if you want it."

There was a faint *clink*, as if from setting the plate and glass down on the wooden floor. Immediately afterward, he moved away again. A minute later came the soft *thud* of the front door shutting.

Good. We needed some distance between us. Miles, preferably.

Why, then, did I feel so abandoned?

———

He'd been gone almost half an hour before I cracked the door open and cautiously peered outside. No one, not even Mary Mullen the ghost. I snagged the plate and water, and then closed the door again. Instead of going to the table to eat, however, I stayed where I was, back against the door as I ate the sandwich bite by deliberate bite. It was good, too, rich and plain, with just a bit of an interesting spread— aioli?—to keep it from being too bland. I figured if nothing else, I needed to keep my strength up.

I'd need that strength to keep myself from having flashbacks to the way Connor's hand had wrapped around my wrist, the heat of his flesh against mine, the way I had wanted to give in. It was the worst ache I'd ever felt, that need for him.

And it didn't seem as if it was going away any time soon. If ever.

Time ticked by. The clock on the table told me it was now past one. Connor probably had enough to keep him busy, I supposed. After all, it was only four days until Christmas. Outside, people were probably navigating the icy streets looking for those last-minute gifts, or getting together with friends, or shopping for their holiday meals, or any one of a number of things people did while getting ready for the big day.

Dimly, I realized it was my birthday.

No, you will not cry, I told myself. *It's just a day, one out of three hundred and sixty-five. No big deal.*

Easy to say, I supposed. But the more I tried not to think about it, the more my thoughts kept tugging themselves back to the plans Sydney and I had made. I was going to meet her in Cottonwood for some girl time and manicures, and then that night we'd go with Adam and Anthony to the Hoppy Grape Lounge in Sedona for drinks and appetizers. It would have been safe; I would have been with Adam by then, no longer a target for Damon Wilcox's plotting.

Instead, here I sat.

I bit my lip. Hard. Not enough to draw blood, but it began to ache as soon as my teeth let go. But at least the pain kept me from giving in to the tears that threatened to fall.

Below me, I heard the door bang open, followed by a heavy stomping of feet on the stairs. "Connor!" Damon's voice bellowed.

Oh, shit. I scrambled to my feet and backed away from the door, grabbing the empty plate and glass as I did so. Frantically I looked around, but of course there was nowhere I could go. Even if I'd wanted to climb out the window, there was no way I could do that, spelled as it was.

"Connor!"

More than any other time in my life I wished my McAllister blood had given me a power stronger than speaking with the dead. Teleportation sounded pretty damn good right about now.

The doorknob rattled, then again, stronger this time. Out in the hallway I could hear Damon curse, and the next thing I knew there was a blast of searing light and a burst of acrid-smelling smoke, and the door swung inward. The Wilcox clan leader stood in the frame and glared at me, and I had to force myself to stay where I was, to not take a step backward. That would only be an admission of weakness.

After an entrance like that, I halfway expected Damon to be wearing his black robes from the night before. Actually, he looked pretty much like what you'd expect from a man out and about on a freezing Saturday afternoon—black overcoat, jeans, heavy-duty dark shoes that weren't quite hiking boots but were close.

"Where's Connor?" he demanded.

"I don't know," I said, as steadily as I could. Upset as I was with Connor, in that moment I really, really wished he were there to act as a buffer between me and his clearly crazy brother. "Down in the gallery?"

"I checked." For the first time his gaze moved past me to the narrow bed—made up, yes, but hastily. It was pretty clear that I had slept there the night before, and the open duffle lying at its foot with my toiletries sitting on top only further proved that I'd taken up residence in this room and not Connor's. Damon's mouth tightened. "Made yourself at home, I see."

I didn't dare more than a lift of my shoulders. Even though I knew I was safe enough from being bound to Damon Wilcox, that didn't mean I wasn't still afraid of him. He'd already shown that he had very little regard for anyone's well-being other than his own.

As he opened his mouth to speak, I heard footsteps on the stairs once again, hastening upward as if they belonged to someone fearful of what they might find. A second or two later, Connor appeared in the doorway, features tight with worry. They cleared somewhat as he spied Damon standing a safe distance from me. Well, more or less safe. It was clear he could do quite a bit of damage from several feet away.

"Where the hell have you been?" Damon demanded, rounding on his brother.

"Out," Connor said shortly.

"I can see that. We need to talk." His gaze flickered toward me and then back to Connor. "Downstairs."

"Okay." By his apparent air of unconcern, it was clear he had a lot of experience managing his brother's rages. He shot me the briefest of glances, as if trying to ascertain for sure that I was all right. I gave a tiny nod, then went and sat down on the bed, trying to appear as collected as he was.

They both left, Damon not giving me a second glance as he shut the door behind him. I forced myself to remain sitting on the bed for a moment to give them enough time to get downstairs, but I knew I couldn't stay there. I had to find out what had sent Damon hastening over here, clearly intent on confronting Connor about something.

After I thought a safe interval had passed, I got to my feet and opened the door. The knob was still warm to the touch, the lock clearly blasted beyond repair. I shivered. And that was just something Damon had done hurriedly and in anger. I really didn't want to think about what he was capable of with a chunk of preparatory time behind him.

The hallway was empty, of course, but I hadn't expected to see them up here. I tiptoed down the corridor, then paused at the top of the stairs. The place wasn't so big that I couldn't hear them from this location, and I didn't dare get any closer.

Damon's voice, tight with rage. "...were you thinking, leaving her alone?"

"The wards you set are working just fine. She couldn't get out."

"Yes, they're working to keep her in the apartment. But she still managed to do a good bit of damage. You know who I just had a visit from?"

Silence. Maybe Connor had shaken his head, but since I couldn't see him, I didn't know for sure.

"The elders of clan McAllister...accompanied by Maya de la Paz."

"Oh."

"I'm going to leave aside the fact that they came to my house. Maybe that's better—at least because it's Saturday, they couldn't come barging into my office on campus. Do you want to know how they figured out that they should come straight to me?"

Another pause, and then Connor replied, "Well, it's not that big a leap to think of you when their *prima* goes missing, is it?"

"Maybe not. But I doubt they would've worked quite this fast if the girl's aunt hadn't gotten an email forwarded from a friend, an email saying that Angela McAllister was here in Flagstaff."

"Oh."

"Stop saying that. You sound like an idiot. Of course, who but an idiot would let that girl roam around freely so she could lay her hands on his laptop and get a message out to her family?"

Despite myself, I felt almost sorry for Connor. Maybe he'd been careless, but he didn't deserve to have his asshole brother calling him an idiot. And Connor was right—of course everyone's suspicions would've landed right on Damon Wilcox when I disappeared. It might have taken them a bit longer to put two and two together, but....

I was sort of impressed by how quickly they'd gotten here, though. It had been not quite three hours since I'd sent that email, and it took almost that long to get here from Phoenix even in good weather. Maya de la Paz must have hit the road almost the minute she got the call from my clan. I wondered if it had been Aunt Rachel who'd made the call, or whether one of the elders had contacted the de la Paz *prima*. Not that it really mattered. The important thing was that they'd come. Maybe rescue was closer than I'd thought.

Voice even, as if he'd suffered this sort of abuse many times before and no longer cared, Connor said, "So what did you tell them?"

"Nothing. I said I didn't know what they were talking about, and that they were trespassing on our land and breaking the pact to stay out of one another's territory. What proof do they have, really?"

"None, I suppose."

"Exactly. And I put out the call as soon as they appeared, so Marie and Lucas and a few others showed up to lend their support. The McAllisters had to back down, even if they did have Maya de la Paz with them. She's too shrewd to start an all-out clan war, although she did tell me this was not the end of the matter."

"So it's all okay, then."

"No, it's not okay. I'll ask again—what the *hell* were you thinking? And you clearly left her alone again after that...not to mention that it's obvious you didn't do what was expected of you and seal the deal."

You didn't have to be a rocket scientist to figure out what he meant by "seal the deal."

For the first time, Connor's voice held a touch of anger. "I'm handling it, okay?"

"Are you? It doesn't look that way to me."

"I'm handling it."

A silence that felt painfully long, although I knew it only had to be a second or two. Finally, Damon said, "You'd better be. If you can't rise to the occasion, then maybe I should step in."

My blood went cold, even as Connor replied, his tone as frosty as the ice-covered streets outside, "You're not her consort. I am. Leave it alone."

Another one of those agonizing pauses, until Damon said, "I will...as long as you don't."

Then I heard the door slam. At the same time, a weight I hadn't even noticed up until that moment seemed to lift from my chest. The *primus* was gone.

And here I was, standing at the top of the stairs, just waiting for Connor to discover me. I hurried back to the guest room and closed the door, then went to the bed and sat down.

A minute later, I heard his voice outside. "It's okay to come out."

Since I didn't know what else to do, I got up and opened the door. Connor stood a foot or so away, clearly making sure I had enough room to get out without having to brush past him. I said hesitantly, "He sounded...upset."

Those sculpted lips, the ones I had to try very hard not to think about kissing, tightened briefly. "Yes, he was, but I have a feeling you listened to the whole conversation, so no need for me to go into the gory details."

I opened my mouth to protest, saw the warning look in his eyes, and decided I'd better quit while I was ahead. Instead, I told him, "I didn't mean to get you in trouble. I just—"

"You just wanted to let your family know you were all right. It's fine." He hesitated, as if he wasn't sure what he should say next, then lifted his shoulders. "Actually, I hoped you'd find my laptop and get a message out to them. Not that it would make this all better, but at least they'd know you were alive, right?"

"You—" The words couldn't quite assert themselves, I was so flabbergasted by his remark. After

taking a breath, I asked, "You *meant* for me to contact them?"

"Like I said, I didn't want them to worry. I wasn't
really expecting them to drag Maya de la Paz into
this, but—"

Right then the cell phone in his pocket went
off. He dug it out of his jeans—it was a sleek silver
iPhone—answered with a brief "hello?", then listened as a frown dug itself into his brow. "Okay," he
said finally, "I'll be down in a minute."

"Your brother?" I asked.

"No. That was Joelle, my assistant in the gallery.
The client I was wooing all morning came back and
is about to buy the piece, but he wants my assurances
as to its potential to appreciate in value." Connor
shook his head. "The guy's supposedly buying it as
a Christmas present for his wife, but he still wants
to make money on it. Anyway, I need to go handle
things. Make yourself at home—but you've already
sort of done that, haven't you?"

Without giving me a chance to reply, he turned
and hurried down the stairs, leaving me alone.

Again.

CHAPTER THREE

Turquoise

STRANGELY—MAYBE BECAUSE I'D BEEN FAIRLY CAUGHT using Connor's laptop—I had no desire to do any more snooping. Instead, I wandered downstairs, found a glass in one of the cupboards, and filled it up with water through the refrigerator door. He seemed to prefer bottled water, but I'd always drunk water like this when I was at Sydney's house and didn't see the harm.

A clock of burnished copper on one wall told me it was now almost two-thirty. I wondered how long the transaction at the gallery was going to take. As long as it took, I supposed. Since I'd just purchased several large original pieces myself, I knew Connor wasn't talking about a few hundred dollars here.

I knew I should just sit down on the couch and turn on the TV, and try to disengage my brain for a while.

The wards on the apartment were too powerful for me to overcome, and I'd already contacted my family. My available options weren't what you could call vast.

But that visit from Damon had filled me with nervous energy, and so I went to one of the two large windows on the street side of the room and looked outside. The day was still bright, although I noticed the sky had begun to be dotted with large billowy clouds. More snow on the way? I didn't know enough about the weather patterns in Flagstaff to say for sure. All I knew was that it was much colder here than in Jerome, and the city got consistent snowfall, whereas in Jerome it was still something of a special event when it snowed and actually stuck to the ground for a while.

The streets below were even busier than they'd been that morning, which made sense. All the shops would be open now. I saw people carrying a lot of bags and packages. Strangely, I didn't notice much in the way of decorations. In Jerome there were holiday lights everywhere, with a good many of the houses with a single lighted "Ho" in their yards or attached to walls and fences. Just our silly in-joke, a crack about the town's bustling red light district back in the day.

I realized then that I'd never asked Maisie what she thought about all those "Ho"s with the Christmas lights attached to them. Probably just as well.

But here in Flagstaff I didn't see much sign of holiday cheer, except in the people themselves, who appeared festive and happy enough. They had friends and families to shop for, places to go, people to be with. It all looked so normal. Then again, the vast majority of the city was normal. I was sort of hazy on Flagstaff's actual population, but it was of course many, many times the size of tiny Jerome. There, half the residents were McAllisters. Here, even if there were a good many more members of the Wilcox clan than there were in my own family, they'd still constitute a tiny minority.

They could probably get away with a lot, using the anonymity of a large population to conceal them.

Seeing all those people intent on their own business didn't cheer me up, though. Sighing, I went and sat down on the couch. In that moment, I could only think of the clan elders, returning to Jerome empty-handed, and how disappointed my aunt and Adam and so many others must be. I didn't see how they'd thought they could ask Damon Wilcox to just hand me over. Maybe they'd thought they could get reason to prevail. Unfortunately, he was the polar opposite of reasonable.

And what now? I had no idea. Damon had said Maya wouldn't risk a clan war, and if she wouldn't, that meant the McAllisters' hands were effectively tied. There was no way they could take on the

Wilcoxes without allies. But Maya had also said this wasn't the end of it. What did that mean?

Once again, I had no answer. There had been clan wars back in what Aunt Ruby had referred to as "the old country," but she'd been very vague about what such warfare actually entailed. "We left those things behind," she told me once when I tried to press her on the matter, and that seemed to be the end of it.

However, it wasn't too difficult to figure out that a war between witch clans would no doubt attract a lot of attention, the sort of attention we all—even the Wilcoxes—tried very hard to avoid. So maybe Maya and the elders were trying to see if there was another way to get me back, one that wouldn't involve magical pyrotechnics. But did they even know where to find me? They'd obviously known where Damon lived, but Connor could be an entirely different story.

As if thinking of him had somehow summoned his return, the door to the apartment opened, and he came in, stopping a few paces away from where I sat on the couch. I still wouldn't call his expression or posture exactly relaxed, but he did seem a little less tense than the last time I had seen him.

"You made the sale," I said.

"I did." He pushed his hair back from his brow. I found myself wondering what those sleek, heavy locks would feel like slipping between my fingers, and once again my heart sped up.

This was getting ridiculous.

"Congratulations, I guess."

"Thanks." He stood there watching me for a few seconds, then added, "I'm surprised you're not watching TV or reading or something."

"I was people-watching," I replied, with an off-hand gesture toward the window.

"Maybe you saw my client, then. Uptight-looking jerk in a gray coat, drove off in a silver Audi SUV?"

Despite myself, I smiled. "No, I must have missed him."

"You didn't miss much." Turning from me, he went into the kitchen and got himself some water.

I watched him—*really* watched him, trying to study his expression, his stance. He was still doing that thing of looking at me without actually looking at me, and while I understood his reason for doing so, it still felt odd, as if he were only partially present in the room.

"This isn't going to work," I said.

That did make him raise his head. For a second his eyes met mine before he glanced away. "I don't know what you mean."

"I think you do." I got up from the couch and moved toward the kitchen, although I stopped in the dining area. That way there would still be a safe distance between us. "Maybe it could have worked, if you'd been honest with me from the beginning." At that comment his eyebrows lifted, and I said, "Okay, maybe not from the *very* beginning. I can see why you wouldn't want to admit you were a Wilcox at the Halloween dance, right when you were smack in the middle of McAllister territory. But you could have told me in Sedona. That's neutral ground."

His expression was more than a little dubious. "Yeah, right. I can see that going over really well— me telling you I was actually a member of the Wilcox clan when you were there with your posse of McAllister witches."

"And you didn't have a posse of your own?" I retorted.

"No, I didn't. I really was there with just a friend. My friends—the civilian ones—don't know anything about…all this."

"Really?" It was my turn to raise an eyebrow. Not that I had a bunch of civilian friends, but of course Sydney knew the score when it came to the McAllisters. I couldn't imagine having not even one person outside my clan to confide in. It would mean an almost unbearable pressure to keep everything in, to never allow anyone to know the truth about you or your family.

"Really," he replied, his tone flat.

I decided to leave that aside for the moment, because once again I was starting to feel sorry for him. He didn't deserve to be felt sorry for, not when he had lied to me and been complicit in my kidnapping. "Okay, whatever. But maybe you could've said, 'Hey, I know this is going to sound crazy, but I'm the man you've been dreaming of for the past five years, and let me drop this illusion so you can see my eyes are really green and that I'm a member of a witch clan just like you. Sorry I'm a Wilcox, but I'm sure we can work this out.' Maybe if you'd done that, we actually could have. Worked it out, I mean."

The look on his face had shifted from dubious to outright disbelieving. "That's a nice fairytale, Angela, but don't tell me that's really what would have happened."

I said softly, "I guess we'll never really know, will we?"

"I guess not." He stared at me for a long moment, one in which I didn't even dare blink. Was he going to move toward me?

Apparently not. He glanced away, then said, "I need to check my email and handle a few things. You know where the TV is." And he took his water and went upstairs, leaving me to watch his departure and wonder how on earth we were going to survive being thrown together like this.

———

I really didn't feel like watching TV, but I didn't have a heck of a lot of choice. Trying not to sigh—loudly—I resumed my seat on the couch and started channel surfing. He had the full cable lineup, with HBO and Showtime, and Netflix and Amazon Prime video to boot, but I still couldn't find anything to hold my interest. How could I, when I was here under an even worse house arrest than I'd suffered back in Jerome?

But since Connor didn't show any signs of reappearing any time soon, I settled for a re-watching of *Last Holiday,* since I liked the movie and had only missed the first ten minutes or so. Maybe it would help me to escape for a few hours. Maybe.

It actually did take my mind off my worries, so much so that when it ended I was surprised to see Connor standing at the edge of the living room, watching the last of the credits roll. I was also surprised to see that it was dark outside; he must have flipped on the light in the kitchen without my even noticing.

"Good movie?" he asked.

I nodded.

"It's almost six. I thought I'd go around the corner and grab some tapas for dinner. I don't cook much."

I reflected on the irony of him having a three-thousand-dollar Jenn-Air stove and not actually cooking anything on it. All I said, though, was, "What's tapas?"

A flicker of surprise crossed his face. "They really did shelter you, didn't they?"

I crossed my arms and scowled at him.

Appearing to relent, he replied, "It's Spanish food. 'Tapas' just means small plates. You get a bunch of different small things to eat and share. It's good."

"Okay," I said, my tone guarded. Not what I would've chosen for my birthday dinner, but....

No, I wasn't going to go there. I'd almost managed to make myself forget it was my birthday. And he was trying to make a gesture, however small.

"That sounds good," I added.

"I'll be back in a while, then." He paused at the closet in the hallway and put on a black peacoat and buttoned it up, then wrapped a scarf with gray, black, green, and white stripes around his neck. For some reason the ensemble just made him look that much more gorgeous, and I had to swallow and look away, pretending to be intent on finding something else to watch.

Without saying anything else, he let himself out of the apartment and closed the door quietly behind him.

Since he'd said he'd be a while, I assumed waiting for the food to be prepared, I wasn't sure what I should be doing. One movie had been enough for me, and though I supposed I could have gone back upstairs to steal more time on his laptop—maybe checking what those all-important "emails" he'd been reading all that time had been—that didn't sound like such a great idea.

No, if he was going out to get food, I thought maybe I should do what I could to get the table set for us. Otherwise, our dinner could get cold while he was trying to get everything put together. That seemed like a valid reason. I didn't want admit that I might be trying to help him out in any way.

I already knew where the glasses were, so I pulled out some clean ones. The next cupboard over contained the plates, and a drawer directly underneath held place mats. In the drawer next to that was the silverware. It didn't take much time for me to get the table set.

When I was getting out the glasses, I'd also seen wine glasses, but I left those inside the cupboard. Connor hadn't made any mention of having anything stronger than water to drink. Probably just as well. Sharing a bottle with him might have unforeseen consequences...even though I felt like I could use a glass of wine or two after that confrontation with Damon Wilcox.

Once I was done with the table, I went back to the living room and shuffled through the cable channels until I got to the music-only ones. Judging by what he'd been listening to when I woke up this morning, Connor wasn't exactly a Top-40 kind of guy, and classic rock didn't feel right, either. But then I found a station with instrumental guitar music, and since we were eating Spanish food, that seemed like a good fit to me. I turned the sound down a little so it wouldn't be too intrusive, then waited for him to return.

He seemed to be gone a long time. Maybe the restaurant was busy; it was Saturday night, after all. But eventually, almost a half hour after he'd left, he returned carrying several bags of food, and with a wine bottle tucked under one arm.

Obviously he didn't have the same reservations about drinking wine that I did.

A flicker of surprise passed over his face when he saw the table, but he only said, "Thanks for getting everything ready. That'll make things go faster." He set the bottle down on the kitchen counter and then started pulling small white carry-out containers from the bag and transferring their contents to an assortment of plates and bowls.

There really was quite a variety. I couldn't tell what everything was, but it sure smelled good.

"Can you start taking this stuff to the table while I open the wine?"

I nodded, again wondering at his ability to act so casual when this was anything but a simple dinner date. But I realized I was hungry, and it seemed best to go with the flow for the moment. Better that than starting a silly argument that wouldn't solve anything and would only let the food get cold.

Carrying everything to the table made me realize how much food Connor had actually brought. This seemed enough for four people, tapas portions or no. But it did keep me busy, and by the time I'd set down the last bowl—filled with an amazing, spicy mushroom dish—he was done opening the wine and had come to the table with the bottle and a pair of oversized red wine glasses.

The easiest thing to do was sit down, put my napkin in my lap, and act perfectly normal. I left the place at the head of the table for Connor and took the spot to his left. That way I was facing out into the apartment. The windows now were two black mirrors, filled by the fast-falling night of midwinter.

"Ever had malbec?" he asked, pouring some for me.

"Yes," I replied, and allowed myself a small smile at his expression of surprise. "We take wine very seriously in the Verde Valley, you know."

"So I've heard." He tipped an equal amount into his own glass and then set down the bottle. "I just didn't think you grew malbec grapes there."

"We don't. But Grapes—that's a restaurant in Jerome—serves all kinds of wine from all over the world. I've tried pretty much all of them."

"I'm impressed. When I was your age, most of the girls I knew were more into Jell-O shots or rum and Cokes or maybe mojitos if they were being really sophisticated."

"'When I was your age'?" I lifted the glass and sipped; the malbec was good, big and fruity, with a velvety feel on the tongue. "What are you, a whole five years older than I am?"

"Something like that." He raised his glass to me. "Happy birthday."

I wished he hadn't reminded me. Was that the point of this elaborate spread, to try to soften the blow of my being here with him and away from my family and friends on my birthday? I almost told him to go to hell, but for some reason I couldn't force the words past my lips. It was pretty obvious he was doing his best to make things as easy for me as he could, and equally obvious that, while he'd behave as his brother asked up to a point, he certainly wasn't going to force me into any intimacies I didn't want.

If only I could convince the hungry, lustful side of my brain that I really *didn't* want those intimacies. At least not with a Wilcox.

"Thanks," I replied, after a pause I was sure he noticed. "So what are we eating?"

Something in his posture relaxed, as if he'd been wondering if I was going to make a scene. If only he knew how close I'd come. "Those are bacon-wrapped dates," he said, pointing with his free hand, "and this is the tortilla española, which is sort of layers of potato and egg, and those are mushrooms with red peppers—"

"Okay, slow down," I broke in. "Where do I start?"

"Try a date."

I pulled the toothpick out of the morsel, decided it was a little too big to stuff in my mouth all at once, and instead cut it in half and lifted a bite to my mouth. "Holy crap," I said after I was done chewing.

"You like it?"

"It's amazing."

And so was pretty much everything else he'd brought. It might not have been the birthday dinner I'd imagined, but it was certainly better than I had hoped. For a while we just talked about the food, which seemed like a nice, neutral subject. I was careful with the wine, too, making sure I took sips of water in between sips of wine so I wouldn't lose my head and get tipsy. That, I thought, sneaking a peek at Connor's black-lashed green eyes as he was focused on setting a slice of manchego cheese and ham on my plate, could get me in a lot of trouble.

Then I asked, "So how long have you had the gallery?"

"About two years."

"And the paintings?"

"Mine," he said shortly.

I supposed I should have guessed, but for some reason his reply took me by surprise. On the wall behind him was a study in reds and corals and dark olive, a bent tree surrounded by stark rock. Somewhere near the Grand Canyon, I thought. Like every other painting in the apartment, it was strong and sure, a study of color and light.

"You're really good," I said honestly. "I mean, *really* good. Do you sell your work in the gallery?"

His mouth tightened. "No."

"Why not?" I asked. "People would eat this stuff up. Do you show in other galleries, then?"

"No. I paint and I hang them here. When I run out of room, I shuffle them around. A bunch are in storage."

That didn't make any sense to me at all. Why on earth would he be hiding his paintings away instead of showing them to the world? "But they're so good—"

"They're just for me, okay?"

Somehow I got the feeling that wasn't the truth, or at least not most of it. I didn't know either of them very well, but I'd already gotten a sense of the dynamic between Connor and Damon Wilcox. "It's your brother, isn't it? For some reason he doesn't want you to paint?"

Silence for a few seconds. Connor reached out and poured himself some wine, then refilled my glass. The bottle was already more than halfway gone. Finally he said, "You don't miss much, do you?"

"I try not to." Ignoring my previous caution, I allowed myself a large swallow of wine. "I guess I'm trying to understand why he'd have a problem with your painting. I mean, if you weren't any good, okay, but—"

"The *primus*'s brother is supposed to be as successful as he is," he cut in. "Gallery owner is fine. Starving artist? Not so much."

"As good as you are, I doubt you'd be starving." I took a bite of ham and cheese, then pointed my fork at the spread in front of us. "Case in point."

A reluctant grin touched his mouth...his lovely, lovely mouth.

Eyes back on your plate, Angela! I scolded myself. At least there was plenty on that plate to keep me distracted.

"It's...complicated."

"It always is, isn't it?" I speared the last bacon-wrapped date with my fork—hey, it was my birthday—and dropped it on my plate. "I get that he's the *primus* and everything, but I'm having a hard time figuring out this whole 'when he says jump, you ask how high' thing with you two."

The grin disappeared. "I don't want to talk about it."

Of course he didn't. I hesitated, trying to decide if I should push it, but a second glance at the flat line of his mouth told me it was probably better if I left it alone…for now. But he'd have to open up eventually if he thought he was ever going to have a chance with me.

A *chance*? What the hell was my brain doing? I shouldn't be thinking about whether I should be giving him any chances—I should be thinking about what steps my clan members were going to take next, and whether there was any way for me to circumvent the fiendishly strong wards that had been put in place on Connor's apartment.

"Have it your way," I said, and recklessly poured the remainder of the malbec into my glass.

A pained expression crossed his face, but whether that was because I'd taken the last of the wine for myself or because he was still irritated with my line of questioning, I couldn't be sure. In silence he set aside his napkin and rose from the table. For a few seconds I thought he was walking away because he was upset, but then I realized he'd simply gone to the kitchen to fetch another bottle. Not a malbec this time, though; the sunburst on the label was familiar. Arizona Stronghold.

He yanked out the cork and refilled his glass. "Did you email anyone while I was out?"

Talk about your abrupt shifts in conversation. "No," I said.

One eyebrow lifted slightly. "Why not?"

"Well, the damage was already done, according to your brother. I didn't see the point."

It was obvious he couldn't quite figure out what to do with that statement. He fiddled with the cork, which he'd left sitting on the table, before swallowing some of the wine he'd just poured. To tell the truth, I still wasn't quite sure why I hadn't sent another email, except that my family already knew the most important thing—that I was all right—and I didn't really know what to say besides that. I wasn't ready to let them know that Connor was my consort, the man I'd been dreaming of for the past five years. Goddess knows what their reaction would be to that little bombshell.

Maybe I could've tried confiding in Sydney, but she really didn't have a grasp on the politics of the situation. She probably would have asked me why I hadn't jumped Connor's bones already. Some part of me was trying to figure that out, too—the part that seemed to go into heat every time I stared too long at any one portion of his anatomy.

He set down the wine cork. "I'm having a hard time figuring you out, Angela."

"You're not the first," I said with a shrug, trying to lighten the moment. "I drive my friend Sydney crazy sometimes."

A nod, and the beginnings of that smile once again. I hoped it wouldn't disappear quite so quickly this time. "Full?" he asked, nodding toward my plate.

I actually was. That last date had pretty much done me in. "I think so."

"Well, I hope you saved a little room. I got some dessert, too."

I always had room for dessert. "I could probably squeeze that in somewhere."

"Good." He got up and began gathering up the plates, and when I began to stand so I could help, he waved me off. "It's okay. You stay put."

Whether he was being extra conscientious to make up for his brusqueness earlier or because he was trying to make nice on my birthday, I wasn't sure, but I stayed where I was and allowed him to clear the table. He busied himself in the kitchen for a few minutes, and then he came back out with two slender slices of what looked like flour-less chocolate cake on fresh plates. A lumpy white bag was shoved under one arm.

He put the larger of the two slices in front of me. "I don't have any candles, but—"

"It's fine," I said hastily. The last thing I wanted was for him to start singing "Happy Birthday" to me or something similarly corny. "The cake looks great."

"There's a bakery around the corner. I went and got the cake while they were working on my order at the tapas place." As he sat down, he extricated the white bag from under his arm and set it on the table-top. A brief hesitation, and then he pushed it toward me. "I got you something. I know it can't make up for not being there with your family on your birth-day, but...."

Mystified, I set down my fork before I had even taken a bite of cake. He'd bought me a birthday present? When would he have even had time for that? I surmised that maybe he hadn't actually been at the gallery all the time he was gone. But still, that he'd gone out and gotten something for me—

"You didn't have to." The spiteful part of me wanted to say that he couldn't make up for kidnap-ping me by buying me a birthday present, but I held my tongue. He was doing the best he could. It wasn't his fault that he'd gotten sucked into his brother's crazy schemes. It seemed clear enough to me that he was doing everything in his power to make sure I didn't suffer any more in the aftermath of those plans.

"I wanted to."

Now I was the one who looked away first. I'd seen need in those eyes, and desire…but hesitation, too. He wouldn't force me, no matter what. Of course, with the way my body reacted to even his briefest touch, I thought there wouldn't be a good deal of forcing involved.

I reached out and took the bag. It was very heavy.

"Sorry it isn't wrapped or anything. The store was out of gift bags because it was busy today."

"That's fine," I said automatically, then reached inside. Something metal, it felt like, wrapped in tissue paper.

I pulled the tissue paper away and pulled the object out of the bag, then gasped. The silver links gleamed in the low light from the bronze and frosted glass fixture overhead, the turquoise nuggets glowing amidst each of those links. It was a concho belt, the sort of thing I'd always coveted but could never really justify the expense.

Apparently misinterpreting my awed silence, Connor said, "I noticed that you seemed to like turquoise jewelry, so I thought you might like the belt. If you don't—I mean, if you'd rather have something else, I can take it back."

"Oh, no," I told him hastily. "It's perfect. I mean, I've always wanted one, and could never afford it. I just—I'm startled, I guess."

"But you like it."

"I love it," I assured him, turning it over in my hands, admiring the workmanship of the stampings, the smooth bevels around the turquoise nuggets. As I did so, I caught the faint markings on the back of each concho: *.925*. That meant the belt was solid sterling, not the nickel silver I'd assumed it had been made of. Those kinds of belts were expensive enough, but one of solid silver? It had to have cost him at least a thousand dollars, if not more.

How could I accept such a costly gift from him? But I somehow knew if I refused it, he'd be upset. It would be a refusal of him as well. I couldn't make myself do that. Despite my best efforts to harden myself to him, to not let him wiggle his way into my heart, I had a feeling he was doing that very thing.

"I'm glad," he said, and went to take a bite of his cake, acting as if it was no big deal that he'd spent more on that one gift for me than anyone had ever spent on me in my entire life.

I murmured, "Thank you," and followed his lead, picking up my fork and helping myself to the cake, which was rich and moist and velvety. My head was still spinning, though.

What was the catch phrase from that old *Star Trek* show?

Resistance is futile.

I was beginning to understand that all too well.

CHAPTER FOUR

Home Cooking

AFTER DINNER WE WATCHED SOME TV, THEN WENT TO bed early. Still strange, still so mind-bendingly odd how we could be so casual about saying our goodnights and retiring to our separate rooms. The lock on my door was blasted to hell and back, and yet I knew that really wasn't going to be a problem. Connor was giving me my space, letting me do with it what I willed.

What that would be, I had no idea. To say I was confused by the situation would be an understatement. He was friendly one moment, completely closed off the next. Not that I had to search too hard for the reason why he'd shut down when he did—no, that was all about his brother. What was going on there, I had no idea. Damon obviously had some strange power over Connor, one that seemed to go far beyond merely being his brother. I wouldn't go so far as to say it was a kind of mind control, since that one confrontation I'd overheard had told me Connor was willing to stand up to his brother when the occasion called for it. But he also showed no inclination to talk about their relationship...and I had to believe something lay there that would explain everything, if he would only open up about it.

The odds of that seemed roughly on par with the likelihood of Damon showing up at the apartment and announcing that I was free to go back to Jerome. As I lay down to sleep that night, acutely aware of Connor's presence just across the hall, I wondered what it would take to get him to talk, and whether I even had the ability to pry open that particular oyster to get at the pearl inside. I had to believe I did. The situation couldn't go on like this indefinitely.

I just didn't know what I would do when it did finally change.

———

The next day went a little more smoothly, mainly because at least I knew what to expect. Connor let me know that he'd be working—"the gallery usually isn't open on Sundays, but it is this weekend because of the holidays"—and I spent my day being bored out of my mind watching TV. I would rather have read, but he didn't seem to have many books around except art books and some leftover textbooks, and there was nary an e-reader or tablet in sight. Since he'd left his laptop behind, I supposed I could've downloaded an app to access my books, but somehow that seemed too invasive.

I debated emailing Sydney, then decided against it. It just felt too strange to open an ongoing dialogue like that on someone else's computer, and I didn't have the faintest idea how I would even begin to explain the situation. Maybe now that my aunt knew I had the avenue of communication open, she'd be checking her email more often, but again, I didn't even know what to say to her.

Hi, Aunt Rachel, I'm captive in Connor Wilcox's apartment, but it's okay because he's taking really good care of me. I'm not sure I even want to come home. Hope everyone is having a wonderful Yule!

Yeah, right.

That night it was pizza and chianti.

"You weren't kidding when you said you don't cook," I told Connor as he set the pizza box down on the dining room table. "You know, I could make something."

"You could?" he inquired, looking dubious.

"I was raised by Rachel McAllister. She would have thought she was being derelict in her duty if she didn't teach me how to cook."

It was true; while I wouldn't go so far as to say I was as good a cook as she was, I definitely knew my way around a kitchen. And making dinner would at least give me something to focus on. Something complicated that would take up a large chunk of the day. That sounded like a great idea.

He was still looking at me with that one raised eyebrow. It was an expression he appeared to have mastered...and one that only intensified his good looks. I forced in a breath, making myself think of possible dishes to make the following day and not how much I wanted to reach out and touch him, feel the fine, sculpted bones of his face under my fingertips.

I shivered, then said quickly, "How about tamales? We usually make up a big batch around the holidays. That, and some homemade black beans."

"How big a batch?"

"Well, the recipe I know makes about fifty."

"Fifty?" He'd turned slightly away from me, and was in the middle of transferring a piece of pizza to his plate when he stopped and gave me a look that told me he thought I'd taken leave of my senses. "Isn't that a lot for two people?"

"We usually share. You can freeze some, or wrap some up to take to your clan members. Don't you do anything for Yule?"

Studiously glancing away, he put together a plate of pizza for me before sitting down. "There's usually a dinner on Christmas Day. Kind of a potluck thing. Damon actually hates it, but it's a tradition, so it keeps on happening. I just figured I wouldn't be going this year."

Because of me, I mentally finished for him. He probably didn't dare risk taking me out of the house before our bond was complete, but on the other hand, he was just enough of a nice guy that he didn't want to leave me alone on Christmas. I almost told him he didn't have to worry about that, but I decided to leave it for now.

"Well, even if you don't go, you can still provide something for the potluck. Consider it a peace offering from the McAllister clan to the Wilcoxes."

"Maybe."

That was all he seemed willing to give me for the moment, so I let it go and concentrated on my pizza and wine. The pizza was decent—nothing gourmet like I'd get at Grapes or at Bocce down in Cottonwood—but it was rich and laden with cheese, so I couldn't complain too much.

"But it's okay if I make tamales?"

He sighed, and reached out to take a drink from his glass. "Sure. Give me a list, and I'll try to get out and go shopping tomorrow morning before the gallery opens."

His tone was still not all that enthusiastic, but I decided to ignore it for now. Maybe he just wasn't looking forward to braving the crowds at the supermarket, where everyone would be fighting over the last bags of fresh cranberries and Jell-O mix or something. He'd probably be even less thrilled when he saw some of the specialized items I'd need, but I'd have to risk that.

At least I had a plan.

———

Having asked for a pencil and paper the night before, I was able to hand over my shopping list the next morning. The lengthy list of ingredients and tools provoked another raised eyebrow, but he didn't say anything until he got to the part where I'd drawn another line across the page and written down another, smaller list of more items.

"Duck...port...dark cherries?" he inquired. "That doesn't sound like any tamale I've ever had."

"It's not for that," I replied. "It's for Christmas Eve. I don't have to make it, though—maybe I should have asked if you had plans with Damon or something."

"Damon?" he repeated, and shook his head. "Hardly. Damon's not exactly the holiday spirit type. Anyway, he doesn't recognize Christmas as a holiday. He just does the potluck because it's a family tradition. We do celebrate Yule, of course, although that was sort of...disrupted...this year."

Because of me. Well, to be more precise, because of their kidnapping of me. I sure wasn't going to feel guilty for screwing up their Yule celebrations.

"Well, we McAllisters never pass up an opportunity for a party, so we do Christmas, too," I said. "And there are members of the clan who do go to church, so it's something a little different for them."

"Church? Really?"

I lifted my shoulders. "As Aunt Rachel likes to say, a visionary is a visionary, whether he's Jesus, Buddha, or Mohammed. Why not celebrate his birth? It doesn't run counter to our other beliefs, more like… alongside them."

To my surprise, Connor actually nodded. "I kind of like that. And duck for Christmas Eve is fine, if you really want to go to the trouble. But I need to get going if I'm going to scrounge all this stuff before the gallery opens. Luckily, there's a Bed, Bath, and Beyond in the shopping center next to Safeway, so I hope I can do it all in one stop."

"I hope so, too." Now I was starting to feel a little bad for making him go get all those supplies. On the other hand, it wasn't my fault that I was stuck in his apartment with nothing to occupy myself.

He just nodded and went to the hall closet to retrieve his overcoat and scarf, then let himself out. Although I was more used to being alone in the place by now, it still felt empty and echoing without him.

Man, two days in this place and you're already losing it, I scolded myself. Then I went into the kitchen and started pulling out the things Connor did have already, like a glass measuring cup and a set of measuring spoons, and wiping down the counter in preparation for the process of making the tamales and beans. His kitchen wasn't large, but it was laid out well, unlike the cramped space in Aunt Rachel's apartment. The kitchen in my big Victorian was much larger, naturally. However, since it hadn't been updated yet, it still left a lot to be desired. This place had a much better setup for my first solo tamale flight.

I'd just have to hope I didn't screw it up.

———

Connor came back about an hour later, laden with so many boxes and bags he had to make two trips up from wherever his vehicle was parked to unload it all. "And now I've got to get down to the gallery. It's already past ten-thirty."

"Sorry," I said, and I did actually mean it. I hadn't intended to make him late to work…and also, seeing all those supplies spread out on the kitchen counter and dining room table made me realize how much I'd asked him to buy. "I didn't realize it would be so much."

"It's fine." He didn't smile. "I'll leave you to it, then." And like that, he was gone again.

I looked out at the grocery bags and the boxes with the new pans and gadgets, and took in a breath. Time to get to work.

And work it was, but I found myself enjoying it. Chopping things and stirring things and watching the clock to make sure everything is cooking more or less at the desired rate keeps you busy but doesn't overtax the brain. By the time I had the pork roast in the dutch oven—newly purchased—and the beans in the crockpot—also new—I realized it was almost one o'clock. My stomach growled, and I wondered if Connor was going to bring me lunch the way he had before, or whether he'd decided he'd bought enough groceries that I should be able to scrounge something.

I probably could have, but he showed up a little past one with more sandwiches and an apology for running late.

"It's been crazy busy," he told me as he bit into the Italian sub he'd just unwrapped. "Which is good, I guess. I've already paid off your little shopping expedition this morning." He paused then and lifted his head to take an appreciative sniff. "That smells good. What is it?"

"Pork roast in the oven and red chili sauce on the stovetop. Oh, and beans in the crock, but I don't think they've really had time to 'work' yet."

"Who knew you were so domestic?"

"I could have told you, if you'd asked." *Or if your brother had been interested in anything about me besides me being the* prima, I thought. But that seemed like I was treading on dangerous ground, so I hurried to add, "My aunt always made cooking fun, so I like doing it. Now, cleaning toilets? Totally different."

Another one of those heart-wrenching grins pulled at his mouth. "No worries there. I have a cleaning service."

And how are you going to explain me to them? I wondered, but didn't ask. Considering how spotless the place was when I showed up—especially for a bachelor's apartment—I had to guess they'd been here recently and probably wouldn't be back until after the holidays.

I only said, "Thank the Goddess!" and then took a bite out of my sandwich. He seemed to recognize that I was trying to keep the conversation light, so he ate along with me in silence until we were both done.

"Back to the salt mines," he commented. "The gallery's open until six, so I'll be up a little later than yesterday."

"That's fine," I replied. "I'm shooting for dinner around seven."

"Sounds good."

If our relationship had been different, this was the moment where he should have bent down to kiss me goodbye before he left. But we weren't there. Not by a long shot.

He left, and I went back to work.

———

Around two-thirty I took a break, as I was waiting for the broth from the pork roast to cool so I could skim off the fat. The day had gradually begun to darken, but not because of approaching night. Not that early. No, I could see gray clouds gathering outside. It had done the same thing the day before, but no snow had fallen, so I wasn't sure what the lowering skies really meant.

I went to the window to look at the weather and the streets below. Not that much had changed, although they didn't seem quite as crowded as they had been the day before. Well, that made sense, since today was a Monday and probably a lot of people were at work. But it was still busy enough, and once again I found myself wishing that I could be down there in the fresh air, window-shopping and enjoying myself. Making tamales was a welcome distraction, but it didn't exactly provide much mental stimulation.

As I watched, a sleek black Range Rover pulled up to an empty spot at the curb just below the apartment and in front of the gallery. The door opened, and a tall dark-haired man got out. Almost at once I recognized him as Damon Wilcox, and I pulled in a worried little breath, wondering if he was going to come up to the apartment again. I really didn't want to imagine what his reaction might be if he barged in here and found me playing domestic goddess in his brother's kitchen.

But as the minutes ticked by and he didn't appear, I realized the apartment must not have been his destination at all. He must have gone to the gallery.

While I would have liked to have been a fly on the wall for that conversation, I didn't possess the sort of clairvoyance that would allow me to eavesdrop on the two brothers from up here. All I could do was wonder what it was that Damon wanted. Scratch that. I had a pretty good idea of what he wanted. I was just surprised that he'd approach Connor in his gallery. It might be owned by a Wilcox, but it was still a public place that most likely would be filled with civilians doing their last-minute holiday shopping.

"My, you've been busy," came a voice from behind me, and I jumped. Literally jumped. Maybe just an inch or two, but still.

My heart resumed a more or less normal rhythm when my brain registered that the voice was feminine, and definitely didn't belong to Damon Wilcox. "Hi, Mary," I said.

The ghost trailed her way from the living room back to the kitchen, where she cast an appreciative eye over the visible evidence of my industry. "What are you making?"

"Tamales."

She looked confused. "I don't think I know what that is."

"It's a Mexican dish. A lot of people make it around the holidays."

A ghostly finger trailed over the glass top of the crockpot. Anyone else would have jerked her hand back right away, since the crock was plenty hot even on the low setting, but of course Mary Mullen was far removed from any such concerns. "I'll bet it smells good."

"It does," I assured her. Then, since she didn't seem inclined to do much more than wander around the kitchen, I asked, "Is there something you wanted?"

"No," she said absently. "That is, I thought I'd check in when I heard all this clatter in the kitchen. Connor barely uses it, except to put things in *that*." A condemnatory finger was thrust in the direction of the microwave.

It seemed she and Maisie had a good deal in common when it came to modern contrivances. "I know. Fancy kitchen, and he hardly sets foot in here. I thought it was time that stove was put to good use."

"I knew you'd be good for him. That I did. I was always a good judge of character. None of those other girls ever came in here and cooked for him."

"About those girls," I began, but she shook her head.

"Oh, that doesn't matter. You're here now. And I've been thinking about it—you know, after you asked me how long it had been since the last girl was here. I thought hard, and looked at the calendar he has pinned to the wall there, and I think I figured it out. Two months, just about. Not since Halloween."

Halloween. When we'd come face to face for the first time. Of course I hadn't known who he was, not then, but he certainly knew I was Angela McAllister. He'd met the girl he'd been dreaming of, and hadn't been with anyone else since then.

I could try to tell myself that it really didn't matter, but it did. It mattered to me…a great deal.

"You're sure it was Halloween?" I asked.

A little frown puckered her plucked brows. "Yes. There were people going up and down the streets wearing funny costumes and laughing. You know" —her voice lowered— "like they'd been drinking too much."

I almost wanted to laugh at her reticence, but then I realized she must have passed away when Prohibition was still in effect. Public intoxication must have been a very big deal back in her day.

"Thank you, Mary," I said sincerely. "That's really good to know."

"I'm glad. It had been bothering me. I can stop worrying about it now."

And before I could tell her it wasn't something she needed to have been fretting about, she disappeared. I supposed it could be disconcerting, if you'd never seen it before, but by then I'd been talking to ghosts for twelve years. It took a good deal to faze me.

Well, when I was dealing with ghosts, at least.

———

Connor came back around six-thirty, later than I'd expected. In a way it was good, because by then the tamales were already more than halfway through the steaming process, and I'd set the table and even put out some candles I'd found tucked away in one of the cupboards. The aged-bronze pillar holders were still in a gift bag, as if they'd never been touched. A gift from one of those girlfriends? Maybe. If they were, they didn't appear to have ever been used, so apparently he wasn't entertaining those girls here.

No, he was probably taking them out on the town and showing them a good time since they didn't have to be locked up in this damn apartment.

I squelched that thought. What he'd done in the past was none of my business. While the idea of being free to go out and have Connor show me around Flagstaff was definitely appealing, as places to be stuck in durance vile went, his apartment wasn't half bad.

Then I had to shake my head at myself. So now I wanted to stay here, get to know the city? This was getting nuts.

Luckily, I was able to abandon that line of thought because Connor came in then, carrying a brown bag with a bottle of wine.

"Tempranillo," he offered. "I thought it would go well with the tamales."

"Where is all this wine coming from, anyway?"

A gleam came and went in his green eyes. "Don't you know that Flagstaff is a very cosmopolitan city? There are several wine shops within walking distance."

"Ah, now I know why you chose this apartment."

When he'd first come into the kitchen, he'd looked tense and preoccupied, and again I wondered what kind of exchange he'd had with Damon. Now, though, he smiled, the shadows momentarily leaving his eyes.

"Can I help with anything?"

I shook my head. "No, I think I've got it. I'll just get some of this dished up and will be out there in a minute."

He surveyed the kitchen for a second or two, saw how the pots I'd used previously were already scrubbed and put away, how I had a serving bowl and plate ready to go for the beans and tamales. A smaller bowl held some crumbled white Mexican cheese for the beans.

"Obviously, I'm in the presence of an expert," he said with a little bow, then got a couple of wine glasses out of the cupboard before beating a retreat to the dining room.

I allowed myself a smile before picking up the tongs and beginning to transfer a stack of tamales to the plate. Even allowing for us to eat more than was probably good for us, there were still going to be a lot of leftovers. That was okay, though; I'd leave them in the steamer until it was time to package them up. Connor could decide if he wanted to freeze them or contribute them to the Wilcox Christmas potluck.

Wow, there were three words I never thought I'd be stringing together.

After I'd ladled a good portion of the beans into the bowl I had waiting, I picked it up and the smaller one holding the cheese and took them out to the dining room. Connor had the wine open, and a good measure poured into each of the glasses. The candles flickered in the center of the table, and I noticed that he'd used the dimmer to turn down the lights overhead.

Are you trying to seduce me, Mr. Wilcox? I thought, and then realized I wasn't as put off by the notion as I probably should be. Uh-oh.

Giving myself a mental shake, I went back to the kitchen and got the plate of tamales, and turned off the lights before returning to the dining room. I noticed he'd been busy, too; more of that instrumental guitar music played in the background.

"Who are these guys?" I asked as I sat down. "I could have sworn I've heard them before, but...."

Connor replied, "Black Forest Society. You've heard of them?"

That was it. I'd only been able to catch one of their shows because they traveled around the state a lot, and the one time they'd played the Spirit Room when I was there, they didn't even have a CD available yet. "I saw them once in Jerome about six months ago, I think." Yes, that sounded right. It had been a warm summer evening, with the doors of the bar open to the streets and people coming and going. Back then I'd thought I'd have plenty of time to find my consort.

Instead, he'd found me.

Connor put a tamale on his plate, then picked up another one and set it on mine. I murmured a thank-you as he said, "They play up here in Flag off and on. One club they play at is just a couple of streets over from here. I've always liked their music, so I was glad when they finally got their CD out there."

"I didn't even know they had one. It's good."

A pause as he took a bite of tamale. His eyes widened. After he was done chewing, he said, "And these are amazing. I'm surprised your aunt runs a shop and not a restaurant."

I didn't bother to ask how he knew that. It was pretty clear to me that the Wilcoxes knew a lot more about us McAllisters than we did about them. Or at least, than I knew about them. There'd been a lot of secret-keeping back in Jerome, and I still didn't have any clear idea as to how much I'd been kept in the dark.

Connor seemed to realize his slip-up, because he glanced away from me and took a sip of his wine. Because I was feeling slightly irritated, I only said, "Thanks," then added, "so what did Damon want today?"

Of course he didn't answer right away. He took another bite of tamale, shut his eyes as if savoring the taste, then answered my question with another of his own. "You saw him?"

"Yes, I was taking a break and looking out the window, and I saw him drive up."

Now it was Connor's turn to look annoyed. "Nothing. Just checking in."

"He doesn't have a phone?"

"Doesn't trust them for the important stuff."

Wow, he really was paranoid. Then again, what with our own government sniffing through our phone calls and emails, I supposed that was one thing I couldn't really give Damon Wilcox much grief over.

"I think he needs a hobby," I remarked, and finally sipped at my tempranillo.

It was on off-hand remark, the sort of thing I'd said about more than one person on occasion, but Connor didn't appear amused by it. "Oh, he has hobbies. I'm just pretty sure you wouldn't approve of them."

"So why don't you tell me about it?" I said the words as a challenge, not expecting to get an honest answer.

To my surprise, Connor seemed to take my question seriously. Maybe the tamales had loosened him up. "You know he's a physics professor, right?"

"No. I mean, I knew he was a professor of some sort at Northern Pines, but I didn't know what he taught." I did my best to keep my tone neutral. I didn't want to say anything that might keep Connor from talking.

"Well, he's been using his work to aid him in altering spells, making them stronger, making them do things no one else has been able to." He spooned some beans onto his plate and then handed the bowl to me. I took it from him with a slight smile, but remained silent so as not to interrupt. "I'm not an expert, so I can't begin to explain half of it, but he tells me that spells are energy, *will* is energy, and he's learned to work with that energy in ways no other *primus*—no other warlock—ever has. So neither you nor anyone in your clan should beat themselves up too much over being bested by Damon Wilcox, because it's hard to defend against something you never even knew existed."

"That's…impressive," I said after a pause. Well, that was one word for it, anyway. "Frightening" was another that came to mind, but I didn't say it out loud.

Connor shrugged. "He's driven. It's good for the clan, I suppose, but it's…a little tiring."

I could imagine, even though I didn't really want to think too hard about what it would be like to have Damon Wilcox as my older brother. But since Connor seemed to finally be talking, I thought I'd better see if I could get anything else out of him. "So…." Now that I thought I had an opportunity to ask questions, I didn't even know which one to ask first.

"So why do I put up with it?"

I nodded.

"It's complicated."

"You told me that before." I picked up the tongs and set another tamale on his plate, since he'd already finished off the first one. "You just didn't tell me why."

The green eyes seemed to darken almost to black. "You really don't want to hear all this."

"Actually, I do."

He poured some more wine into his glass, then topped mine off as well. "Why?"

"Because...." I had to stop myself from saying, *Because I think I'm starting to like you a lot more than I should.* Instead, I told him, "Because I think it will help me to understand what's going on here a little better."

Another pause. The steel-string guitar played in the background, fast and intense, accompanied by equally intense drumming. Connor let the music spool out for a moment, then sighed as he reached for his wine glass. "It's not a pretty story."

"I figured it probably wasn't. You want mine first, just to break the ice?"

He gave me a smile with little humor in it. "I already know it—at least, about your mother dying when you were a baby, and how you don't know who your father is." His fingers tightened around the stem of his glass. "There are times when I wish I had that luxury."

I remained silent, waiting for him to go on. My heart, though, had begun to beat a little more quickly.

"Do you know about the Wilcox curse?" he asked abruptly.

"A little."

"Then you know the marriages in the direct line aren't exactly happy ones."

Mouth tightening, I nodded again.

"For a while it seemed like it might be different for my father and my mother. She was an artist, too—did a few shows, I guess, but she mostly liked to paint for herself."

"Those are hers, aren't they?" I murmured.

"What?"

"The paintings in your room. They don't look like your work. They're hers?"

"Yes." He drank some more wine, a large gulp, but I wasn't about to give him grief over that. Not when I could tell how difficult this must be for him. "She had Damon, and everyone started watching her carefully, because usually once the *primus*'s wife has a son, the trouble starts. But she seemed fine. She *was* fine, for years and years. Then she got pregnant again." He gave me a humorless smile. "Me. Damon's almost ten years older than I am, and everyone thought it was a sort of miracle, and maybe for some reason the curse had finally been broken. Then...."

The word trailed off and I held my breath, wondering if this was where he would stop, if this was the point where he couldn't make himself say any more.

But then he drank a little more wine, a much more measured swallow this time, and continued. "It started with little things. At least, that's what Damon tells me. I didn't notice that much at the time. I mean, I was barely three. But she stopped painting, and then there were days when she couldn't even be bothered to comb her hair or get out of bed. One of the women from the clan started coming over to help with meals and tidying up and all that, since my mother just…stopped doing it."

All this was said in an almost expressionless voice, as if he were relating events that had happened to someone else, but I could see how tense the fine lines of his jaw were, how he couldn't quite look at me. I wanted so much in that moment to reach out and touch his hand, to give him some kind of reassurance, but that would only cause a whole new set of problems. I could only wait and hope that he would go on.

Which he did, although he had to take another fortifying sip of wine before that happened. "It was sometime in late spring. I remember that because Damon was at Little League practice."

Despite everything, I had to smother a smile at the thought of a thirteen-year-old Damon Wilcox in a baseball uniform. I didn't think the Wilcoxes ever did anything that normal. Then again, I wouldn't have believed they had Christmas potlucks, either, if

Connor hadn't told me. But again I didn't comment, only waited for him to continue.

"Deirdre was the one who was supposed to be watching me that day. She was there for a while, but then she got a phone call and had to go out. Some kind of emergency, Damon told me later—her own son was out riding his bike with some friends and fell and broke his arm, although I guess when she first got the call, she didn't know it was that serious. I suppose she figured she could go handle it, get him to the healer and then come straight back, but instead she ended up spending hours at the ER because the coach had taken Ethan to the hospital directly and she couldn't get him out without stirring up too many questions. Anyway, I was left alone in the house with my mother. And for some reason she decided that was a really good time to take me down to the garage and have us both sit in the car with the engine idling."

"Oh, no," I said, putting my hand to my mouth.

"Oh, yeah," he said. His expression held only a kind of weary resignation. "She stuffed rags in the tailpipe to concentrate the carbon monoxide. Damon came home, saw that there was no one in the house, and heard the car in the garage. He ran out and grabbed me—I was already unconscious at that point, I guess, because I don't remember any of it—and then went back to try to get her. But she'd locked all the car doors while he was rescuing me. Of course he called 911, but by the time they got there, it was too late. They rushed us both to the hospital, and I was okay after they administered some oxygen, but...." He pushed his hair back from his brow. "She was in a coma for three days and then just...went. The Wilcox curse strikes again."

I stared at him in horror. "Connor, I am so, so sorry—"

A shrug that was chilling in its detachment. "We're used to it. But maybe now you can see why I put up with Damon's crap. If it weren't for him, I'd be dead."

And with that, I did see. At least, I thought I did. I couldn't quite understand owing that kind of debt to someone, as I'd never been in that position, but the bond Connor and Damon shared was far, far greater than what two brothers might normally have.

"Your father?" I asked then, since that was the last piece of the puzzle. The Wilcox brothers weren't so old that their father shouldn't still be alive.

"Heart attack when I was fifteen," Connor replied briefly. "Definitely Type A, just like Damon. The healers had been working on him for years, keeping him going, but as you know, spells aren't always infallible."

No, they weren't, especially when it came to something as fluid and unpredictable as healing spells. Not that I knew from personal experience, as the McAllister clan's one healer had passed away several years ago, and we didn't have a good replacement. Like the rest of the mere mortals in the Verde Valley, we relied on regular medicine or certain forms of alternative and holistic healing.

"I'm sorry," I said. It was an automatic response, the sort of thing you were supposed to say when you learned of such an untimely passing.

"Don't be. He was a first-class bastard."

Like father, like his son Damon, I thought then, but I held my tongue. It was one thing for Connor to be passing judgment on his relations. I didn't think I was yet in a position to do so.

"Well, that's enough ancient history," he went on. "Now can we talk about something more pleasant so I can actually enjoy this food you made?"

"Of course," I replied immediately. "Do you think it's going to snow? Those clouds looked pretty ominous."

He actually cracked a grin at that. "The weather? Seriously?"

"Do you have something better to talk about?"

"Not really."

After that we really did talk about the weather, how much snow Flagstaff usually got, how he liked to go cross-country skiing with his friends, how the snow would stick on Mt. Humphreys long after it had melted down here in town. Normal things. Someone eavesdropping on the conversation would never have guessed that just a few minutes earlier, Connor had been relating the Wilcox equivalent of a Greek tragedy to me.

But I knew. And I'd never look at him in quite the same way again.

CHAPTER FIVE

A Midnight Clear

I WOKE THE NEXT MORNING WITH CONNOR'S REVELATIONS still rattling around in my head, but because he was acting almost studiously normal, I decided I had better let it go. If he wanted to tell me more, he could. That was his decision, though. I wouldn't be the one to force it.

Because it was Christmas Eve day, I sort of thought maybe he'd close the gallery early, but I thought wrong. When I asked, he gave me his trademark raised eyebrow and said, "No, I'll close at five. Gotta catch all those last-minute desperate men buying things for their wives."

"I wasn't aware paintings and sculptures were such a hot item with procrastinators."

He grinned and shook his head. "They aren't, but we also sell jewelry from local artisans, and that is the sort of stuff that tends to fly out the door at four forty-five. Besides, Joelle does need to leave early so she can head out to Winslow to be with her family. So I've got to close up."

My disappointment must have shown in my face, because he made an odd little movement, as if he'd been about to reach out and brush my hair away from my cheek, and then realized that wasn't a very good idea. "You won't be alone on Christmas Eve. I'll be here by five-thirty."

I wanted to tell him I hadn't been thinking that at all, but it would have been a lie. "Okay," I said, then added, "Sorry I don't have anything to give you for Christmas. I haven't been able to get out much lately."

"Very funny," he remarked, and then gave me a half-wave and headed out the door. I'd noticed that he never put on an overcoat when going straight to the gallery, so there must have been an inside hallway or something that connected the apartment to the shop on the ground floor.

Unlike the tamales, the dinner of duck with port cherry sauce and wild rice I had planned wasn't something that was going to take up my entire day. And even though I knew that technically I wouldn't be alone on Christmas Eve, I still had a very long stretch ahead of me with not much to do in it.

Although I wished I could push the thoughts away, I couldn't help brooding over what was happening back in Jerome. Yes, the solstice and Yule were big deals, but we sort of let Yule blend into Christmas in a week-long excuse for parties and dinners, and caroling along the town's steep streets. Cheerful lights and Aunt Rachel's melt-in-your-mouth butter cookies, and standing rib roast on Christmas Eve. Would they be doing any of that this year, or were they too busy worrying about me?

No, I didn't think that would be the case. I was their *prima,* but my not being there shouldn't be a reason to keep them from enjoying their holiday. They had to be worried, not knowing exactly what was going on with me, and I realized I'd been selfish to not stay in contact more. Connor had already basically told me it was all right for me to use his laptop. So shouldn't I use it now to give my family the only thing I could give them this holiday—the knowledge that I was okay?

I went upstairs then, to Connor's room. Just like the last time I'd entered it, the place was scrupulously clean, the bed made, no dirty clothes strewn around the way I'd always imagined the room of a guy who lived on his own must look like. The laptop still sat on the table, power cord connected.

Once again, I knew an email to Aunt Rachel wouldn't get read right away, but this time I didn't let that stop me. I went to Gmail and opened up a new message, then wrote quickly, *Aunt Rachel, I'm not sure when you'll get this, but I just wanted to wish you and everyone back home a very happy holiday. I don't know if you'll believe this or not, but I'm being treated well (except for not being able to leave). I'm safe. I know that sounds crazy, but I really think I am. Love you all. Angela.*

I sent it as soon as I was done writing it so I wouldn't have second thoughts. Maybe it would upset her to hear how I was trapped here. And maybe she would think that the Wilcoxes had made me write the email. No way to prove that, so I could only hope she'd detect the truth in my words.

My gaze strayed to the Facetime icon in the dock at the bottom of the laptop's screen. Aunt Rachel didn't have any iThings, as Sydney liked to call them, so using Facetime to try to get in touch with her directly wouldn't work. Adam had an iPhone, though....

On second thought, that probably wasn't such a good idea. Things were strange enough between Connor and me right now that I didn't even know what I could say to Adam. I certainly couldn't admit I was developing feelings for Connor, feelings no McAllister should have for a Wilcox. Saying anything on the subject would only hurt Adam. True, I could ignore the topic completely, but Adam would want to know where I was, who I'd been staying with.

Once it got out that the "Chris Wilson" he knew was actually Connor Wilcox....

Bad idea. Bad, bad idea.

But Sydney had an iPhone. Things were probably crazy at her house, since I knew her parents generally hosted the family parties because their house was the largest in their extended family. Her father was an engineer at the cement plant in Clarkdale, and her mother a supervising nurse at the local medical center; they were doing all right, especially by local standards. Cottonwood, Arizona, wasn't exactly Beverly Hills when it came to the average income of its residents. However, I also knew that Sydney was not exactly the same whiz in the kitchen I was, and tended to stay out of the way after the obligatory table-setting and bathroom cleaning was done. Anyway, it was worth a try.

I entered Sydney's email address in the Facetime app and waited, unconsciously crossing my fingers while it made the odd little ringing sound as it attempted to connect. Just when I was sure she wasn't going to answer, that her mother had made her put her phone away so she could play nice with the relatives, she picked up, her face sort of swinging into view as she angled the phone toward her.

"Hello?" Her eyes widened. "Angela! OmiGOD, where are you?"

"Flagstaff."

I didn't think her eyes could get any wider, but somehow she managed it. "But I thought you never went *there*. I mean, you were gone, and Adam had this shiner like you would not *believe*, and no one was telling me anything, and I was starting to wonder if you guys had gotten in a bar fight and you'd been kidnapped by *bikers* or something, and—"

"It's sort of complicated."

"Try me. I've got nothing but time."

"You do? I thought your relatives would be coming over."

She rolled her eyes. "They'll be here at six. My mother's gotten enough slave labor out of me today. I came up to my room for a breather because I couldn't take it anymore. I cannot *wait* until Christmas is over, actually." Seeming to recover herself, and realize that I was waiting patiently for her to finish, she said, "Okay, enough about that. So you're in Flagstaff. *Why* are you in Flagstaff?"

"Is Adam okay?"

"Why wouldn't he be?"

"You just said he had a black eye."

"Oh, that. Yeah, I mean, it was a black eye, but it's not the sort of thing that sends you to the hospital or anything." She tilted her head and squinted at me, and I realized she was trying to get a glimpse of my surroundings. "So you're in Flagstaff. Where? That doesn't look like a hotel room."

"It's not." I hesitated. "You know how I said there were things I couldn't really talk about?"

"Yes." Her eyes lit up. "So are you going to talk about them now? Spill it."

"I don't have time to go into everything, but… let's just say that not all witch families are on the best of terms with one another. And the clan here in Flagstaff, the Wilcoxes—well, they've always been our enemies."

"But you're there now." One hand went to her mouth. "Oh, God, you *were* kidnapped, weren't you? But…now you're using Facetime like it's no big deal? I'm confused."

Get in line, I thought. "I told you it's complicated. Yes, they did bring me here, and I'm not exactly free to leave, but Connor has been very nice to me."

She must have detected a change in my tone. "Connor, huh? Is he cute?"

"Well, you thought so."

A blank stare. "Huh?"

"Turns out Chris Wilson and Connor Wilcox are the same person."

"Holy *shit*. Seriously? Is that where you are now—his place?"

"Yes."

"So…" She drew out the word as if trying to process the situation. "You're, what, just staying there?"

"Basically." I took a breath. "Actually, it turns out that *he's* my consort."

"Are you serious? He's the man of your dreams?"

"More or less."

"Boy, did you luck out."

I couldn't help laughing. "'Luck out'? I wouldn't exactly call getting kidnapped from my room in the middle of the night 'lucking out.'"

"Well, it could have been worse. It could've been bikers. Big, hairy bikers. But Chris—I mean, *Connor*—is seriously hot."

"He's also the brother of the leader of the Wilcox clan…the man who planned the kidnapping. He thought he was going to make me *his* consort, but it sort of backfired."

"Because Connor is your real consort."

"Yes."

She paused. I could practically see the wheels in her head going around. "So…do you *like* him?"

"I—" I floundered for a second. "Sydney, his brother *kidnapped* me."

"I know, you told me. That's not what I asked. If it wasn't Connor's idea, why is there a problem?"

"Well, he didn't do anything to stop his brother."

That halted her for a second. Then she said, "*Could* he have? Stopped him, I mean."

Good question. The truth was, even if Connor had tried to argue against the plan—and for all I knew, he had—he wasn't strong enough to stop Damon.

No one was, apparently.

"Probably not," I admitted.

"Well, then," she said. "Come on, Angela, you're shacked up with the man of your dreams, and you've admitted that he's your consort, so I don't see what the big deal is. Get moving and tap that ass."

"Subtle, Sydney. Real subtle. Did you not hear what I told you earlier? His clan and mine have been enemies for generations."

"Oh, don't hand me any of that Montague and Capulet crap."

I blinked. I had no idea she paid that much attention when we read *Romeo and Juliet* in English class. "It's not crap."

"It is. If he's your consort, and you like him… what's the problem?" Her eyes narrowed. "Does he not like you? Because if that's what's going on, I'm going to have to drive up there and give him a lecture on his taste in women."

Oh, for Goddess' sake…. "No, that's not the problem. I think…I think he doesn't want to do anything that feels like he's forcing me, I guess."

"Would he be?"

Time to own up to that one. "No, not really."

"Well, then." From somewhere off in the distance I heard a disembodied voice yell, "Sydney! Get down here! Your cousins will be here any minute!", and she grimaced. "I'm being summoned. Look, you're going to do what you're going to do, and I get that. But don't let this history between your families get in the way. That's just dumb. I mean, Dad isn't that thrilled about Anthony being Native American—"

"Seriously?" I broke in. "What year is this?"

"I know, right? But anyway, I'm not going to let that get in my way, because it's stupid. Just like this McAllister/Wilcox feud or whatever it is shouldn't get in *your* way. Just be Connor and Angela. The rest will work itself out."

"*Sydney!*"

"*Coming!*" Another eye roll. "Jesus. Anyway, I really have to go. Just think about what I said, okay? And Merry Christmas."

"Merry Christmas to you, too," I replied.

She winked and then shut down the app, and the screen went dark.

I sat there for a minute, then glanced up at the time display in the upper right-hand corner of the computer screen. Five fifteen. Close enough. It was about time to get down to the kitchen and rev up my domestic goddess routine.

As I closed the laptop and got up, I thought again about what Sydney had said. *Just be Connor and Angela. The rest will work itself out.*

Maybe it was time to give that a try.

———

The table was set, the duck roasting away in the oven. I'd planned dinner for seven, just to be safe, but by now it was past six and still nothing from Connor. If he was closing the store at five, then what in the world was taking him so long?

Maybe a customer had come in at the last minute. Even so, it shouldn't be taking this long. I turned on the oven light and peered in, but I was still far from having to worry about overcooking the bird; it had only been in there for half an hour. No, my checking on it was nerves more than anything else.

For a minute I contemplated running upstairs to check my hair and makeup, but I hadn't done anything to mess up either of those, so that was just me coming up with a way to kill some time. I didn't have any footwear except the riding boots I'd picked out at Nordstrom Rack what felt like eons ago but I knew was only two months past. But with dark skinny jeans tucked into them and that gorgeous concho belt riding my hips, and a dark teal sweater over a lace-trimmed cami, I thought I was looking better than usual. Whether Connor would notice was a different story.

Then I heard a sort of *thump*-pause, *thump*-pause coming from the corridor outside the front door. Frowning, I left the kitchen and headed to the entryway, then stopped. It wasn't as if I could open the door to see what was going on out there.

As I was wondering whether I could press my face up to the peephole without getting one of those nasty magically induced shocks, the door swung open. Connor stood on the threshold, gripping a gorgeous Noble fir with a look of grim determination on his face.

I stared at him, mouth slightly agape, and he said, "I thought we should have a Christmas tree," before tightening his grasp on the tree and coming inside.

At once I moved out of the way so he could take the tree past me and on into the living room. I noticed that it had a plastic water bowl already attached to it, most likely put on by the people at the tree lot.

"How in the world did you get hold of a Christmas tree that nice at five o'clock on Christmas Eve?"

The green eyes glinted. "Magic."

I tilted my head. "Magic." I didn't know Connor all that well yet—heck, I wasn't even exactly sure what his talent was, although I figured it had something to do with illusion—but I did know his was not the type of magic that controlled minds or involved any other sort of coercion. No, that was more up Damon's alley.

"Okay, a judicious bribe. Anyway, I had to go by our storage unit to dig out the box of Christmas ornaments, so it took me a little longer than I thought." He sniffed the air. "That smells awesome."

"Well, fingers crossed that it'll taste as good as it smells."

"I'm not worried about it." He adjusted the scarf around his throat, and I noticed he was still only wearing a sweater and shirt. It seemed way too cold outside to not have an overcoat. "I have to run back down to the car and get the box. I'll be right back up."

He went back out—leaving the front door slightly ajar. I stared at it for a long moment. It couldn't really be that easy, could it? I could just walk out of here and....

And what? Leaving aside the impracticality of wandering around sub-freezing Flagstaff on Christmas Eve in only a thin sweater and a camisole, was I prepared to do that? Walk out and leave?

I realized I wasn't. Right now, this was where I wanted to be.

Maybe it was a test. Maybe he wanted to see if I would leave. That seemed more like something Damon would do, though, not Connor.

He came back with a large cardboard box in his hands. I was watching him carefully to see what he would do when he realized the door was open already and I hadn't bolted, but beyond the slightest lift of his brows and maybe a small shrug, I didn't notice anything. Once he was inside, he pushed the door shut with his foot, and that was that. No more chances at freedom.

Not that I'd really wanted them.

After setting the box down in the living room, he turned and glanced back at me. "How much time until dinner?"

"A half hour or so."

He nodded. "Think we can get this decorated by then?"

"Maybe. Some of it, at least. We can always finish up after dinner."

"Sounds like a plan. Let me get a fire started, too."

I'd noticed the fireplace, of course, but despite the chilly weather, he never seemed to use it. Now, though, he went over, opened the glass doors, and touched one finger to the wood stacked inside. A spark touched the bottom-most log and spread out quickly. Soon the entire stack was crackling away happily.

So he had that power as well. It was a minor skill, one Adam possessed, too, but I did find myself wondering how many others Connor had up his sleeve, since he seemed to studiously avoid using magic whenever possible.

"I need to get back in the kitchen in about fifteen minutes," I warned him as I came into the living room.

"That's fine. We'll do what we can. I'll get these lights on at least."

The box of ornaments was very organized, the white lights wrapped neatly around spools instead of thrown into the box in a jumbled mess the way the ones Sydney's family used always were. I'd been at their house once or twice for their tree-decorating, mostly because Aunt Rachel never got a tree and I felt like I wanted to participate in the holiday at least a little bit. Also, a plate of her holiday cookies was usually all I needed to bribe my way into the Hodges' family tree tradition.

Connor plugged the lights in. A whole section was dark, and I shook my head, wondering how long they'd been kept in storage. At least twenty years, probably, if everything had been packed up after his mother died.

"No worries," he said, and touched the wire connecting the lights. At once the whole thing lit up.

"That's handy. My friend Sydney's family would love to have you around when they're decorating their tree. I swear, every year they have to stop the whole process and have someone run off to Walmart to buy a new set of lights."

"They probably don't put them away properly. It looks like my father is the one who boxed all this up. He always was anal about keeping things organized."

Connor sounded casual enough when he mentioned his father, so I thought maybe I could try asking a question or two. "From what you said about him, he didn't exactly sound like the Christmas type."

"He wasn't. The tree was something my mother wanted. It's one of my earliest memories, actually... reaching out to try to touch the ornaments on the tree and my father yelling at me about it." His expression darkened, and I wished I hadn't said anything. "Since that was before things got bad, I'm guessing I must have been around two. Anyway, all this stuff went into storage after she died. No more Christmas trees in the Wilcox household."

As he said this, he was studiously looking away from me, intent on winding the lights around the pretty little tree. It wasn't very big; he stood several inches taller than it did.

"We never had a tree, either," I said, hurrying in to break the silence. "My aunt was fine with other people in the clan celebrating the holiday if they wanted to, but she always said she certainly wasn't going to bother, since she wasn't Christian. I did get one this year, since it was my own house and I could do what I wanted, but...."

This time he did pause. His eyes met mine, and I felt a little shiver go through me. There was something naked in those green depths, worry and regret, and something more. Longing?

"I'm sorry about that," he said. "I'm sorry we took you away from your home, from your family."

The words *it's all right* rose to my lips, but I didn't say them. As much as I felt myself softening toward him, what his brother had done was definitely not all right.

"Well, we have a tree now. I don't care if it's commercial and Christian and not what witches are supposed to do—I *like* Christmas trees."

"I had a feeling. That's why I got it."

Once again our eyes locked, and I could almost feel the flow of energy between us, the pull of the bond so strong that I took a half-step forward before I realized what I was doing. I froze, then forced myself to drag my gaze away from his and made myself look up at the clock.

After clearing my throat, I said, "I need to get back in the kitchen."

He blinked. "Sure. I'll just finish with these lights and then come open the wine. We'll do the ornaments after we eat."

"Sounds good."

Pulse racing, I went back to check on the duck. Bending down to peer inside the oven gave me a chance to at least attempt to pull myself together. I'd known this would be hard, but I hadn't realized how hard. It was easy for Sydney to tell me to ignore all the "Montague and Capulet stuff," as she put it. She hadn't been raised to think of the Wilcoxes as the big bad. I wanted Connor; I wasn't going to deny

that. But I knew what a break it would be with everything I'd been taught if I gave myself to him. I could
only wonder what cruel fate had determined that
he should be the bond of my blood, the consort to
make me complete.

I took a deep breath, then another. The fate of
the clans did not have to be decided tonight. I just
needed to pull myself together and get this dinner
finished.

Which I did, letting my training with Aunt Rachel
kick in so that I managed to get the duck, the cherry
sauce, the wild rice, the salad, and the rolls all to
the table more or less when they were supposed to.
Connor had turned down the lights and lit the candles at the table, and the fairy lights on the tree and
the warm flicker of the fireplace in the living room
only enhanced the feeling of quiet, of intimacy. We
were in a little island of warmth and comfort. Just
the two of us.

That was the problem.

We both sat down, and Connor paused. "I suppose this is where people are supposed to say grace
or something."

"Probably," I agreed. "But I wouldn't exactly call
this a normal Christmas dinner, so…."

"You're right, of course." He picked up his napkin and put it in his lap. "Even so…." After stopping
for a second, as if to gather his thoughts, he said, "I'd

just like to say thank you for what you've done since you came here. These dinners, and…." Once again his words trailed off. He seemed almost nervous, which for him felt out of character to me. I'd seen him diffident, closed off, quiet, but never nervous. "'Grace' is actually a good word for it. You've shown a lot of grace these past few days. So thank you for that."

I stared at him, words seeming to flee my mind as I tried to think of a way to respond. Never had anyone said anything like that to me. Finally I managed, "Well, you have, too. You've made this all… bearable."

There went the eyebrow again. "Bearable?"

"Oh, you know what I mean. It could have been horrible, but it's been…all right."

"All right?"

Now I could tell he was teasing me. "I am not going to say that I've had a wonderful time being locked in your apartment away from my family, Connor Wilcox." As I said this, I kept my tone light so he'd—hopefully—know I was teasing him right back.

His face went still, though, and I knew I'd said the wrong thing. "If I could have sent you back, I would have."

And would I have wanted to go? A few days ago I would have known exactly how to answer that question. Now, though….

"I know you would have, Connor." I forced myself to meet his eyes. "I know this isn't your fault. I just wish I knew what you expect me to do."

"I don't *expect* you to do anything." Finally he reached out for the bottle of wine and poured some into my glass. To my surprise, it was a soft, deep pink. "Anything more than you already have. Actually, I didn't even expect that."

"I haven't done that much," I said. "I made some tamales."

He shot me a sideways glance. "You've done more than that, and you know it. But those tamales have definitely been appreciated."

"Good." After I'd packaged them all up, Connor had taken most of them over to his cousin Marie's house as his contribution to the Wilcox potluck. Of course he still said he wouldn't go, that he wouldn't leave me alone on Christmas Day, even though I'd told him I really didn't mind. Maybe I did, a little; sitting here alone while he was off at a get-together didn't sound all that appealing. But I didn't want to be the reason he avoided going. Truthfully, I sort of wished I could go, too, if only for the anthropological curiosity of seeing a bunch of Wilcoxes in their natural habitat.

Even as I thought this, though, he said, "This all looks too good to let it get cold. So I'll just say thank you to the universe for everything we have, and leave it at that. Sound like a plan?"

"Sounds like a great plan," I replied, relieved that he wasn't going to push things any more on that front.

For a while we were quiet as we ate our salads. After that came the duck carving, which Connor did a decent enough job of. Good thing, because it was a skill I definitely lacked. I just wanted to cook the birds, not have to cut them up afterward.

He took a bite and let out a sigh. "This is incredible. Better than anything I've ever had in a restaurant."

"Thank you," I said, feeling my cheeks flush. It shouldn't be that hard to accept a compliment, should it? Especially since I didn't feel as if I'd done anything that special. Aunt Rachel had done most of the heavy lifting in teaching me how to cook, and after that it was really a matter of following directions more than anything else.

We ate and drank, and again talked of anything except the Wilcox clan and Damon's plots. The gallery, and how he was preparing to set up a new installation of an artist who worked in bronze and fused glass, and how he was excited about that. That led into my talking a bit more about jewelry making, and how I'd tried working with dichroic glass once but found it very difficult. And so on.

Through it all, however, I couldn't help but be conscious of his gaze on me, the way he watched me. Something in that direct green stare made the heat within me flare up again, and I had to fight to keep my hand from shaking as I lifted my fork to my mouth or reached out to grasp the stem of my wine glass.

I want you, that stare said.

And Goddess, how I wanted him. For the first time I had the barest inkling of what it must feel like to be an addict, to have that need ache along every vein, every artery, through every cell in your body until you feel as if you're going to cramp up forever because of it. But I couldn't let myself give in to it. I couldn't betray my family that way.

On the other hand, since Connor was my consort, wouldn't I be betraying the very forces of fate by trying to ignore the bond between us? There had to be a reason why he was the one…didn't there?

"Any more?"

I blinked. "What?"

A faint trace of a smile at the corner of his mouth, as if he might have guessed why my thoughts were wandering so much. "I was asking if you wanted any more duck."

"No, thank you. I'm getting full, and I made cranberry tarts for dessert."

That trace of a smile turned into a full-fledged grin. "Well, in that case, I think I'll stop, too. Cranberry tarts? When did you squeeze that in?"

"They're easier than they look," I replied, which they were. Quickie cheesecake on graham cracker crusts and topped with a sweeter version of cranberry sauce. Easy peasy.

"I'll have to take your word for that. As you know, I don't cook."

"I kind of got that impression." This time it was my turn to shoot him a sideways look. "Which makes me wonder why you bothered with all those top-of-the-line appliances."

He shrugged. "They're the best."

I didn't really have an answer for that. Maybe I shook my head slightly. But since we were done, I just gathered up my plate and Connor's, and took them into the kitchen, while he picked up the remaining serving pieces and set them down on the counter.

When I reached out to turn on the water to start rinsing off the dishes, though, he said, "Just leave them. I'll clean up later. It's the least I can do. Besides, we've got a tree waiting for us."

Fine by me. Cleaning up afterward was always my least favorite part of cooking. I followed him into the living room, where he went back to the box of ornaments and started pulling out smaller boxes filled with beautiful decorated glass balls and what looked like icicles of hand-blown glass, and so many other things—drops of mirror and brass, jingling bells in red and green and gold, strands of tinsel.

Everything looked almost brand-new, and carefully chosen to coordinate well.

Connor's mother obviously had very good taste. Maybe it was her artist's eye that had led her to choose these things, so different from the cheerful chaos of eclectic ornaments that decorated Sydney's family's Christmas tree.

By some unspoken agreement, Connor and I started hanging up the larger glass balls first, using them to create a sort of framework that we could fill in later with the smaller pieces. We worked without talking, focusing on the task at hand. Earlier he'd put on what sounded like a New Age holiday station, and the music played quietly in the background, mingling with the crackling of the fire.

As I moved I was far too conscious of him only a few feet away. We took care to maintain a safe distance between us, as if we both knew that a single touch would cause us to flare up hotter than the fire blazing in the hearth on the other side of the room.

I'd just reached up to hang one of those glittering mirrored ornaments from a high branch when a flicker of movement outside the window caught my eye. Lowering my hand, I squinted into the darkness outside. There it was again, a pale splotch against the black night. Then another, and another.

"It's snowing!" I cried, and ran to the window, ornament still dangling from my fingers.

"You sound like a kid hoping for a snow day," Connor said, hanging up the bell he held before coming to stand next to me and peer outside. "It's just snow. We get a lot of it around here."

"Well, we don't in Jerome," I replied, watching as the white flakes drifted down, swirling in a wind I couldn't feel. It wasn't entirely dark outside, of course; there were street lamps at regular intervals, and occasionally a car would go past, presumably running late to some Christmas Eve get-together or another. "It snows every once in a while, but it doesn't last long. And Adam—that is, our weather-worker tries not to meddle with it too much. A couple of years ago, he tried to give us a white Yule, and the snow piled up so high it actually broke some basement windows."

Connor's lips twitched. "Well, it definitely snows here. Tomorrow morning you'll get to see it piled up on every street corner."

"You sound so jaded."

"I was born here." He shook his head. "Come on—we're almost done with the tree. And then there are those tarts to eat."

Truthfully, I couldn't see as much as I would if it were daylight, so I let myself be persuaded to go back to the tree decorating. A few more minutes, and then it was pretty much done, except for the star to go on top.

That was a beautiful piece, made of cunningly twisted brass wire in delicate filigree designs, the sort of thing that looked as if it had been purchased from a local artisan. You didn't see ornaments like that at your local big-box store. Connor had pulled the star out of the box earlier and set it aside. It was sitting on the coffee table, waiting to be set on the top of the tree.

We both reached for it. Maybe I could have pulled my hand back in time…maybe not. It was as if some part of me didn't want to stop…wanted this to happen.

Our fingers touched. That same heat rushed over me, flooded every limb, every vein, sent the pulsing desire into raging life right in the center of me, into that emptiness I wanted filled. Filled with him.

For a second our eyes met. His seemed to glow almost as bright green as mine, and then we were falling to the rug, his weight on top of me, his mouth on mine. I opened to him, let him taste me, tasted the faint sweetness of cherry sauce and rosé wine on his tongue. My arms tightened around him, and I felt his hand drift up my waist, cup my breast, his touch so warm, even through my bra and camisole and sweater.

And then he paused, gaze locked on mine. His breath came harsh and ragged, just as it had that first night he had kissed me and awakened our bond. "Angela…are you sure?"

I didn't have the power of speech in that moment. I only knew that I needed him, wanted him, and I didn't have the strength to fight it anymore. Moving away from him then was as impossible as escaping the pull of a black hole.

Wordlessly, I nodded.

"Then I don't want to do this here." He let go of me, but only briefly, just so he could scoop me up in his arms and lift me from the floor, carry me up the stairs to his room.

It was colder there, away from the fire, but that didn't matter, as the heat was still pounding in my veins, seeming to burn me from the inside. He set me down on the bed, and then he was on me again, mouth so sweet against mine, hands moving down my body so he could pull off the cardigan and lift the camisole over my head, unhook the fastener on the front of my bra.

His mouth closed on my nipple, and I cried out then, arching against him, feeling the heat and the need build even further. He reached down and fumbled with the heavy concho belt, trying to get it undone.

"I'm regretting buying you this thing," he muttered.

I laughed and unerringly found the latch on the buckle, let the belt drop away and fall with a metallic thud to the rug-covered floor. He let out a little growl, and undid the button and zipper of my jeans, pulled them down, taking my underwear with them.

Then I was naked beneath him, no embarrassment at being completely exposed to him like this, nothing at all except the need to have him be as naked as I was. I reached up and grabbed his sweater and the T-shirt he wore underneath it, and pulled them over his head. His body was as beautiful as I'd imagined it must be, firm with muscle, stomach flat, skin smooth and warm-toned, a gift from that long-ago Navajo ancestor, perhaps.

But I didn't have any more of a chance to admire him, because he lowered himself to me, trailed kisses down my neck, swirled his tongue around one nipple, then the other. I gasped, burying my hands in his heavy hair, holding him against me, even as I felt his fingers trace their way up the inside of my thigh, caressing me, coming closer, closer....

There. A groan forced its way from my throat as he stroked me, touched the heat in my core and made it flare up higher, higher....

Even with the response he was able to evoke from my body, I hadn't expected I would come that fast. But I did, wordlessly crying into the darkness as he gave me the release I'd been denied for so long.

And he didn't stop there, but moved slowly down my stomach, kissing his way over my flesh, until his tongue found the dampness between my legs, kissed and suckled me there, as I whimpered and gasped and felt the pulsing need build in me again, heat rising, until yet another orgasm rocked its way through me. My fingers tightened in his hair, holding him there until the last little ripples had finally worked their way through to my fingers and toes.

Then I realized he was still wearing his jeans, which just seemed wrong, so I found his belt buckle and undid it, and went to the buttons of his Levi's and more or less tore them free of their buttonholes. Just as he'd done with me, I grasped the waistband of his jeans and the boxer briefs he wore underneath and pulled them down as one. He sprang free, large and hard...*ready*.

I wrapped my fingers around him, felt the silky smoothness of his skin and the rigid strength of the flesh beneath. My hand moved up and down, and up and down again, and he moaned, letting me touch him, bring him to the brink.

"God, Angela, you're killing me," he groaned.

"That's the last thing I want to do," I whispered. I stopped, fingers still holding him, but not moving.

"I want to...be in you."

"I know," I replied. Beneath the waves of heat I felt the slightest shiver of apprehension. Or was that anticipation?

"And you're—you're ready?"

Not trusting myself to speak, I nodded.

He took in a breath, then shifted away from me. I let go of him, wondering what he was doing. The answer became clear as he yanked open the top drawer of his nightstand, pulled out a little foil packet.

I almost protested. After all, a witch didn't really need that kind of protection; my Aunt Rachel had taught me a simple charm to prevent an unwanted pregnancy. It was something all young witches learned, although I hadn't needed it up until this point.

But then I thought of all those young women Mary Mullen had mentioned, the ones who had been here before me...here in this very same bed. Probably Connor had been careful with them, too, but why take the risk? At least, not until he could get tested and we'd know for sure.

These thoughts flickered through my mind, oddly not killing the desire I felt for him, but only increasing it, as if I needed to forge this final bond with him so the specters of those girls who'd come before me could be banished forever. I waited, time seeming to hang, suspended, as he opened the packet and then slid the condom over his shaft.

He moved back toward me, slipped between my legs. Once there, though, he paused, staring down at me, as if to reassure himself that I wouldn't stop him.

I knew I couldn't do that, not now when we'd already come so far. This would change everything, and we would have to deal with that, but for now I wanted nothing else but Connor against me, *inside* me.

"Please," I said.

The softest of sighs escaped his lips, and then I felt him moving against me, his tip pressing against me, and then into me. For the briefest second there was a flash of pain, and I shut my eyes. But then he was within me, moving slowly and steadily, pushing his length into my core, filling me. And the heat was there again, pulsing stronger and stronger, as we rocked together, breaths mingling, no sound at all except our ever-increasing gasps for air, driving into one another, taking our two halves and making them a whole.

Then at last the climax, rushing over us, pulling us along with it, two hapless swimmers struggling against a current we could not control. In that end-less, weightless span of time, I felt the bond that had begun with a kiss finally fuse into a link I couldn't begin to describe, only that I no longer knew where my soul ended and his began.

And within me the power of the *prima* flared up, a new strength glowing within me, bringing with it at last the knowledge that within me was the ability to do so many things I'd never even dreamed of.

I had come into my own.

Connor stared down into my face the way a man dying of thirst might gaze on the oasis of his salvation. He bent and kissed me, and the tenderness in that kiss was enough to make me want to weep.

"I love you, Angela," he whispered.

"I love you, too, Connor," I whispered back.

For in that moment I knew I did love him, that I'd loved him for longer than I wanted to admit.

What it all meant, I had no idea.

I only knew that there would be no turning back from this now.

CHAPTER SIX

New Day

WE LAY IN EACH OTHER'S ARMS FOR A LONG TIME, savoring the warmth of one another's flesh. Finally, though, I stirred and said, "Did that work up an appetite for some cranberry tarts?"

I saw his teeth flash in the darkness as he grinned. "For those…among other things. But I suppose we can go for tarts and then come back here for round two later."

My body flared with heat at the thought. "That sounds perfect to me. But let me run over to the other room so I can get my jammies."

"I like you better the way you are now."

"It's cold, Connor." And it was; despite the building's heat, I could practically feel the night's chill seeping in around the window frame. "Besides, if I put my pajamas on now, that means you get to take them off later."

"Point taken. Okay, I'm down with that." He pushed himself off the bed and walked across the room to the dresser. Fine by me, as I got to see his well-muscled thighs and backside that way. All that hiking and skiing obviously had worked their own magic on his physique.

I could feel the damp heat stirring between my legs as I stared at him, but somehow I managed to force myself up and across to the guest room, where I pulled some clean underwear out of the duffle and then got into my flannel pajama bottoms and thermal top. After this I had a feeling I wouldn't be sleeping in here ever again. And what would that be like, to close my eyes with Connor beside me, to know that I could reach out in the darkness and feel his warmth, his strength, just where I needed it?

When I came back to the master bedroom, he was wearing a pair of godawful plaid pajama pants and a Northern Pines University sweatshirt. He looked so adorable like that, with his hair mussed and his bare ankles showing under the too-short pajama bottoms, that I almost wanted to laugh.

I didn't, though. "Ready for that tart?"

"You bet." He flashed a smile at me. "And I have a surprise."

"Haven't we had enough surprises for tonight?"

"You'll see."

He reached out and wrapped his fingers around mine, and a tingling heat moved up my arm. Would it always be like this? Would every touch from him make me want to throw myself against him so he could fill me yet again?

In a way, I hoped not. It would be awfully hard to get anything done.

But for now I was all right with that unnerving warmth moving through me, the throbbing between my legs that told me I wasn't done with him, not by a long shot.

We went downstairs hand in hand. Only when we reached the kitchen did he let go and reach for the refrigerator door. Opening it, he peered inside, then pulled out the tray of tarts I'd put in there to chill earlier. He wasn't done there, though; he bent down and got something out of the door.

"Champagne?" I asked.

"Can you think of a better excuse to drink it?"

"Not really."

He retrieved some rather dusty flutes from one of the higher shelves in a cupboard, then pulled out some plates for the tarts. I handed him a dish towel so he could wipe down the glasses, which clearly didn't see much use.

The dirty dishes from dinner were still stacked next to the sink, but otherwise I hadn't done too bad a job of tidying up. Although in the past it had sometimes irritated, now I was glad of the way my aunt had trained me to clean up as I went along so I wouldn't be faced with a huge mess in the kitchen at the end of the evening.

Or in the morning, I thought, eyeing the bottle of champagne. I had a feeling neither of us was going to be in the mood for dish washing tonight.

I transferred the tarts to the dishes and got out some forks, and then we both headed into the living room. The fire had banked down, smoldering into coals, but after setting the champagne and the glasses down on the coffee table, Connor placed some fresh wood in the hearth. The flames, newly energized, licked up against the logs, bringing some welcome warmth to the room.

Outside, the snow still fell. I wondered if it would do that all night.

"Want to make a wish?" he asked as he retrieved the champagne and began working the cork free with his thumbs.

"Is that what you're supposed to do? Make a wish? The only times I've had champagne were at weddings and things like that."

"You've never had anyone open a bottle of champagne, just for you?"

I shook my head.

"Well, I'm glad I'm the one to correct that oversight." For a second his gaze met mine, and I shivered, remembering what it had felt like to have that beautifully sculpted mouth kissing my lips, making love to every inch of my body. "You don't have to make a wish...it just feels like something we should do now."

"Okay," I said, thinking it over. I'd already had such an amazing wish granted, just being here with him like this, I wasn't sure what else I could possibly ask for.

"Almost there," he muttered, still working the cork with his thumbs. He angled the bottle slightly so the cork would shoot off toward the high ceiling, and not at a window or something else breakable.

Better think of something fast. Just as the cork popped out of the bottle with a sharp *crack!*, I said, "I hope that you and I can always be as happy as we are right now."

"That's a good one. Now give me your glass fast, because this thing is about to spill over."

Hurriedly I reached for one of the champagne flutes and handed it to him, and watched as he poured it about halfway full, pausing so the bubbles could flutter almost up to the rim of the glass before they subsided. He did the same with the second flute, then held it out toward me. We clinked them together, and he added, "May your wish come true."

"It already has."

He leaned down and pressed his lips against mine. Oh, how I wanted to sink down to the rug with him right then and there. But we'd have time for that soon enough. Besides, from what I recalled, that Navajo rug was fairly scratchy.

So I kissed him back, tasting him once again, and then we pulled apart and each took a sip of champagne. It was good, light and fizzy, practically dancing off my tongue.

"So do you have a habit of keeping champagne in your fridge, just in case?"

A quick, flashing grin. "No. I bought it because a friend of mine—a civilian friend—had just gotten engaged, and I was going to give it to him and his fiancée. But then they had a blow-out fight over something and called the whole thing off. I didn't think a bottle of champagne was particularly appropriate, given the situation, so it's just been sitting in there for the last six months."

"Ouch," I said, and hoped that didn't mean the champagne was cursed or something.

"I thought that, too, but then it turned out she was cheating on him with one of her exes, so I supposed he dodged a bullet." He waved a hand. "But enough of their drama. I don't keep champagne around just so I can seduce women when I bring them up here to show them my etchings."

"Oh, is that what you call it?"

"Very funny." He swallowed some more champagne and then put down his glass, reaching for one of the plates with a tart on it. "Dessert?"

"Thank you." I took the plate from him and settled myself down on the couch.

A second or two later, he sat next to me with his own helping of tart. He picked up his fork and took a bite, and his eyes shut, heavy black lashes startling against his cheeks. "Wow…that does taste like Christmas."

"Since when are warlocks experts on Christmas?"

"When they grow up with it, I suppose." His eyes opened, and his expression sobered. "It's probably different for you there in Jerome. You McAllisters have your own little enclave—"

"It's not only witches in Jerome," I pointed out.

"No, but about half the town is, and that makes a big difference. There are a lot of us Wilcoxes here in Flagstaff and all the way out to Winslow and so on, but you mix five hundred people into a pot with more than sixty thousand in it, and you get kind of lost. We do what we have to in order to blend in. Yes, we're clannish, but so are a lot of tight-knit families. Most people don't look all that closely."

I took a bite of tart. It was good, the tartness of the cranberry topping contrasting and then mixing with the creamy sweetness of the cheesecake underneath. "I never would have thought of Wilcoxes blending in. I mean, you guys were always the boogeyman to me."

He cracked a smile at that. "Do I look like the boogeyman?"

No, but your brother sometimes does. Of course I didn't voice that thought, instead remarking, "Connor, if I'd thought the boogeyman looked like you, I wouldn't have done such a good job of making sure he was locked up tight in my closet when I went to bed."

Before he said anything else, he ate some more of his own tart and washed it down with a swallow of champagne. "Believe it or not, we Wilcoxes don't spend our days boiling babies and kicking puppies."

His comment was so off-the-wall I just had to grin. "I didn't really think you did."

"Well, I just wanted to clear that up."

All right, maybe there was no puppy-kicking or baby-boiling involved, but that didn't mean the Wilcox clan didn't engage in some bad juju if the situation warranted it. It was more like...we McAllisters set limits on our magic, both to be safe and to avoid inviting unwanted attention. Delving into the darker side of things had consequences we really didn't want to face. The Wilcoxes didn't seem to have the same concerns, although it did sound as if they didn't want people scrutinizing their doings all too closely.

"I can't excuse some of what we do," he went on, appearing to correctly interpret my silence. "But we don't all behave that way. In fact, most of us don't."

"So what do you do?" I asked. "I mean, if you're not casting hexes or whatever."

"We live our lives, same as you do. You'll see, when you come with me tomorrow."

"Come…with you?"

"To the party. There's no reason you have to stay trapped in here any longer. That is, we're…."

Well and truly bonded. I hadn't even stopped to think about it, but it was true. Now that Connor and I had been together, his clan would see it as me throwing my lot in with theirs. I no longer needed to be a prisoner in this apartment. The strange thing was, I didn't feel any different. Oh, I felt different in the way that most young women must feel after they've lost their virginity. I'd stepped over a threshold. I wasn't a girl anymore.

Even with that, though, I still felt like me…which meant I was severely disinclined to do anything that would make life easier for the Wilcoxes, no matter how much I cared for Connor. And I had to admit it puzzled me, because according to what I'd heard from my aunt, the *prima* must bond with her consort on her home territory, so her powers might remain connected to her own clan.

Figure it out later, I told myself. *At least for the moment, you haven't turned into the Wilcox equivalent of a Stepford wife.*

Anyway, I had more pressing things on my mind. "You want me to come to the potluck? That just feels...weird."

"You'll have to meet them sometime," he said, his voice coaxing. "Really, they don't bite."

I recalled the avaricious gleam in Damon's eyes when he'd looked down at me when I was helpless on that makeshift altar a few days ago and thought, *Well,* some *of them, maybe.* "Okay," I replied, then asked, tone wary, "Will your brother be there?"

"Yes. It's always held at his house. The *primus* and all that."

Who knows what look of terror must have flashed in my eyes. Something that must have been fairly obvious, because at once Connor set down his plate and took my free hand in one of his. "It'll be all right," he said. "He knows you're with me now. He's not going to try anything."

"But to go to his *house*—"

"Where there'll be tons of people. I swear it will be fine. Don't you trust me?"

Maybe I shouldn't. After all, I didn't know Connor all that well...we'd been around each other for only

four days. But it was the frightened part of me thinking that, the McAllister girl who'd been taught that
all the Wilcoxes were pure evil. It sounded as if it
might be a bit more complicated than what I'd been
told. And somewhere deep inside I knew I could trust
Connor. The bond between was too strong, golden
and glowing and pure. I could tell he had no agenda
here. He only wanted me to meet his family.

I stared into his face, taking in the deep green
eyes with their heavy fringe of lashes, the longish
nose and high cheekbones, the beautiful mouth and
strong chin. It was a face I loved very much, and the
spirit and soul behind it even more.

"Yes, Connor," I said. "I trust you."

<hr>

We finished our champagne and dessert after
that, growing drowsy and satisfied before the fire,
with the Christmas tree glowing in the background.
Sometime around one we deposited our empty
plates and glasses in the kitchen and went back
upstairs. Moving quietly and smoothly, in contrast
to our frenzied coupling of earlier, we fell into bed
together, pajamas falling in a heap on the floor as
we pressed bare flesh against bare flesh, joining in a
way that once again made me feel as if I no longer
knew where he started and I began. And afterward

we slept, twined in one another's arms, breaths coming as one.

Pale morning light peeking through the blinds woke me. I blinked up at the ceiling, thinking of how I had awoken in this apartment just a few short days ago, and how much had changed in the intervening time. For there was Connor sprawled next to me, the white wintry daylight casting his perfect profile into sharp relief. I'd no longer have to sleep alone. He'd always be there next to me.

I saw his eyelids flutter, and he shifted, letting out a little groan as he stretched. "What time is it?" he asked.

There was a clock identical to the one in the guest bedroom on his nightstand. "Seven-fifteen. I'm sorry I woke you."

He pushed himself to a sitting position and ran a hand through his hair, making various locks stand on end, and in the process making him look even more adorable. "No, it's fine. I'm not a late riser. Besides, there's something I want to show you."

"Oh, yeah?" I inquired in suggestive tones. "I thought you showed me that last night."

"Very funny. Seriously, get into some clothes. We can shower later."

I didn't miss the "we" in that sentence and wondered if I was finally going to find out whether that big shower really did work well for two. But I figured

I could leave that for now, so I retrieved my clothes from where I'd tossed them over a chair last night, right before collapsing into bed, and climbed back into them. Connor did the same, putting on his underwear and jeans, then a T-shirt and sweater. He pulled on his socks and shoes, heavy quasi-hiking boots similar to what I'd seen Damon wearing a few days earlier, while I slid into my riding boots.

"Come on," Connor said, and I followed him downstairs, running my fingers through my hair and wishing I had an elastic band to pull it back. It felt like a snarled mess.

We paused at the coat closet. He reached in and handed me a beautiful knee-length wool coat in a deep shade of green. Stuffed into the pockets were a pair of flannel-lined black leather gloves. I gave him a questioning look.

"Well, we kind of hoped you wouldn't be stuck in here indefinitely. Marie picked that out when she was buying some other things for you. Does it fit okay?"

"It's perfect," I said, slipping it on and buttoning it up.

At the same time he was getting into his charcoal-gray peacoat. "Good. Let's go."

He opened the front door, and I followed him into the hallway, eyeing my surroundings with interest. After all, when I was brought here, I'd been blindfolded and hadn't seen anything of the place except the interior of Connor's apartment. The hallway was a short one, with a door directly opposite the one we exited now, and then a staircase leading down. The floor was wood, the walls brick. And it was cold in here, much colder than inside the apartment, which led me to believe that no one bothered to heat the interior corridor.

"What's over there?" I asked, pointing at the door across the landing. "Another apartment?"

"Well, it was, but I bought the whole building, with the gallery and both apartments. I use that one for my studio now."

As I pondered that, we went down the stairs to the ground floor of the building, and through another short hallway that opened directly outside. As soon as Connor opened the door, a gust of freezing air hit my face, and I blinked, then quickly pulled the gloves out of my coat pockets and pulled them on.

Connor didn't miss much. He saw what I was doing, and remarked, "A little colder than Jerome?"

"Just a little," I replied, trying to keep my teeth from chattering and only partially succeeding. Actually, I was sort of shocked by how much colder it was here, considering that Jerome in December wasn't exactly sunny Palm Beach, either. But this was the kind of cold that actually made your teeth hurt. I wondered what the temperature was.

"I'll get the heater going once we're in the car. It's just over here."

I noticed that an alley backed up to the brick building, and behind the building were a few spots with little "reserved" signs in front of them. In one of those parking spaces was a shiny dark green Toyota FJ Cruiser, the kind of vehicle I'd secretly coveted for a few years, even though I'd known it was silly to want a second vehicle when my Aunt Rachel and I did perfectly well sharing the Jeep.

Connor pulled out his keys and used the remote to unlock it, while I trailed after him and then went over to the passenger side. I couldn't help wondering how much money the Wilcoxes really had. Sure, we McAllisters were definitely comfortable, but we didn't flaunt our wealth. After seeing Damon's Range Rover, and noting the way Connor didn't seem to particularly care how much things cost, I had to think that they were doing okay. More than okay, actually.

I waited until we were both inside and he'd gotten the engine going and the heater running before I asked, "Just how rich are you?"

He let out a sound that almost sounded like a snort. "Whoa. Are you after me for my money, Angela?"

I shot him a pained look.

"We do all right," he replied as he backed the SUV out of its parking spot and then headed down the alley. Just after that we turned onto a one-way street, and then another, until we were out on the main road.

The side streets hadn't been plowed yet, and I noticed Connor had engaged the four-wheel drive and then kept it slow.

We cut through an area of mixed residences and small businesses, then turned onto Highway 180. Well, it called itself a highway, but as with 89A back in Jerome, it was really a two-lane road. Here there were heaps of snow piled up along the sidewalks, and I couldn't help pitying the poor snow plow drivers who had to get up at o'dark-thirty on Christmas morning to make sure the streets were clear. At that point we were heading out of the town, toward the snowy peaks to the north and west of Flagstaff proper. I wondered where we were going, and hoped Connor wasn't planning to take me cross-country skiing or something.

"Just all right?" I pressed.

Although the highway was plowed, it was still slick and treacherous. He didn't take his eyes off the road as he replied, "What does it matter?"

"I'm just curious. I mean, the McAllisters are certainly comfortable, but we're not riding around in brand-new Range Rovers, either. Just part of the whole flying-under-the-radar thing."

"Let's just say we have a different attitude about that." He paused at a stop sign, then turned right. Here, the road wasn't plowed, and we were back in four-wheel drive as we headed up the steep, narrow lane. "If people in our clan have the power of seeing, then we don't have a problem with using that power to…help things out a little."

Which I supposed was his way of saying that there were people in his clan who could see the future and use that knowledge to play the stock market or bet on horses or whatever it took to generate some extra income. One could say it was a victimless crime—I mean, I sure wasn't going to shed any tears over someone taking advantage of a few Wall Street types—but that just wasn't how we McAllisters did things.

Oh, well, Dorothy, you're not in Jerome anymore. I shrugged and said only, "Well, it seems to be working for you."

He grinned. "What, no lecture on the immorality of us Wilcoxes using our powers for selfish gain? You must be tired."

I stuck my tongue out at him and turned to look out the window. Dark pine forest surrounded us now, the branches of the trees only lightly dusted with snow, but the ground beneath them was obscured by what looked like at least two feet of drifts.

The badly paved lane gave way to…nothing. Well, I supposed in the summer it was probably gravel, or maybe even dirt, but right now we were just plowing our way across virgin snow. I gripped what Sydney liked to call the "Jesus handle" on the roof of the SUV and hoped that Connor knew what he was doing.

To my relief, he stopped the Cruiser a minute or so later. "I'll come around and open the door for you," he said. "The footing can be a little tricky."

I didn't protest. The last thing I wanted was to climb out of the SUV and slip and slide down the mountain. Or hill, I corrected myself; off to my left I could see the top of Humphreys Peak, probably several thousand feet above where we were, wisps of cloud sitting on it like a halo, and so I knew we weren't on a mountaintop. Not technically, anyway.

Snow crunched as Connor came around the back of the vehicle, then paused on my side and opened the door. "Here you go," he told me, reaching up to take my hand and help me down to the ground.

Those rubber-soled boots had been more a prescient purchase than I'd imagined. Even with his strong fingers holding mine so I wouldn't lose my footing, I could still feel my feet begin to slide and then catch as the treads on my boots finally gained a purchase. I clung to him as we walked a few paces away from the Cruiser, then asked, "So what are we doing here, exactly?"

"Look," he said, and used his free arm to make an expansive gesture toward the pine woods around us, the looming San Francisco Peaks, the glistening snow banks. Here, you would never think you were close to a city of sixty thousand. We might have been the only two people in the world.

"It's beautiful," I murmured. Funny—I never thought I'd use that word to describe the home of the Wilcox clan, but it was true. This didn't look like Mordor at all.

"I like to come up here to get away from things. Walking in the woods helps to clear my head. Down there"—he jerked a thumb somewhere to the south and east—"things can intrude too much. But up here I don't have to think about being a Wilcox or the *primus*'s brother or any of that. I guess that's why I wanted you to come up here with me. Because whatever comes next, remember that it's only a small part of the picture."

Following his gaze, I looked at the ponderosa pines looming around us, the purple-indigo of the mountains, the aching blue of the sky. There were the faintest, thinnest streaks of clouds painted against that sky, like the traceries in a stained-glass window, and somehow I felt as if I stood in a cathedral, hushed and quiet and holy.

Movement caught my eye, and I held my breath. From within a stand of pine a large mule deer buck stepped forth, then paused. His antlers were sharp and dark against the snow-covered branches around him. For the longest moment he stood there, black eyes fixed on Connor and me. Then he dipped his head, as if acknowledging us, before turning and heading back into the forest.

Connor's gloved fingers tightened around mine. He was silent for a few seconds, watching the spot in the trees where the buck had disappeared. At last he expelled a breath, which wisped up into the frigid air, then said, "Well, it appears as if the lord of the forest has given us his blessing."

"I - I guess so."

He bent and kissed me, his mouth warm even though the air was bitterly cold. "I don't think there's any way to top that. Besides, your lips are starting to look a little blue. I'd better get you back and get some breakfast inside you."

Breakfast sounded wonderful. Christmas dinner had been a very long time ago. "Are you cooking for me?"

"Since I don't want to poison you, no. I'll take you someplace that makes the best omelettes you've ever had."

"And they're open on Christmas?" I asked. Somehow I found that hard to believe.

"Three hundred and sixty-five days a year," he replied as he opened the car door for me, then helped me in.

My stomach growled, and in that moment I didn't really care that I had snarled hair and no makeup on and was wearing the same clothes I'd worn the day before. "Sounds fabulous."

———

Well, it wasn't exactly fabulous, just a little diner off Highway 180 on the way back to town, but they were open, and the food was good—although I wasn't quite ready to admit that their omelettes might be just as good as Aunt Rachel's—and nobody seemed to give a damn what I looked like. The waitress gave Connor a hearty hello and took our orders promptly, and returned even more quickly with some much-needed coffee.

I waited until she was gone, then asked quietly, "Does she know?"

He seemed to guess right away what I was really asking. "No. This place isn't a Wilcox hangout. My friend Darren brought a group of us here once when we were going out to do some cross-country skiing, and I've been coming back ever since. Sometimes it's nice to be in a place where no one knows much about you."

That made a lot of sense. Being the brother of the *primus*—especially when that *primus* was Damon Wilcox—couldn't have been too easy. Anonymity had its attractions.

"Okay," I said. "Then it looks like it's back to the weather for a convenient topic of conversation."

He shook his head, then replied in resigned tones, "If you must."

I laughed. He'd been right—it did feel good to be away and out, someplace where no one knew who you were or what crazy circumstances had brought you there.

Too bad I knew that sensation of ease couldn't possibly last.

CHAPTER SEVEN

Enemy Territory

AFTER BREAKFAST WE WENT BACK TO THE APARTMENT. By then it was nearly ten, but we still had plenty of time; apparently the potluck didn't start until two. And I could tell exactly what Connor had in mind when he pulled off his sweater and T-shirt, then asked, "Ready for a shower?"

Without waiting for a reply, he undid the buttons on my cardigan and eased it off my shoulders, then drew my camisole over my head. Already heat was beginning to swirl through me in anticipation of him touching me once again. Goddess knows I wanted to touch him as well, draw my fingers over that smooth skin of his so I could feel the muscles beneath, then take him in my hands and feel his rock-hard arousal.

"Almost as ready as you," I replied, and brushed my fingertips against the bulge in his boxer-briefs, then laughed as he gasped. He reached for me, but I slipped out of his grasp and ran up the stairs, with him only a pace or two behind.

We burst into the bathroom, and he caught me and pulled me against him, kissing my mouth, my neck, moving down to my breast. Impatiently, he grappled with the hooks on the back of my bra, then flung it away in the general direction of the clothes hamper. His hands moved over my naked breasts, squeezing the nipples ever so slightly.

I gasped. "I thought we were taking a shower," I told him, words too breathless to constitute a true rebuke.

"I'm getting to it." He released my nipples and tucked his thumbs in the waistband of my panties, yanking them down and tossing them to land on top of my discarded bra.

Not to be outdone, I did the same with his boxer-briefs, although a little more gently, easing them over the erection straining the fabric.

"Now we shower," he said, and turned away from me so he could get the water going.

I already knew it heated up fast here, much faster than back in Aunt Rachel's apartment or the house I now owned, so when he picked me up a few seconds later and carried me into the shower stall, at least I didn't have to worry about getting hit by a blast of freezing water. No, it was already hot, steam beginning to curl up toward the ceiling.

He grabbed the bottle of shampoo and poured some into the palm of his hand, then began working it into my hair. Although I'd had other people wash my hair before—most notably Sydney, who tended to use me as her guinea pig when it came to practicing cosmetology techniques—never before had it felt so completely sensuous. His powerful hands kneaded into my scalp, and I closed my eyes, almost moaning at the contact.

"Your turn," I said, once he lifted his hands away and I had rinsed the shampoo out of my hair. I put some in the palms of my hands and reached up to massage it through his heavy locks. His eyes closed, and I watched as the water caught in his long lashes and glittered there like diamonds. It was a reach for me, since he was a good deal taller than I, but I didn't mind too much—I stood close enough that my breasts brushed against his chest, and he let out a groan.

"Okay, enough of that," he growled, and tipped his head back so he could wash away the shampoo.

Then he was reaching for me, mouth finding mine. With one hand I took hold of him, felt how hard he was, how ready. I stroked up, and down, and he moaned. After what he had done for me the night before, it seemed the most natural thing in the world to go down to my knees on the tiled floor, to touch my tongue to his tip as the water sluiced over me.

He gasped, and I pulled him into my mouth, sucking on him, taking in as much as I could manage, then slowly slid back down to his tip before moving upward again.

"I was right," he gasped. "You McAllisters are trying to kill me."

In response, I moved my tongue down the length of his shaft and tried not to giggle.

"Evil, evil witch." And he pulled me off him, lifting me up so that suddenly my back was against the tiled wall of the shower stall and he was pushing up against me, almost sliding in. Then he stopped. "Shit."

"What?" I gasped.

"Should've brought a condom in here with me."

Logically, I knew that was the best way to handle this. But I didn't want to stop, didn't want anything to ruin this moment. "It's all right," I told him. "I have a spell that'll handle it. The pregnancy thing, I mean. As for the rest of it—" I paused. "I know I'm not your first. But you've always been safe, right?"

"Always," he said at once. "Even when they didn't want to. I figured my life was complicated enough."

"Then we're fine." I shut my eyes, murmuring inwardly, *Blessed Goddess, now is not the time. Bestow your blessings elsewhere.* As Aunt Rachel had said, simple. But it was effective…at least, that was what she had told me. Tiny Jerome would have been completely overrun with McAllisters if we hadn't been mindful of such things. And sometimes, the reason for using the contraceptive spell was even more serious than that. For all her other strengths, Great-Aunt Ruby did not fare well in childbirth, and made sure to only have her two sons.

"We're more than fine," Connor said, and kissed me on the mouth, tongue touching mine, even as I felt him push against me, thrust inside, filling me once more. I wrapped my legs around his narrow hips and moved with him, the sensation of him being within me even more delicious now that we had nothing separating us. It was only flesh to flesh, Connor and Angela, the heat and the need building, building until we cried out as one, our bodies crashing through the climax at the same time. I felt him stagger, but then his grip on me tightened, still holding me in place, until the last ripples of the orgasm faded away.

We were both silent for a minute, breathing heavily. Then he smiled and pulled away from me before lowering me ever so gently to the shower floor. His chest moved up and down, glinting as the hot water still fell upon it, but he seemed to recover himself and shot me a wicked grin.

"Conditioner?" he asked, reaching for the bottle.

———

A few hours later we were back in the FJ, heading out of the downtown section of Flagstaff and up toward the hills, going in the same direction we had that morning, although we passed the turn-off that had led up into the woods and continued to follow the road as it wound through the rolling landscape on its way out of town. By then there were more people on the highway—possibly heading to their own holiday parties. However, I sort of doubted most of them were going to the kind of get-together that lay at the end of our route.

I don't know if I was fidgeting or what, but Connor lifted one hand briefly from the steering wheel to give my fingers a reassuring squeeze before redirecting his attention to the icy road. "It'll be fine," he said. A quick glance over at me, and he added, "You're beautiful."

Despite my nerves, which felt as if they had all been twisted into a knot and then dumped somewhere in my stomach, I had to smile. After we'd emerged from the shower, laughing and tingling, I'd gotten serious as soon as I contemplated having to face a horde of Wilcoxes. Guessing my mood, Connor had left me to primp, a process that took much longer than it normally would. I didn't have much to work with, my wardrobe here consisting of five camisoles, three pairs of jeans, and three sweaters. I had to recycle one of the sweaters I'd worn over the weekend, but I had to hope it would be enough. Then of course I berated myself for caring what the

Wilcox clan might think of me. It seemed I couldn't win either way.

"I'm still trying to wrap my head around this potluck thing," I told him, trying to keep my tone light even as I stared out the window at the snowy woods passing by and wondered how far out of Flagstaff proper Damon lived. The houses were set far apart here, and getting bigger. It looked as if the Wilcox *primus* lived in what Sydney liked to refer to as "Richie-Rich Land."

"It got started back during World War Two, from what I've heard," Connor said. "The Wilcoxes actually marry civilians a good bit, and I guess one of the wives got this idea that everyone should do more together as a family. There was some rationing during the war, so they decided to pool their resources and make it easier on everyone that way. And the tradition just sort of kept up after that."

That all sounded perfectly pleasant and innocuous...or would if you didn't know anything about the Wilcoxes and their history. However, what Connor had just related to me did jibe with what Margot Emory had revealed during our talk, that the Wilcox clan, having a smaller pool of family members to work with in the beginning, often married civilians to keep themselves from getting too inbred. I wondered how they selected these people. Did they truly care for them, or simply choose those who were attractive, intelligent, resourceful…whatever qualities might do best to improve their "breed"?

It was a question I decided I really didn't want to ask Connor. Not when I was about to meet a bunch of people who were the result of such matches, anyway.

We turned off the "highway" and onto a smaller lane that curved around past some eye-popping mansions, then pulled into a wooded drive already choked with cars. Apparently even here the clan was following protocol, though, since there was still room to maneuver, and a choice spot left open right in front of the multi-bayed garage. The house itself was massive and sprawling, its peaked roofs heavy with snow.

I stared at it, wide-eyed. "Okay, and no one thinks it's odd that a college professor lives in a place like this? I mean, I know they make a little more than minimum wage, but this looks like something from one of those shows on HGTV where they give you tours of celebrity houses. My friend Sydney loves those."

A shrug as he turned off the engine. "We just say it was our father's investments. He owned property all over town, so no one thinks it's that strange."

"It still seems like a lot of house for just one person," I replied, then unfastened my seatbelt.

He shot me an unreadable look. "Well, he hadn't really planned to be living here alone."

No, I suppose he hadn't. I realized then that this was where Damon Wilcox would have brought me, if he'd succeeded in his mad plan and actually forced a consort bond upon me.

For a long moment, I said nothing, only stared at the house. Connor reached out and took my hand in his. "You don't—don't regret anything, do you?"

At first I couldn't quite understand what he was saying. Then I realized he was uncertain, was wondering if some part of me wouldn't have rather been here in this mansion than in his apartment, which, while very nice, was an order of magnitude removed from this place. "Goddess, no!" I replied with such vehemence that he startled a bit. "I would rather be stuck in a drafty single-wide with you than be here with your brother."

"Well," he said, sending me a relieved grin, "I wouldn't exactly call my apartment a single-wide."

"No, of course not. I love your apartment. It's cozy and warm, and just right. Besides," I added, recalling the open countryside we'd just driven through, "I have a feeling you'd have to go a lot farther to get some decent tapas in this place."

He actually laughed at that. "You're right. I can't guarantee you tapas today, but we usually put on a pretty good spread. So let's go. I'm hungry...we used up all that breakfast."

That we did. I'd actually begun to feel a bit peck-
ish right before we left the apartment, although now
my appetite seemed to have taken a back seat to
nerves. "Okay," I said reluctantly. I'd agreed to this,
so sitting in the car and not moving at this point was
a little silly. The time for protests was long past.

I wrapped my fingers around the door handle,
opened it, and got out. The biting air was all around me,
although a little more bearable now, since the sun had
been up for hours, and the temperature had warmed a
bit. Most of the snow had already melted off the tree
branches, although it was still thick on the ground.

Connor paused at the hatch to the Cruiser's cargo
compartment and got out the two bottles of wine we
were contributing to the potluck. His cousin Marie,
whoever she was, had supposedly already brought
up the tamales I'd made, but at least this way we
weren't walking in empty-handed. Then he came up
to me and took my hand with his free one.

"Ready?"

I nodded. No, I wasn't ready—talk about walking into the lion's den—but I certainly couldn't back
out now.

He squeezed my fingers. "It'll be fine. Like I said,
we don't bite…much."

Even in the freezing air, I could feel my cheeks
flush. I'd done my best to arrange my hair so it covered some of the more obvious bite marks on my

neck, but they were still there. The little supply of makeup I'd been given hadn't included foundation or cover-up; I didn't know if that was a vote of confidence for the quality of my complexion, or that whoever had been buying the stuff didn't trust themselves to get me a correct match. Either way, I'd been pretty limited in what I could do to make it look as if Connor and I hadn't spent the last eighteen hours jumping one another's bones.

I'd asked him if he could do anything about it, just a little camouflage spell or something, but he'd shaken his head. "No, I can only alter my own appearance. I can't do anything about those." And he'd reached out to brush his fingers against the smudged-looking bruises on the side of my neck.

Just that light touch was enough to ignite the fire within me once more, but somehow I'd managed to push it away. I certainly didn't have time for another shower at that point, and I was already nervous enough about facing the Wilcox clan without walking into Damon Wilcox's house reeking of sex.

Now I saw that someone had swept the snow off the walk leading to that house, so the footing wasn't as treacherous as I'd feared. I still clung to Connor's hand, just to be safe. Or maybe that was just me trying to get whatever reassurance I could.

The oversized door had an equally oversized pine wreath, complete with red bow, hanging from it. I wondered if Damon himself had put it there, or whether one of his relatives had hung it to give the place a more festive look. Somehow I just couldn't imagine Damon Wilcox being the cheery holiday-decorating type. Then again, I never could have imagined him hosting a potluck, either.

Connor opened the door and led me in. I suppose he didn't see the need to knock, as it was his brother's house. Or maybe it was locked against anyone who wasn't a Wilcox. All I knew was that I didn't intend to touch the door handle to find out. Those magical shocks were strong enough that I'd still be able to feel them even through my gloves.

When we entered the place, my first impression was of sound and light—people talking and laughing, pale winter sunlight shining through the pine trees that surrounded the house and slanting through the enormous floor-to-ceiling windows in the room opposite the entry, windows that surrounded an equally enormous stone fireplace. Logs crackled and snapped within. I pulled in a breath and wished I knew a good invisibility spell. Or one for teleportation. That would do just fine, too.

Neither of those spells was at my disposal, however, so I followed Connor's lead and took off my coat, then hung it on one of the overcrowded racks clustered by the front door.

"Connor!" an unfamiliar voice called out, and I saw a tall dark-haired man smile and wave. He had the Wilcox look about him, with his sooty hair and eyes and high cheekbones, but his expression as he approached us was far friendlier than I imagined Damon's could ever be.

"Lucas," Connor said, "I want you to meet Angela."

The man came to a stop even as his eyes widened. I could see the astonishment in them, that I would be here at all. But then he seemed to gather himself, and he smiled at me. "Angela. It's so very good to see you here. I'm Lucas Wilcox, Connor's cousin."

"Fourth, right?"

"Something like that. Who's counting?"

I couldn't help smiling a little, recalling how I'd always thought of Adam that way. Third...fourth... five times removed...when the connection got that tenuous, it started to not matter very much exactly what degree it was. Thinking of Adam probably wasn't wise, though, because then all I could do was wonder who else among these dark, handsome people had been wearing a hooded cloak that night, and had been there when the Wilcoxes invaded my home and stole me away.

Although my smile had faded, I still managed to say, "It's very nice to meet you, Lucas."

His dark eyes twinkled a little, as if he guessed I was only uttering the words custom expected me to say. But his only comment was, "Don't even try to remember all our names, because it's impossible. Just smile and nod...and make sure Connor keeps your glass filled. Assuming you drink, of course."

Oh, I drink. Right now I want to drink...a lot.

I gave a foolish sort of nod, not knowing exactly how I should reply. Connor rushed to my aid, saying, "Looks like I'm already falling down on the job in that department. Angela, let's get these bottles over to the table in the family room—that's where we set up the food—and then I'll get us a couple glasses of wine."

"Sure." I allowed him to lead me away from Lucas, who seemed to watch me as I went, a speculative look on his face.

I couldn't figure out what that meant, though, because once we were moving through the living room we were approached from all sides, people saying hello and introducing themselves, a blur of smiling faces and names that, as Lucas had said, I couldn't possibly begin to remember. Looking at them, I wondered what their talents were. We had a good deal of variation in Jerome, as there weren't as many of us, and somehow the different skills seemed to get distributed evenly amongst a witch population, but there were so many Wilcoxes it seemed there had to be some doubling up. Not that I could ask; it was one thing to discuss such things privately, but going up to a witch or warlock and asking them to identify their talent was about on par with walking up to a stranger and inquiring about their weight.

We'd just set down the wine bottles when a woman approached and said, "So you were able to make it."

As I focused on her features, it was all I could do to hold in a gasp. This was the woman from that nightmarish scene when I'd first been brought here to Flagstaff, when I'd been held down on a makeshift altar by one of Damon Wilcox's unnamable spells. The Native American blood in her features was far more pronounced than it was in many of the other Wilcox clan members, and I wondered at it.

"Hi, Marie," Connor said. "This is Angela."

Her cool dark gaze slid over toward me, and she smiled, although it didn't quite reach her long-lashed black eyes. "So glad you came. And you really made those tamales Connor brought over the other day? You are quite an amazing cook."

So this was Connor's cousin Marie. He'd mentioned her several times, and she appeared to hold a position of some importance in the clan. If nothing else, she seemed to be one of the few people with the strength to stand up to Damon Wilcox.

Belatedly I recalled that she was also the one who'd done most of the shopping for me, so I said quickly, "Thank you, Marie. And thank you for choosing all those wonderful clothes. They all fit perfectly, and the colors are great."

Another one of those cool smiles. She herself was dressed very well, if simply, in a long black skirt, slim-fitting black sweater, black boots, and some eye-popping turquoise jewelry. My Aunt Rachel would've positively salivated over that squash blossom necklace. "You're very welcome. It's good to see that you've...adapted...so well to things here."

"She really has," Connor put in. "Although I'm hoping after today the two of us can get out to do some hiking or something. If she keeps feeding me the way she has, I'm going to need some way to work it off."

"Better buy me some snowshoes first," I said, trying to keep my tone light. Something about Marie seemed to set me on edge. Maybe it was just that I did clearly remember her from that hideous night when Damon had tried to make me his consort, and couldn't forgive her for the role she'd played. Or maybe it was the faint hint of disapproval that seemed to emanate from her, although I couldn't figure out why. After all, she hadn't seemed all that upset at the time when it turned out I was Connor's match and not Damon's.

Well, this probably wasn't the place to attempt to figure it out. I'd try to pick Connor's brain on the subject later, when we were safely home and away from here.

Home. Funny how I already thought of the apartment as my home, when I'd only spent a few days there. But somehow I knew that wherever Connor was, that was home.

"The snow melts pretty quickly on the lower elevations," he said. "And it's supposed to warm up through New Year's. So I don't think you need to worry about snowshoes."

"Hiking boots, then."

"Not a problem. We've got two hiking stores in walking distance."

I couldn't really argue with that. What I found more interesting was the way Marie seemed to watch our interchange, as if she were carefully studying our interactions. What, was she surprised by the way Connor and I got along? Didn't she know that was how it worked with a *prima* and her consort, that our bond made us more than mere mates, made us lovers who were intertwined on every level, body, mind, and soul?

Maybe she didn't. After all, things were done very differently here in Wilcox territory....

But of course she made no comment, offering another of her Mona Lisa smiles before saying, "There are quite a few diversions here in and around Flagstaff, Angela. I hope you and Connor have fun exploring them." Her gaze drifted away from us. "But it looks as if Taryn is waving me over. You two enjoy yourselves." She moved off into the crowd.

So many questions filled my mind, I didn't know where to start. But I had one thing uppermost in my brain. "I'll take that glass of wine now, Connor."

———

After a few gulps of some local wine—a red blend from Arizona Stronghold—I was feeling a little more in control of myself. So far no one had tried to hex me straight back to Jerome, or turned me into a frog. Then again, why would they? In their eyes, I was one of them now. I'd bonded with Connor, brother of the *primus*. Now we were all just one big happy family.

Well, more or less.

More introductions, more smiling at attractive dark-haired people whose faces I wasn't sure I'd be able to recall the next day. Okay, maybe their faces—I was always fairly good at that sort of thing. But names? As Lucas had advised me, I didn't even try.

We ate and drank, and then drank some more. I felt as if I were in a sort of dream, as if all the introductions were happening to someone else, someplace else. I couldn't be in Damon Wilcox's house, chatting with his relations, talking about the weather and the food in downtown Flagstaff (not that I was an expert, except for the tapas Connor and I had shared my first night here), and talking about my aunt's cooking and providing tips on making tamales as if doing so was the most natural thing in the world.

Through all this, I wondered where the man himself actually was. I hadn't seen anything of him since we'd entered the house. Was he avoiding Connor and me, not wanting to see the two of us together, not wanting to look at the prize he'd had taken from him?

No, that was ridiculous; I shouldn't flatter myself. The place was huge, after all; laughter and chatter echoed from the open area on the second floor, which looked like a game room of sorts, and there were many other rooms down on the ground floor that I hadn't even seen yet. Connor seemed to understand that I was more comfortable staying here in the family room, close to the food and the wine. Everyone flowed in and out of the space anyway, since they needed to refill their own glasses and plates.

We'd been there for a little more than an hour when Connor leaned down and murmured in my ear, "I need to go to the bathroom. Will you be okay here for a minute or two?"

My first reaction was to say no, I wouldn't, but that would be childish. Setting aside the off-putting undercurrent in Marie's reaction to me, everyone else had been very friendly. Maybe too friendly, because of course it didn't take much for me to start wondering just *why* they were being so nice. I'd worry about that later, though. I was certainly in no imminent danger, except maybe from indigestion after eating my way through everything from chili cornbread to Swedish meatballs.

"I'll be fine," I said, and hoisted my plastic cup in his direction. "You just gave me a refill, remember?"

"Right." The corners of his eyes crinkled as he smiled down at me, and he bent and kissed me quickly, a soft touch of his lips at the edge of my mouth. "Don't eat too much, though. I don't want you so full that we can't have a repeat engagement when we get back to the apartment."

"Not a problem," I said. "I'll have, what, a whole twenty minutes to digest even if we left right now?"

He shook his head and moved away, heading toward a hall I'd noticed earlier, although I didn't know which rooms branched off from it. The bathroom at least, obviously. Or one of them, as a place this big had to have at least three or four.

I took a few steps toward the fireplace. This room had its own hearth, not as grand as the one in the living room, but still imposing, made of more stone and reaching up to the wood-paneled ceiling. The crowd had ebbed away, most people seeming content to let the food they'd eaten settle a bit before they came back for seconds or thirds.

"Enjoying yourself?"

Damon Wilcox's voice. Something in those silky tones sent an icy shiver down my spine. My fingers tightened on the clear plastic cup I held, and I had to tell myself to relax before I crushed it and spilled wine everywhere.

I took a breath, then forced myself to turn around. He stood a few paces away, watching me, black eyes hooded. He wore a gray houndstooth jacket over a white button-down shirt and jeans, an outfit that seemed calculated to present the perfect image of a college professor relaxing at home.

"Very much," I said coolly. "You have a beautiful home."

"You like it?" he inquired. "It could have been your home as well."

My heart thumped uneasily, and I told myself it was fine. He couldn't do anything to me here in front of all these people.

What, the same people who stood by and watched while he tried to force the primus *bond on you?* my brain mocked me. All right, maybe the presence of the Wilcox clan members wasn't as big a safeguard as I'd thought.

But Connor had just gone down the hall and would be back at any second....

"I'm fine with Connor's apartment, actually."

"Are you?"

I paused, then forced myself to meet those piercing black eyes. *He can't do anything to you now,* I reassured myself. *You're bonded to his brother. You're useless to him. He's just messing with you because he can, and because he's still pissed that he didn't get what he wanted.*

"More than fine. I mean, I have everything I could possibly want. My consort has turned out to be the man I've been dreaming of for years. What girl wouldn't be thrilled by that?"

His lips thinned. "Sometimes dreams can be nightmares."

"I know that," I retorted. "Because you sure did your damn best to screw up mine, didn't you?"

At least he didn't try to deny that he'd been meddling with my dreams. "It was an interesting experiment, that's true. Dreams have…a fascinating energy."

At that moment I saw Connor approaching from behind his brother. Judging by the look on his face, Connor was not exactly thrilled about the *primus* swooping down on me the second I was left alone. "Damon," he said, his voice tight.

Damon allowed his gaze to linger on me for another second before he turned to greet his brother. "Oh, hello, Connor. Angela and I were just having a nice chat."

Jaw tight, Connor moved past Damon to stand next to me. "Were you?"

No way was I going to challenge Damon here on his home ground. Besides, I'd always been taught that causing a scene at a family get-together was in extremely poor taste. "Oh, yeah," I said airily. "I was just complimenting Damon on his lovely house. Wasn't I, Damon?"

Instead of looking annoyed, he merely smiled and said, "Yes, you were. Connor, it seems your little *prima* here appreciates the finer things in life. You might want to reconsider that cramped apartment of yours."

Hearing this, Connor looked irritated enough for the both of them. "Actually, I think we're fine where we are."

"Oh, definitely," I chimed in, and wrapped my arm around his waist, snuggling up against him. "I wouldn't want a place so big that I didn't have this guy within arm's length at all times."

That shot seemed to have found its target. "Oh, so now you're in *love*, are you?" Damon sneered. "Well, enjoy it while you can."

He left us to stew over that as he stalked off toward the living room. As I watched, I saw a young woman around Connor's age approach him and smile. She stood out amongst the Wilcoxes, her hair a warm honey blonde, unusual in this crowd of brunettes. Damon glanced down at her, seemed to hesitate, then offered her a smile before reaching out and winding his arm around her waist.

I didn't really want to know what that was all about. Then again, having someone else around for the *primus* to focus his attention on could only be a good thing.

Connor noticed, too—I could tell by the slight narrowing of his eyes as he watched his brother. However, puzzling over the young woman's identity wasn't enough to distract me from what Damon's words—"enjoy it while you can"—had meant. It was a horrible truth I'd kept buried at the back of my mind, since I hadn't wanted to acknowledge it, acknowledge that I might one day share the same fate as all the other wives of Jeremiah Wilcox's line.

Connor's green eyes seemed to glow with anger. He stood there, body hard and unmoving under the arm I still had wrapped around his waist. Very slowly he pulled away from me, then said, "You want to get out of here?"

Relief flooded through me. "I thought you'd never ask."

CHAPTER EIGHT

Revelations

FOR THE FIRST FEW MINUTES AS WE DROVE AWAY FROM Damon's house, Connor was silent. It was still light out, but the sun had begun to slip behind the hills to the west. It would be dusk by the time we got back to the apartment.

Finally he let out a sigh and said, "He wasn't always like this, you know."

"Don't tell me you're going to try to defend his behavior."

"No." His gloved fingers tightened on the steering wheel. "I'm not going to do that. But you don't know what he's been through."

"What, besides losing his mother at thirteen and his father twelve years later? You went through the same stuff, and it didn't turn you into a raging asshole."

He almost smiled. Almost. "Thanks for the vote of confidence. Okay, that's true, I suppose. But have you ever wondered *why* he kidnapped you, wanted to make you his consort?"

Of course I had. It was one of the roughly ten thousand questions I'd wanted to ask Connor but hadn't quite dared to. I knew it had something to do with my being *prima*, but I'd never been able to figure out why he though that was so important, other than the obvious benefit of adding a McAllister *prima*'s stock to the Wilcox gene pool. "You mean it wasn't my outstanding beauty and charm?"

This time he really did grin. "Besides that."

"All right, yes, I did wonder. That is, I figured it was partly to try to do what Jasper hadn't succeeded in doing with my Great-Aunt Ruby. And that all of it was to increase the powers of the Wilcoxes by bonding a *primus* with a *prima*."

"That might have been Jasper's reasoning, but it wasn't Damon's...at least, not the primary reason. No, he thought that by joining with a *prima* he would finally have the power to break the curse."

A better reason than creating a race of über-warlocks, I supposed. "So that's supposed to make me forgive him?"

"Of course not." Connor tapped his fingers on the steering wheel, then slowed to a stop as we came to a four-way intersection. There wasn't anyone around for miles, or so it seemed, so after the barest of pauses, he pulled out onto the two-lane road that would lead us back to town. "It wasn't his first attempt at breaking it. I think after what happened with our mother...." He let the words die away and hang in the air for a moment. "Anyway, he knew that would be his fate as *primus* if he didn't make some attempt to change it. So when he got married—"

"Wait," I interrupted. "You mean he was married once?"

"Yes."

I digested that for a moment. No point in asking what had happened to her, either. Fate wasn't kind to the wives of Jeremiah's line.

"They met in grad school," Connor went on. I noticed that he'd flicked on his headlights, even though there was still plenty of light to drive by. "She was a civilian."

That did shock me. "Seriously? I can't imagine a Wilcox *primus* stooping to marry a civilian. I mean," I went on hurriedly, since I could see Connor beginning to frown, "I know a lot of the people in your family marry civilians. Actually, the McAllisters do, too, and probably for a lot of the same reasons. But never the *prima*. I just figured you had sort of the same...traditions...in your clan."

"Normally, we do. But Damon got it in his head that maybe having a civilian wife would change things, render the curse ineffective."

"So he just picked some poor civilian girl to be his guinea pig?"

"She wasn't a guinea pig." Connor's tone was faintly reproving. "She was smart and beautiful, and he loved her. He did. Not that he came out and told me that, because, well, we didn't have those sorts of conversations. I was in high school when they got married. Felicia. She was getting her master's in psychology, and she worshipped him."

I had a hard time imagining anyone worshipping Damon Wilcox. Then again, if he and this Felicia had gotten married when Connor was still in high school, all this had happened some time ago. "Did she know about the whole...magic thing?"

"He told her. That's a pretty big secret to keep from your wife, and he knew she wouldn't be able to have much contact with the clan if he didn't tell her. But she seemed to take it in stride. I don't think he told her everything about the curse, though...just that there had been some tragedies in our family. But you could probably say that about most families."

I thought that was pretty hard on Felicia, and not precisely fair. She deserved the truth, deserved to know what lay in store for her. I didn't say anything, though, because I wanted to know what had happened to her. Well, the details. Since she wasn't around now, it was pretty clear that the curse had hit her, just as it had every other wife of a Wilcox primus.

"Everything seemed fine for a few years. She was getting a practice going as a family counselor, and Damon got the associate professorship position here at Northern Pines. I was off at school in Tempe by then, so I wasn't around to see them much except for a weekend here and there, but they seemed happy. Then Felicia got pregnant."

Uh-oh. That did seem to be the death knell for the Wilcox wives.

Connor stared straight ahead as he spoke. I didn't know if he was avoiding my gaze so he couldn't see my own worry, or whether what was coming next was so painful that the only way he could tell it was without looking at me.

"It was January. I'd just gone back to ASU after winter break. I got a phone call one evening. I think it was a Thursday." A shake of his head. "Like it matters what day of the week it was. There'd been a car accident. The roads were icy. She was driving home from her office when some tourist lost control at an intersection and T-boned her car. Just slammed right into the driver-side door. They got her to the hospital, but there wasn't much they could do. She was gone, and the baby."

My fingers tightened around the purse I held on my lap. A wave of pity rolled over me. Feel sorry for Damon Wilcox? In that moment I did.

"He changed after that. Sold the house they'd been living in, bought this place, and moved way out here. And he started obsessing over how he could end the curse forever."

I reached over and squeezed Connor's arm. Briefly, not enough to distract him from his driving, but merely to let him know I was there.

For just a second or two the tight set to his mouth softened a bit. But then I could see his jaw tense again as he said, "That was when he started obsessing about you. The first time he brought it up—it was over the summer, about five years ago now—I told him he was crazy, that he needed to let it go. I mean, bad enough that he should contemplate such a thing at all, considering you were only sixteen at the time and he was past thirty."

"Definitely disgusting," I agreed. It actually made my flesh crawl to realize Damon Wilcox had been thinking of me that way even when I was underage.

"Pretty much what I said. And he told me that modern scruples shouldn't be coming into it, and besides, of course he wouldn't touch you until you were twenty-one and your *prima* powers had begun to awaken. Then he sort of dropped it for a while, and since I was busy with school, I let it go as well."

At last he looked over at me. Quickly, so he wouldn't endanger us while driving or anything, but enough so I could see the warmth in his eyes. "Besides, soon after that I began dreaming of you, and I realized that eventually Damon's plans were going to come crashing down around him anyway."

"So you knew all along who I was?" I demanded. "That's not fair. I *never* got to see your face in my dreams. Not that I would've known who you were, even if I'd been able to get a good look at you."

"Well, I did know what you looked like, since Damon had people surveilling you for some time."

Now, *that* was creepy. "You're kind of freaking me out, Connor."

"I thought you should know the truth."

Just another way he was so very different from his brother. Damon seemed to have only a casual acquaintance with the truth, as far as I could tell. "So, um…surveilling me how, exactly?"

"No family members. Your elders would have sniffed out a Wilcox the second he or she crossed the wards you have set up. But being a college professor does give you access to a bunch of civilians, students who go on day trips all over the place, including Jerome. It didn't have to sound sinister or anything— he could do something as simple as mention he was thinking of vacationing there, and could they take some photos so he could make a decision that wasn't based on a B&B's website marketing copy? You were out in plain view, working at your aunt's store on the weekends. It was easy to get a picture."

I thought of the groups of kids around my age who'd come in and out of the store, who'd joked and messed up our stacks of T-shirts and taken loopy Instagram pictures with the javelina figurines in the background. How many of them had been Damon's unwitting spies?

"That's messed up, Connor."

"You think I don't know that?" The area around us was becoming more populated as we headed south, and he had to slow abruptly as a Dodge truck pulled out almost in front of us. I felt the tires slip a little on the icy road before they caught again. "Asshole," he muttered under his breath.

My fingers had unconsciously tightened on the edge of the seat. Driving in these kinds of road conditions was not something I enjoyed, even though Connor clearly knew what he was doing. Something he'd said nagged at my mind, though. "So if our wards should have alerted us to your presence, how did Damon and his little band of commandos get past them?"

"You'd have to ask him that. I told you he's been experimenting with spells, changing them, making them stronger, altering them. I don't know the details." He lifted his shoulders, and a frown creased his brow. "I do know he's frustrated because, although he's done some amazing work with spell-craft, he hasn't made any headway with the curse. He made a comment not too long ago about investigating alternative magic, but when I tried to get him to tell me more, he said he was only in the preliminary stages of his research, and there wasn't much to tell."

That didn't sound very reassuring. Damon using his physics knowledge to somehow twist spells into something different, something new, was bad enough. But if even that wasn't enough for him, what could this "alternative magic" possibly be?

I shivered, and Connor must have misinterpreted my reaction, because he added, "Anyway, I didn't even go with him to Jerome...I was waiting back at Lucas's house with the others."

So it was Lucas whose house had the basement rec room, the one where they'd turned the pool table into an altar. I wondered why they'd done it there, and not out at Damon's house, which seemed secluded enough. Maybe they wanted someplace that was easier to get to.

And for some reason, I was irrationally relieved that Connor hadn't gone on the Jerome raid. Yes, some people would say he was complicit just by waiting at Lucas's house, but I didn't see it quite that way. He'd known we were meant to be together, that Damon's plan would ultimately fail, but it was still important for him to be there at the moment of truth, so Damon would turn to Connor to make the binding.

Plots and plans, twisting around one another. This latest ploy of Damon's hadn't worked, either, but I couldn't help wondering how long it would be before he came up with something else.

"Are we almost home?" I asked.

Connor's eyebrow lifted at the word "home," but he replied with hesitation. "About five minutes."

"Good," I said. "Because I want you to do everything you can to scrub the last few hours from my brain."

And he did, more or less—when we got in, he scooped me up in his arms, took me upstairs, then laid me on the bed, slowly removing every article of clothing until I was naked, while he looked down at me, still fully dressed.

"You're the best Christmas present I've ever unwrapped," he whispered, voice husky.

"Well, get down here so I can unwrap mine, too," I replied, warmth surging over me at the gleam I saw in his eyes. I should have been cold, since we'd turned down the heat before we left, but all I needed was the raging fire of our bond flooding through every vein, a glow that could defeat even the iciest winter.

He'd already discarded his coat. The rest of his clothing went quickly enough, and soon he was naked as well, bare flesh pressed up against my body. There was no real foreplay this time, save his mouth on my breast, and my hand drifting down his shaft, until he shifted his weight and pushed inside me. I was ready for him, had been from the second his gaze met mine. There was something frenzied in the way our bodies joined, as if he needed to bond with me all over again, just as I wanted him to claim me, to put his mark on me once more so Damon Wilcox could never, ever attempt to make me his.

Afterward, we dozed off in one another's arms, sleeping for an hour or so, then waking up to full darkness. Still, it was early, not much past six o'clock. Despite the various tidbits I'd snacked on at the potluck, I was hungry.

As I stirred, I heard Connor's stomach rumble and couldn't help laughing. "Glad I'm not the only one," I said, sitting up and reaching for my discarded underwear.

"No, I was expecting to eat more, but something about my brother tends to kill my appetite. Please tell me you kept some of those tamales back and didn't send all the leftovers for the potluck."

"Of course I did." I reached over and brushed a lock of heavy black hair off his forehead. Having a mind of their own, the offending strands fell forward once again. "You know what we should do?"

He reached for his own underwear. "I thought we just did that."

I gave him an eye roll, and he laughed. "No," I said severely. "I don't mean that. I think we should go downstairs in our jammies and eat leftovers and watch that cable station that plays *A Christmas Story* over and over again in a continuous loop. You know, something normal people would do on Christmas."

"Deal." He paused, then added, "Well, as long as we can sneak a viewing of *Scrooged* in there somewhere."

I happened to love *Scrooged*, so that was no hardship. "Deal," I agreed.

And that's exactly what we did. Ate, and laughed, and leaned against each other, basking in the warmth of the other person and the glow from the fireplace. No more talk of Damon Wilcox and his plots, no tragedies, no spells or hexes or curses from beyond the grave. Only Connor and me, and the comfort of one another's company. I didn't know what was coming next, but at least I would have these few golden hours with him.

The next morning after we'd gotten up and showered—another long, slow, delicious shower, where we took turns scrubbing one another down and which ended with me up against the wall once more as Connor drove into me with hard, deliberate strokes until I cried out in ecstasy—he came downstairs holding his laptop open, an amused expression on his face.

"I think you're being paged," he said. "I was catching up on my email, and the Facetime app kept going off. Your friend Sydney, I think."

Oops. "Sorry about that," I said, taking the computer from him. "You'd think she'd have the sense to wait until I got back to her."

"Judging by how many times she pinged me, I have a feeling patience isn't her strong suit."

I couldn't help chuckling. "Well, that's true."

He wandered off to the kitchen to pour himself another cup of coffee. "Want some?" he asked, lifting the pot in my direction.

"Yes, please," I replied. I'd had fun with my Keurig coffeemaker back in Jerome, but Connor was hardcore about his coffee—used a French press and everything. That stuff was amazing.

After setting a mug down in front of me on the coffee table, he said, "I'm going over to my studio. Just come across the hall when you're done."

I'd been itching to see inside that place ever since he'd mentioned it, so I was feeling a little impatient when I clicked on the Facetime icon and launched the app. With any luck, this wouldn't take too long.

Sydney picked up right away. "Holy crap, I've been trying to get you for *ages!*"

"Well, this isn't exactly *my* computer, you know."

"Oh, right." She paused, then seemed to bring her phone closer to her face so she could get a better look at me. "Wow. You look like a girl who's been well and truly fucked."

"Sydney!"

"It's true, though, isn't it?"

My hand went up to the marks Connor had left on my throat. Since it was now safely after Christmas, I was going to make him take me to the mall or the drugstore or something so I could invest in some spackle. This was getting ridiculous.

"Well…yes."

"I knew it! So you took my advice."

"I—" There was a lot more to it than just that, but I figured I'd make her happy. "Yes. And it's—it's great. So thanks for that."

She couldn't exactly clap her hands together, since she was holding her phone in one of them, but she did bounce a little. Behind her I could see pale blue walls, so I knew she was in her bedroom. "So when do I get to meet him?"

"You've already met him, remember?"

A lift of her shoulders. "That doesn't count. We said, like, two sentences to each other. I mean, *really* meet him. Get together and go out."

As fun as that sounded…hypothetically…I wasn't sure how we could possibly make it work. "Well…."

"I wasn't saying come down here," she said. "Obviously. Will Connor get zapped on sight if he shows up in Jerome?"

Good question. "I don't know. Not that it's really an option. I don't see us leaving Flagstaff anytime soon." As I said this, though, I felt a wave of homesickness pass over me. Yes, I loved being with Connor. Being with him in Jerome would be even better, though. How exactly I would make that work, I had no idea.

You should *be able to make it work,* I thought. *I mean, what good is being the prima if you can't get your own way from time to time?*

Hmm….

Sydney said, "We could come up there. It's not like Flag's off-limits to me, you know. And Anthony's truck has four-wheel drive, so even if the weather gets crappy, it's no big deal." She added, her tone almost plaintive, "It would be fun to get out. I had to work *such* shit hours going up to Christmas, you have no idea."

Actually, I did, because she'd complained about it enough. However, I only said, "Well, let me talk to Connor. I don't know if we have anything going on or not." Ha, that was a lie. I had a feeling that, now the Wilcox holiday potluck was safely past, our social calendar was pretty empty. Not that I would know for sure. We hadn't talked about much that was in the future except our next meal.

"Okay. Check with him and then call me, okay? Or at least email, if that's all you've got."

"Probably email, because I don't have a phone." Or a wallet, or my I.D., or…anything. All that had been left behind when the Wilcoxes stole me away. The purse I'd carried to the party the day before had held a tube of lip gloss and a wad of Kleenex, and nothing else.

"God, how do you live?" Then she waved the hand that wasn't holding her phone. "Anyway, let me know. I'll bet he knows all the good places to go up there."

"I will," I promised. "Let me go talk to him, and then I'll get back to you."

"Sounds like a plan. Later, *chica*." The screen went dark.

I closed down the app, then paused, realizing I hadn't had any opportunity to check my email to see if Aunt Rachel had actually replied to the message I'd sent her the day before. As much as I wanted to hurry across the hall and see what Connor had been hiding in his studio, it was silly not to take this opportunity to check my email. So I went to Gmail and logged in. I didn't get much email, but there were still the usual after-Christmas sale ads from a few places where I'd made online purchases. Buried amongst the spam, though, was a reply from my Aunt Rachel.

For some silly reason, my heartbeat began to speed up. Was it mere anticipation of her disapproval, knowing that she would be less than thrilled—to put it mildly—once she found out the true nature of my relationship with Connor?

Maybe. But I couldn't worry about that now. I was an adult now. She would have to figure out how to handle the situation.

I clicked on the link, and the message window opened up.

Angela,

Of course we're all relieved to know that you're all right. The elders have been discussing the situation and are trying to see what can be done. Be strong, my dear. Just hold out, no matter what, and we'll do everything we can to bring you back home.

Love, Rachel

Ah, the guilt. "Hold out"? My resolve had crumpled like wadded-up tissue paper after Connor kissed me that second time. Maybe I could have tried to resist, attempted to ignore the heat of our bond, although I'd never heard of any *prima* doing such a thing. That connection wasn't meant to be resisted, but given into, embraced with every fiber of a *prima*'s being. And the truth was, I hadn't wanted to resist. Not any longer. Not once I'd come to know Connor as Connor, and not a Wilcox. And my family needed to know that, too. I didn't give a damn about traditions and custom and what had happened in the past. Connor was part of my future now, and they'd just have to deal with that.

It seemed clear what I would have to do. The problem was, I had no idea how Connor would react. Only one way to find out, I supposed.

I logged out of Gmail and closed the browser window, then shut the laptop. Of course the front door was no longer barred to me, so I opened it and crossed the landing to the apartment opposite ours. That door was unlocked as well. I twisted the knob and let myself in.

The layout was almost the same, as were the wood floors and the exposed brick of the exterior walls. Here, though, the kitchen was obviously not updated, the counters a chipped tile, an empty space where the refrigerator was supposed to go. The windows were uncovered, letting in the pale winter sunlight.

And everywhere were canvases—finished pieces hung on the walls, and paintings in various stages of completion were propped up below them. All landscapes like the ones I'd seen in Connor's apartment, all with those same strong, sure brush strokes, the same interplay of light and shadow and color. Seeing them all grouped together like this once again reminded me of how talented he really was...and what an ass Damon Wilcox was for trying to squelch his brother's gift.

Connor stood in the middle of the living room, although there was no furniture except a large table littered with paints and brushes, and the large easel where he was standing. His gaze was abstracted as he stared at the half-finished painting on the easel. An absent hand ran through his hair, mussing it, although he turned around at once when the floorboards creaked beneath my feet.

"Did you talk to Sydney?"

"Yes," I replied, stepping forward so I could pause next to him. It was colder in here, and I moved close so I could put my arms around him. At once he reached out to hold me, his body heat mingling with mine. "She wants to come up to Flagstaff to meet you."

"She has met me."

"I told her that. She said it wasn't the same thing. But...."

He must have sensed the diffidence in my tone, because he loosened his embrace, drawing back slightly so he could look down into my face. "What are you thinking, Angela?"

"I—" There wasn't any easy way to make the suggestion, so I just plunged ahead before I lost my nerve. "I want you to come to Jerome with me."

Eyes widening, he shot me an incredulous look. "Just like that. Do you know what you're asking?"

I pulled out of his arms and planted my hands on my hips. "Of course I do. I don't see much difference between you asking me to go to Damon's house and me asking you to come to Jerome. I've braved your family, so why can't you return the favor?"

"I—shit." Again that nervous gesture, his hand running through his hair. "Because they'll blast me with every spell in their arsenal the second I set foot there?"

"They didn't when you came to the Halloween dance," I retorted, then paused, my brows crinkling in a frown. "How *did* you manage that, anyway?"

"Damon," he said briefly. "But I wouldn't have that protection this time."

"No, but you'd have me." His expression was dubious, to say the least, so I went on, "I'm their *prima*—they have to do what I say, even if they don't like it. Anyway, McAllister magic isn't like that. We don't go around blasting things."

"Maybe not, but I saw that one warlock at the Halloween dance, the one in the Grim Reaper costume. He looked like he could break me over his knee."

I smothered a smile. "Tobias? He's a big teddy bear. He won't hurt you, and neither will anyone else. But don't you see, Connor? How can we make anything right, move forward from this and try to mend the rift between our clans, if we don't start here and now?"

That made sense to him, I could tell. He reached up and rubbed his chin; he hadn't bothered to shave that morning, and the stubble had him looking distractingly scruffy. Then he shook his head. "Damon will never allow it."

"How's he going to know? Does he have your apartment bugged? Did he plant a witchy tracking device on me so he'd know my whereabouts at all times?"

A grimace. "Not that I'm aware of."

"Well, then." My gaze flickered to the painting on the easel; it was obviously somewhere just outside Flagstaff, since a snow-capped Humphreys Peak towered in the background behind an autumn hill of yellow grasses and blazing golden aspens. Not all the aspens had been filled in, or the deep blue sky, but it was still powerful, half-finished as it was. "And once they find out what an amazing artist you are, they'll love you just as much as I do."

"I sincerely doubt that," he said wryly. "But okay. You're right. It's not exactly fair of me to subject you to Damon and the rest of the clan without me having to suffer your relatives in return."

"My relatives are *awesome*," I replied. "You'll see."

He paused. I wasn't psychic, so I had no idea exactly what was going through his mind, but I could guess. It's never easy, walking into the lion's den. "How long?" he asked.

"I don't know. A couple of days." I thought of the gallery then and asked, "We can wait until the weekend, if you need to work."

"No, that's okay. The gallery isn't going to reopen until Saturday anyway, so this is a good time. It's slow after Christmas for us—Joelle can probably handle the place on her own if it turns out we're going to be away longer than that."

I reflected how much he had changed in just the past few days. When we first met, he'd said he didn't trust Joelle to have the keys to the gallery. Now it seemed he didn't have a problem handing everything over to her.

This was happening fast, but I supposed that was a good thing. That way he wouldn't have much opportunity to back out. "So we can go today."

"Sure, why not?" His tone was resigned. He glanced over at the painting. "Good thing you caught me when you did. I was about to start mixing a fresh batch of oils—everything had dried out. So yeah, let's get out of Dodge before anyone knows what we're up to."

A warm rush of happiness went over me, and I stood on my tiptoes and kissed him, felt his mouth open to mine, tasted him. The need returned, just as it always did, but this time I could control it better. Besides, we'd already made love here in Flagstaff multiple times. The next time I was with him, I wanted it to be in that big king-size bed of mine back in Jerome. About time that thing got some breaking-in.

"It'll be fine," I said. "I love you, and I know they'll love you, too."

Something in his expression told me he sort of doubted that, but at least he didn't argue. "Well, start getting your stuff together, and we can head out after lunch. I'll just close up things here."

Fairly dancing, I kissed him again, this time on the cheek, and hurried back to the apartment to pack a few things. It was hard to believe, but true.

In a few hours, I'd be going home.

CHAPTER NINE

Cleopatra Hill

"So you're leaving?" Mary Mullen asked in resigned tones as I folded the last of my sweaters and put it in the duffle bag.

I hadn't seen her for a few days, and had wondered if she disapproved of the change in my relationship with Connor. Maybe now I was just another one of "those girls." What they used to refer to back in the day as "loose women."

But I didn't see anything particularly condemnatory in Mary's doll-like features, only a slight worry that she was going to be left to haunt an apartment with no one in it.

"Not permanently," I told her. "At least, I don't think so. We haven't quite figured out how this is all going to shake out."

Her head tilted to one side. I reflected that her hairstyle was just another reason why I was glad I hadn't been born back in the day. No way could I have ever managed those perfect finger waves. She asked, "Are you getting married?"

Wow. To be honest, I hadn't even thought about it. Everything with Connor was still so new. We'd only been together a few days. Going from that to marriage seemed like a big leap...or at least it would have been a huge jump under normal circumstances. It was different with a prima and her consort, though. Marriage in that situation was pretty much a foregone conclusion.

"Um...eventually," I hedged. "We haven't really discussed it yet."

"You should marry him," she said. "You're a nice girl. He deserves a nice girl."

I was oddly relieved that she still thought of me as nice, even if I did happen to be a fallen woman. "Right now I'm just taking him to meet my family."

"Oh, that's nice. That's a good step."

I sure hope so.

"Who're you talking to?" Connor asked, sticking his head in the doorway. Immediately Mary Mullen disappeared.

"The ghost," I replied. "She was worried that we were leaving permanently."

"Are we?"

"Of course not." I zipped the duffle and turned to look at him. "I'm going back so I can let everyone know what's going on, have them meet you. That's all. It's important for them to know that I'm with my consort."

"Even if that consort is a Wilcox."

"Yes, even that. Especially that. We're all going to have to learn to live with the situation. Better to start now."

He came to me then and kissed me, long and thoroughly, igniting the slow fire in my veins. I cuddled against him, wanting him. For a second or two, I thought he might press things further, push me down on the bed so we could follow the heat of the moment to its logical conclusion. I wouldn't have minded, except for the delay and the fact that I really wanted our next time together to be in Jerome. But he pulled away, and smiled down at me. "I love you," he said quietly.

I took his hand, pressed it against my cheek. "I love you. And it's going to be fine."

No reply to that, save a soft squeeze of my fingers before he stepped away and picked up the duffle bag. "Let's get going."

Despite Connor's assurances that Damon wasn't completely all-knowing and all-seeing, I couldn't help casting furtive glances over my shoulder as we exited the building and threw our meager luggage— my duffle bag, a beat-up athletic carry-all with the Northern Pines University logo on the side—in the back of the FJ. There were a few people around, going from the parking lot behind the building to the shops and restaurants in a sort of outdoor mall off to one side, but none of them were paying us the slightest bit of attention.

"It's fine, Angela," Connor said, opening the passenger door for me. "I don't recognize any of my brother's spies."

I waited until he had climbed inside and started up the engine before asking, "He has *spies?*"

"Well, okay, any of my relatives." He fastened his seatbelt, and I did the same. "Even if they did see us, what are they going to do? We could just be going shopping or something."

"With luggage?"

"Our 'luggage' doesn't really look that much like luggage. We could just be going for a day trip with those bags."

"Okay, true."

He backed out of his parking space and headed down the alley. After turning down a couple of one-way streets, we emerged on Route 66 and headed east. I frowned, because even though I didn't know

the town very well, I did know that I-17 was in the
other direction.

Connor must have noticed my worry, because
he said, "It feels like we're going out of our way,
but really, it's easier to get to the freeway from this
direction. Otherwise, we have to sit through a ton of
lights."

That seemed reasonable. I nodded, and sure
enough, a few minutes later we were on I-40 going
west, heading to the interchange that would take us
south and toward Jerome. As soon as we were past
the Flagstaff city limits, I could feel my spirits start to
rise. No one had stopped us.

Great snowy pine forests crowded the landscape to either side of the highway. The highway
had been plowed, but Connor kept our speeds down
well below the posted seventy-five miles an hour.
Although I understood his caution, part of me chafed
at the delay. I wanted to be home.

We didn't talk much on that drive. He seemed
calm enough, but I could feel the tension practically
radiating off him. I understood it, of course; I'd been
in a similar situation just the day before. Well, except
that the McAllisters generally tended to be a far less
dangerous bunch than the Wilcoxes. Their outward
normality hadn't soothed my misgivings all that
much. Yes, Lucas and some of the others seemed
pleasant enough, but there were those weird vibes

I sensed coming from Marie, and Damon…well, enough said on that topic.

"The 260, right?" Connor inquired, and I startled. I'd been watching the changing landscape outside the window, watching as the ponderosa forests dwindled to familiar juniper, the snow fading as well until all that was left were patches in the shadows behind rocks or under trees.

"Right," I said, then asked, "But you've been to Jerome before. Don't you remember the way?"

"Actually, my friend Darren was driving. Everyone I came with that night was a civilian. They didn't think we were doing anything except going out and having a good time. Damon wanted to send some family members with me, but I didn't think that was a good idea since it was his first time using that masking spell, and I didn't know how many people he could really handle."

I supposed that made sense. So those had been some of Connor's civilian friends. I wondered what their reaction would be if they ever discovered the truth about his family…or the real reason why he'd come to the Jerome Halloween dance.

That was between them, though. For now I was content to guide Connor up the highway that led us into the heart of Cottonwood, to go through streets that were almost as familiar to me as those of my own little hillside town. After we swung our way through the last roundabout and began heading up twisty 89A to Jerome, I could feel tears beginning to sting at the back of my eyes. I hadn't realized how much I'd missed this place until I saw it again.

By then it was a little past three in the afternoon. Snow still gleamed on the north face of Mingus Mountain, but the roads were clear enough. And in the town itself, everything seemed normal, serene. The usual gaggle of tourists, maybe a little thicker today because it was the holidays and so many people were off from work and school.

I saw Connor wince a little as we passed the town limits and reached out to lay my hand on his leg. "Everything okay?"

"Yes," he said, although his voice sounded tight. "I think we must have just passed one of your wards. I didn't feel it back in October, when Damon cast that one spell. It had to have protected me somehow."

"Are you all right?" I asked immediately.

"I'm fine. It was just a twinge. Maybe being with you eased it a little, or maybe it's not intended to actually hurt too much, just warn someone off."

That sounded about right. The McAllister way was not to bring suffering to others. However, if Connor had felt the ward, that meant the alarm had probably been sounded. We might not have a lot of time before the welcoming committee showed up.

"Where are we going, anyway?" he inquired. "We're about to run out of town."

"Turn left up there," I said. "At the sign that says 'residents only.'"

He followed my directions, and soon we were twisting up the back alleyway that led to my house. It was icy and treacherous, and he slowed to let the four-wheel drive take over. I'd actually only come in this way once or twice, since I didn't have my own car yet and therefore hadn't needed to park in the garage. But I figured it was probably safer, since Paradise Lane was narrow, and the FJ would stick out like a sore thumb if we parked it in front of the house.

Not that it probably mattered, since the people who monitored the wards already knew a Wilcox was in McAllister territory.

We'd just pulled into the garage and were climbing out of the Cruiser when I heard Boyd Willis's voice. "Hold it right there, Wilcox."

At once I stepped forward. "Boyd, it's me."

The look of astonishment that passed over Boyd's craggy features would have been amusing under different circumstances. He wasn't exactly the most expressive of men. "Angela?"

From around the corner of the garage stepped Margot Emory and Henry Lynch. The welcoming committee—in other words, the clan's strongest witch and warlock. Both of them stopped dead when they saw me, although I noticed Margot's eyes tracking toward Connor and then back toward me.

He had stilled as well, standing quiet, waiting, his hands at his sides. Obviously he didn't want to do anything that would provoke a response. I could tell he was waiting for me to take the lead here. After all, we were now in my territory.

I shut the car door. "I think we should all go inside," I said.

———

Although I'd only been gone a few days, the house felt alien to me. Maybe that was just because I hadn't had a lot of time to get used to it before I was taken to Flagstaff, but somehow I thought it was more than that. Being out of Jerome, living with Connor, had shown me just how circumscribed my life was before this past week.

No one said much of anything as I opened the door and led everyone inside. The dining room, with its large table, seemed the logical place to go. Besides, there I could sit at the head of the table, act like the *prima,* even though inwardly I could feel myself jittery and nervous, wondering whether they would listen to me, wondering what I would do if they didn't.

I shot Connor as reassuring a glance as I could and nodded toward the chair to my right as I sat down. The slightest head tilt in return as he acknowledged my silent request. He pulled out the chair and took his seat. After a hesitation, during which Margot, Henry, and Boyd exchanged their own silent and unreadable looks, they all sat down in the empty chairs on my left, facing Connor but not looking at him.

After a long, heavy pause in which I was sure everyone could hear my heart battering away in my breast, I said, "This must look a little…strange."

Margot was the first to reply. She folded her pale, slender hands on the tabletop, glanced at Connor for the briefest of seconds, then tilted her elegant head back toward me. "That's something of an understatement, but yes, it does seem rather odd that you'd bring a Wilcox here."

"He's here with me because" —I drew in a deep breath— "it turns out he's my consort."

"Impossible!" Boyd burst out.

A quelling look from Margot, and he subsided somewhat. He was here because of his strength in spells of protection, of defense, but still she was the only one of the clan elders present, and he had to defer to her authority. Where the other two elders were, I didn't know. Gathering the clan against the possible Wilcox threat?

She shifted in her chair, the first time I could recall ever seeing her make a movement that was anything less than completely self-assured. "You'll forgive us for being...disbelieving."

"Well, I didn't want to believe it at first, either."

Beside me, Connor's mouth twitched in what might have been the beginnings of a grin, as if he were thinking that had to be the understatement of the year. Luckily, he got it under control before anyone else noticed. Boyd's, Margot's, and Henry's attention was focused all on me. Maybe they were hoping that if they didn't acknowledge Connor's presence, he'd just disappear or something.

It didn't work that way, though. I leaned forward, saying, "He's the one I've been dreaming of all these years. I don't understand exactly what's going on, either, why my consort would turn out to be a Wilcox, but it's something you're all just going to have to deal with." The three of them gazed at me, stony-faced, and I added impatiently, "Just look at his eyes. You all know I've been dreaming of a man with green eyes. None of the candidates you found for me had eyes like that. But Connor does."

Reluctantly, they turned and regarded Connor for a long moment. I was proud of the way he sat there in silence, returning their stares coolly but with no sign of hostility. How handsome he was, with the sunlight coming through the windows on the west side of the room and warming his raven hair, show-ing all those translucent layers of sage and slate and moss in his remarkable eyes.

At last Margot let out a long sigh. "I don't know what to make of this. Perhaps the other elders will have some insights. In the meantime, I think you should stay here in the house."

I placed my hands flat on the tabletop. "No."

The winged black eyebrows lifted. "I beg your pardon?"

"*No,*" I said. Where the strength to defy her was coming from, I didn't know. Maybe simply from hav-ing Connor near me, feeling his reassuring presence, even when surrounded by those who should have been his enemies. Something told me, though, that I needed to make a stand, to assert myself. I was the *prima* now, and although she was a clan elder and worthy of my respect, still, mine was the final word. "I've had enough of house arrest. I brought Connor here to meet my family, to see where I grew up. It is not your place, Margot Emory, to tell the *prima* what she can and can't do."

Her face had always been pale, but something about it appeared pinched now, as if she needed all her strength to prevent herself from snapping out a retort.

"Now, Angela, you don't need to be speaking to Margot like that," Henry said in his easygoing manner. Since Great-Aunt Ruby, the former *prima*, had been his mother, maybe he had more experience dealing with someone who intended to get her way. "She's just concerned, that's all."

"It'll be fine." I let my gaze sweep the table, moving from Henry to Boyd and then back to Margot. "I'm here in my home territory. I'm safe, and Connor will be safe. Won't he?"

None of them said anything.

"*Won't* he?"

"Of course he will," Margot said then, her tone quiet but somehow laced with venom. "After all, *we're* not Wilcoxes." A scrape of her chair's legs on the wooden floor, and she had risen to her feet. "Boyd, Henry, it seems we can go. Angela has everything under control."

They looked dubious, but followed her lead, getting up from their chairs and then following her to the front door. She paused there for a moment, even as I stood up to face her. "I hope you know what you're doing," she remarked coldly.

Then they were gone, the door slamming behind them. For a few very long seconds, the house was completely still. At last Connor expelled a breath.

"That was…impressive. And here I thought you were all shy and retiring."

I raised an eyebrow, but, despite my earlier show of strength, my knees felt like jelly. "I don't know about shy and retiring, but I do know I feel like passing out." I didn't, of course, but I did let myself more or less fall back into my chair. At once Connor reached and gave my hand a reassuring squeeze. His fingers were warm and strong, and the heat of our bond had never felt so welcome.

He waited, watching me, as if he could tell I had more to say.

"It was just—somehow I could sense that if I let her tell me what to do, then she'd just keep on doing it. 'Poor little Angela, so young to be a *prima*. Let's keep guiding her since she doesn't know what she's doing.'" I let out a breath of my own, and tightened my fingers around his before letting go so I could push a wayward strand of hair back from my face. "But I'm the *prima*, damn it, and that's not how things are supposed to work. This is my house, and this is my town, and if I want to walk around with my boyfriend—"

An amused glance. "So I'm your boyfriend now?"

I made an impatient gesture with one hand. "Come on, 'consort' sounds so...I don't know. It's one thing when you're talking to other witches, but to anyone else you're just going to sound crazy. So, yeah, 'boyfriend' works for now."

"It's fine. I don't care what label you want to put on our relationship. I'm just glad we have one."

The table was just big enough that I couldn't quite lean over to kiss him. Well, there'd be plenty of time for that later. I settled for saying, "I love you."

"And I love you, O *prima* of the McAllisters."

"Very funny. Anyway, what I was trying to say was that if I want to walk around town with you, stop in for drinks somewhere, get in the car and drive down to Cottonwood to meet Sydney and Anthony and go out, then that's what I'm going to do. If the elders don't like it, they can just suck it."

"Spoken like a true *prima*. Well, except maybe for the 'suck it' part." He got up and extended a hand to me, and I took it and rose from my seat. "Let's get our stuff out of the car, and then you can show me around." A pause, and then he added, "But that drink did sound like a good idea. I could use one."

"You and me both," I replied, and let out a shaky laugh.

———

After that we went and collected our things, then took them upstairs to the master bedroom. I could see the way Connor's gaze flicked toward the king-size bed, and I felt a smile pull at my mouth. *Later, I promise*, I thought.

I didn't say anything, though, just gave him the nickel tour of the house. He was properly apprecia-tive of the place, although he gave the claw-foot tub in the upstairs bathroom a dubious glance. "I think I'm missing my apartment already," he remarked.

"I was planning to remodel all that," I said. "I'll admit that your bathroom has me thoroughly spoiled. So this should reassure you that I'm not planning on staying here forever—I don't think I could put up with that tub for more than a few days, either."

"Thank God," he said casually, and I raised an eyebrow. Here in Jerome we usually swore by the Goddess, but I had to admit the Wilcoxes weren't particularly attuned to the feminine divine. Maybe he used the more conventional form of the deity's name as yet more of the protective coloration his clan employed to hide their true nature from everyone around them.

Just then the doorbell rang. "Great. If it's the elders coming here in force to convince me of the error of my ways—"

"Tell 'em to suck it," Connor suggested with a grin.

I shot him a pained look but headed down the stairs to answer the door. The bell rang again, and I grimaced. Right then I didn't feel like dealing with anyone else. I just wanted to finish showing Connor around the place so we could go out and get a much-needed drink. Or five.

When I opened the door, expecting to see Margot Emory and Bryce McAllister and Allegra Moss, the three clan elders, instead I saw my Aunt Rachel standing on the porch, a scarf wrapped around her neck against the cold and a worried expression on her face. When she saw me, the worry didn't precisely go away, but her eyes went bright with tears.

"Oh, thank the Goddess," she said, moving forward and folding me in her arms. "When the word came down that you were home, I couldn't quite believe it. Since I hadn't heard back from you, I didn't know—"

Her words broke off as she noticed Connor standing a few paces away in the foyer, his figure shadowed, since the light from the narrow leaded-glass windows framing the door didn't reach that far. She let go of me slowly, then took a step backward.

Again, no easy way to do this. I lifted my chin and said, "Aunt Rachel. This is Connor. Connor Wilcox."

She didn't quite gasp, but I still heard her breath go in. "But—"

"He's my consort." Half-turning from her, I gestured for Connor to step forward. He did so, but I could see the reluctance in every tense line of his body. Despite that, he reached out and took my hand in his, held it tightly.

"That's not possible." Like Margot and Boyd and Henry, she wouldn't look at Connor, instead kept her gaze fixed squarely on my face.

"It is. *He* is."

She remained silent, staring at me in a sort of numb horror, as if her brain had frozen and she couldn't get it working to process what I was telling her.

Wanting to fill that horrible, empty pause, I said quickly, "Well, at least now you know why none of the candidates worked out. We just weren't looking in the right place."

The joke fell flat, as I realized it would the second it left my lips. Nothing for it, though. I floundered for something else to say—*anything*, as my aunt was staring at me as if I'd been diagnosed with some sort of horrible, infectious, and ultimately fatal disease.

To my surprise, Connor said gently, even as he took my hand, "We know this sounds crazy. We're still trying to figure it out ourselves. But Angela wanted her family to know the truth. So we're here. And I want you to know that I do love her. Very much."

At last my aunt found her voice. Not that I wanted to hear what she said next. Her brows pulled together, and I saw the same loathing she'd shown when we encountered Damon Wilcox in Phoenix a month earlier. "Love? That's something you Wilcoxes know nothing about."

She turned on her heel then, marching down the porch stairs and along the path that cut through the postage-stamp lawn, now yellow and dead with winter's frosts. I took a step after her, then felt Connor's hand gripping mine, holding me back.

"Let her go," he said quietly. "She has to figure this out in her own time, in her own way. You can't erase a lifetime of hate in just one afternoon."

True words. I knew that, but still I felt a little piece of my heart break as I watched my aunt turn her back on me, on the man I loved. Maybe she'd work through it eventually, but it was going to be a rough road until then.

"Okay," I said at last. "But you know what? I've changed my mind. I don't want to show you around town. I can't take another confrontation like that. Not right now, anyway."

"That's fine. Whatever you want to do." He hesitated, then asked, "So what *do* you want to do?"

"Something normal people would do," I replied, the plan resolving in my mind even as I spoke. "I'm going to call Syd, and we're going to go down to Cottonwood, and we're going to go out and eat and drink and talk about anything except our crazy families. I don't care what. Movies. Politics. Baseball."

"It's football season," Connor pointed out gently.

"Whatever. Let's just go."

"Okay, sweetheart." He bent down and kissed me. "Whatever you want."

CHAPTER TEN

Normal

WE DIDN'T MAKE OUR ESCAPE QUITE AS QUICKLY AS I'D HOPED, mostly because when I called Sydney, it turned out she was working until five. "But Anthony has the night off, so that's something," she told me. "How about we meet you at Bocce at about a quarter to six? It's going to be crazy-busy, but maybe you can get there a little early and get our names on the waiting list."

I said that was fine, and hung up. Since she was at work, she didn't have a chance to really talk, but I could tell she was bursting with questions as to why we were here in Jerome rather than up in Flagstaff. Good question. I'd begun to wonder the same thing myself.

Unfortunately, she'd have to wait a while to get any actual answers, because no way was I going to talk about any of this stuff in front of Anthony. He seemed like a nice guy, but even so, I wasn't going to start blabbing about McAllisters and Wilcoxes and witch clans in front of him. Maybe if this thing with Sydney turned out to be really serious, and it looked like they were going to make it permanent— well, maybe then I'd feel safe confiding in him. Until then, Connor and I would just have to pretend to be another normal couple.

So I took the time to freshen up a little, to change into a long-sleeved white T-shirt and black wool jacket, and fuss with my hair so it wasn't quite as much of a mess as usual. Connor seemed to guess my mood and went down to the study/library to look at the books on the shelves there.

I'd just finished slipping a pair of silver hoops in my ears when he came back into the bedroom, a paperback in one hand. "I hope that's not *Valley of the Dolls*," I said. "I don't want you getting corrupted."

"Too late for that." But he was smiling, so I knew he'd meant it as a joke. "No, hate to disappoint you, but it's just a copy of *The Client*."

"As if I'm going to give you much time to read," I teased.

The smile faded. "We don't have to stay here, you know. We can go out with your friends and just head back to Flagstaff at the end of the evening."

"No," I said at once. "I'm not going to go running back with my tail between my legs. This is my town and my clan, dammit. Sooner or later they'll get their heads out of their asses. I was probably being naïve thinking they were going to welcome you with open arms."

"It just shows you're the better person." He shifted the paperback from one hand to another, then turned it over, as if intending to read the copy on the back. But his gaze remained fixed on my face. "I said I'd do what you want, Angela, and I meant it. But there's no shame in leaving here and regrouping if you're not comfortable."

I hesitated. Never in my life would I have thought I'd consider Flagstaff a place of refuge. And it wasn't, really. Connor's apartment, yes, but I realized that was because it was Connor's. I had him with me here. It was enough. I could do this.

"I know that," I replied. "Let's just go out tonight and clear our heads, and then tomorrow let's see if giving them all a night to think about it has helped any."

"Deal." He glanced up at the clock on the mantel. "Still too early to go?"

It was a little after five. "Close enough. We'll have to wait anyway, and if we get a table before Syd and Anthony get there, it's no big deal. They'll find us. The place isn't that big."

A nod, and then he put the book on one of the nightstands before heading out and down the stairs. I gathered up my purse; my overcoat was hanging in the closet downstairs, so I'd fetch that on the way to the garage. Connor had left his draped over one of the dining room chairs; I assumed he was on his way to get it. Maybe it wasn't as cold here as in Flagstaff, but I could tell it was going to get below freezing tonight.

No matter. We'd be inside someplace warm with friends, and that was all I needed.

———

As predicted, there was already a sizable crowd at Bocce, but Connor and I managed to squeeze in at the bar and order a glass of wine while we waited.

"I had no idea Cottonwood had this kind of night-life," he said, gazing around at the packed restaurant in some amusement.

"'Cause we're just a bunch of hicks, right?"

He gave me a pained look. "That's not what I meant."

I sipped some of my malbec before replying. "No, I was just teasing. Bocce's gotten written up in some pretty big magazines and newspapers, so a lot of people on vacation make a special effort to come here. Kind of sucks for us locals, but what do you do?"

"Go somewhere else?"

"You'll retract that statement once you've had their mushroom pizza."

Green eyes danced at me. I noticed one of the waitresses giving Connor the side-eye as she passed by us, and I refrained from scowling or throwing a random hex in her direction...not that I really knew how to do anything like that. The ogling was something I'd probably have to get used to. After all, he was so very stare-able.

Connor's name got called then, so we squeezed through the crowd to the hostess station, then followed the girl on duty to a cozy table off in one corner. It was better than I'd hoped for, considering how crowded the place was. At least here we'd be able to talk without having to shout at one another.

The two of us settled in on one side of the booth, and I could feel Connor run his hand along my thigh before he reached up to put his napkin in his lap. Heat surged in me, pooling somewhere between my legs, and I gave him a mock-frown.

"It's not fair, getting me all hot and bothered when we're out in public like this."

"Just making sure you'll still be up for it when the time comes."

"Oh, I'll be up for it...as long as you are."

He shot a dazzling smile at me, then bent close to my ear and whispered, "Angela, I'm *already* up for it."

The heat in my core threatened to rage hotter than the wood-fired ovens in the kitchens just a few yards away. "Now you're playing dirty."

"Always."

I heard my name called then, and looked away from Connor to see Sydney and Anthony weaving their way through the tables to our booth. Although of course they'd both met Connor before, if briefly, that wasn't stopping Sydney from giving him a fast appraisal before she mouthed *oh, my God* at me. Good thing she was facing away from Anthony so he couldn't see what she'd just done.

As they got to the table, Connor stood up and extended a hand. "Hi—we sort of met at the Halloween dance, but I don't think we actually introduced ourselves. I'm Connor Wilcox."

He said it casually, as if it really wasn't a big deal, but of course it was. Cottonwood was still McAllister territory. I scanned the restaurant briefly to see if any clan members were there, but I hadn't noticed any on the way in, nor when I gave the place a second look now.

But Anthony certainly didn't know anything about that. He shook Connor's hand briefly. "Anthony Rocha. It's nice to meet you."

"And I'm Sydney, but you already knew that." She spied the two half-empty wine glasses on the table and said, "Looks like you guys got a head start. We'll have to play catch-up."

"That's my Syd, all business," I said, and she plopped down in her chair, grinning.

"Hey, if you'd had to deal with the people I did today, you'd need a drink, too."

Somehow I doubted that managing cranky after-Christmas shoppers was quite as bad as facing down the three strongest witches in the McAllister clan, or seeing the disappointment—scratch that, *dismay*—on my aunt's face when she realized who had been standing behind me in the foyer of my home. Again, though, it wasn't something I could really discuss in front of Anthony. I'd have to wait until Sydney and I had a chance to talk in private.

"Do you want me to shoot up a flare to get the waitress over here?" I asked.

She shot me an irritated look, but luckily a flare or other signal wasn't necessary, as the waitress came over soon afterward. We decided to get a bottle of the malbec—"for starters," Sydney put in—and then ordered some caprese to get the meal going.

We sort of lapsed into silence after that, the guys shooting furtive looks at one another, as if they weren't sure if they should be the ones to get things started. After a few seconds, though, Sydney seemed to spy the lay of the land, because she said, "So, wow. I was not expecting to see you two down here. I thought Anthony and I were going to come up to Flagstaff."

"Change of plans," I said.

"I wanted to see Jerome in daylight," Connor said easily, as if the whole thing had been his idea. "I didn't get to see much when I came for the dance. And since we'd already spent a few days in Flagstaff…."

"We decided to come here," I finished for him. "But we're not going to stay in Jerome for more than a few days, probably, so it's not like you won't have your chance to come to Flagstaff."

"You get a lot of snow up there with this last storm?" Anthony asked.

"A good bit," Connor responded. "But I don't think it's going to last long. They're predicting warmer weather over the weekend."

The comments about the weather seemed to break the ice, and the guys started talking about cross-country skiing and the hiking trails up and around Flagstaff, while Sydney kept darting her gaze between Connor and me as if she wasn't quite sure she believed the evidence of her eyes. I couldn't really fault her for that; it seemed slightly surreal to have him next to me, his warm jean-clad thigh pressed against mine, to hear his warm baritone as he and Anthony kept chatting. What Sydney had told Anthony, I had no idea, but he seemed to be taking the sudden development of a relationship between Connor and me in stride. Thank the Goddess that they hadn't actually exchanged introductions at the dance, or Anthony would probably be trying to figure out the reason behind Connor's name change.

The appetizers came, and we ordered a couple of pizzas and another bottle of wine, since we were already a good bit into the first one. Then Connor said, "Do you two have any big plans for New Year's?"

Sydney and Anthony exchanged a glance. "Well, we've been invited to a couple of parties," Sydney replied. Her blue eyes took on a glint I knew all too well. "Why, do you have something better in mind?"

The corner of Connor's mouth twitched a little. "I don't know about better, but up in Flag they do this pinecone drop at midnight, and it's basically a street party—all the bars are open, of course, and there's a lot of live music."

"A pinecone drop?" Sydney repeated.

"Sort of our version of Times Square," Connor replied.

It was the first I'd heard of it, but then, I'd never bothered researching Flagstaff's various events and nightlife, since I hadn't exactly thought I'd ever get a chance to participate in any of them. "That sounds like fun," I said.

"It does," Anthony put in, "but the drive back could be tough, depending on the weather."

"Then stay up in town."

"Ooh, that would be fun. A hotel on New Year's Eve instead of just going back to your apartment,"

Sydney said. Then her expression fell somewhat. "They're probably all booked up, though, right? At least anyplace worth staying?"

I'd thought of that, too, but Connor shook his head. "It's pretty busy, but I know the people who run the Weatherford Hotel, where the event takes place. I'm sure I can get something lined up for you, if you want to come."

"That would be fab!" Sydney turned to Anthony. "Wouldn't it?"

"It sounds great," he agreed. "But I don't want you to put yourself out or anything, getting a room together for us—"

"It's no problem. Really." Connor shifted in his seat so he could look down at me. His gaze was questioning, as if he wanted to know if it sounded okay to me, if I was all right with not being in Jerome on New Year's.

Considering the frosty reception we'd gotten so far, I was fairly certain that Connor and I wouldn't be partying with the McAllisters anytime soon. The pinecone drop sounded like fun—and it also sounded like the sort of thing the Wilcoxes would stay far, far away from. I couldn't imagine them rubbing elbows with a bunch of civilian hoi polloi on the streets of Flagstaff. No, it could be simply a fun evening out for the four of us, with no one having to worry about driving home.

"It does sound perfect," I said, and I felt rather than saw Connor relax at my words.

Sydney grinned. "Great! Then we're doing it—if you can get the hotel room sitch worked out."

"I'll make a few calls. It'll be fine."

I had to wonder if he was going to call in a few Wilcox favors to have someone hexed into stomach flu or what-have-you to make sure a room was available. Did I want to know? Probably not, but I was going to ask anyway, once Connor and I were back at the house.

Then the pizza came, and we ate and chatted some more about the various bars and clubs in downtown Flagstaff, and which ones were the best. Or rather, Connor and Sydney and Anthony participated in that particular conversation, since I didn't have much to contribute on the topic yet.

After we were done eating, it was still not that late, so, rather than ending the evening, we headed for a bar on the opposite end of the old town section of Cottonwood. It was more or less packed, too, especially since the cold weather prevented people from using the patio outside, but we grabbed a booth as another group was leaving, and put in our order while the table was being bussed.

Even as crowded as the place was, we were able to manage the noise level a little better. I'd mentioned to Connor that Anthony worked at the Fire

Mountain wine-tasting room, and so he asked about that. Anthony, who was fairly quiet—especially compared to Sydney—really opened up on the subject, talking about how he was taking the viticulture course at Yavapai College and wanted to work at a winery one day as a winemaker, and maybe someday in the future have his own vineyards.

As he talked, his dark eyes glowed, and Sydney seemed to glow, watching him. I could already tell Anthony was different from all the other guys she'd dated, partly because they'd made it past the two-month mark and seemed to still be going strong, but it was more than that. Some of her past boyfriends I'd liked and some I hadn't, but none of them had had Anthony's drive, his passion for something beyond watching sports or playing video games or even working on their cars. And I had to shake my head at Sydney's father for not liking Anthony just because he wasn't some white-bread kid who went to high school with us, or whatever.

Stupid prejudices. I allowed myself a quick glance up at Connor's fine profile, dimly highlighted by the frosted glass fixtures overhead. He was amazing in so many ways, and yet my family couldn't seem to see past him being a Wilcox. Maybe in time they'd come around, but it frustrated me that I had to tell myself to be patient. What was so hard about seeing someone for who they were, and not where they had come from?

I was still brooding on the subject after we'd said our goodbyes and gotten in our respective vehicles. Sydney and I had finished most of the second bottle of wine, since the guys were driving. I wouldn't say I was exactly tipsy, but I wasn't as steady on my feet as I could be as Connor helped me up into the Cruiser and then went around and slid into the driver's seat.

We were heading back down Main Street when he said, "You're very quiet."

"Am I?" I watched the shops and restaurants passing by outside the window. "Just thinking about Anthony and Sydney. Her dad doesn't like Anthony because he's Native American. How stupid is that?"

"Pretty stupid." He slowed to let someone cross Main Street from the public parking lot to Bocce, which had a line out the door, even though the thermometer on the FJ's dashboard indicated that temperatures were already down into the upper 30s. "Do I keep going on this street?"

"Yes, until you get to Clarkdale Parkway. Then turn left." I readjusted the seatbelt, which suddenly felt too tight, too constricting. "Just about as stupid as everyone in my family looking at you like you're a leper or something just because your last name is Wilcox."

"Well…"

"Well what?"

Since he was concentrating on the unfamiliar road, he couldn't turn to look at me, but I caught a quick sidelong glance before he focused ahead once again. "It's not as if the Wilcoxes are exactly blameless. I've tried to lead as good a life as I can, but it hasn't always been easy. So your family's reaction is...." He trailed off, drumming his fingers on the steering wheel, as if he wasn't sure of the right word.

"What?" I demanded. "Justified? Okay, I could kind of see them feeling that way if I'd showed up with Damon in my pocket. They have every reason to dislike and distrust him. But you haven't done anything wrong!"

"You know that, and I know that, but they don't. Angela, you've had time to get to know me—"

"—intimately," I put in.

He did crack a smile at that. "Yes, intimately. We've gotten to know each other, learn things about one another. You know I only went along with Damon's whacked-out plan because it would bring you to me. You know I didn't go on that raid on your house. *You* know all these things, but they don't. So I'm not sure you should be judging them as harshly as you are."

"Watch it," I said. "You keep up with that kind of talk, and I might have to nominate you for sainthood."

"I'm serious."

"So am I."

For a few seconds he didn't say anything. We'd come up to the turnoff for Clarkdale Parkway, so he made the left as I'd instructed and then slowed down a little, since we were coming into Clarkdale's tiny downtown area. "Anyway, if I were in their position, I'd probably be feeling the same way. That doesn't mean I'm going to enjoy walking around Jerome tomorrow and having people look at me like I've got horns and a tail, but at least I understand it."

I tried to wrap my wine-muddled brain around his words. On some level, I did get what he was saying. On the other hand, the stubborn part of me kept thinking, *But I'm the* prima. *The clan is supposed to accept my decisions, whatever they might be.*

Apparently there was a line, though, and in being with Connor, I had stepped right over it.

We didn't say much after that, except for me to give him a few terse directions on how to get back to the house. When we pulled up, I halfway expected to see "Wilcox go home" spray-painted on the garage door or something, but the place looked undisturbed. The ancient door was on my list of things to get replaced, but I hadn't done it yet, so I had to slip out in the freezing darkness and lift the heavy thing so Connor could pull into the garage.

After he parked, he got out and met me outside, then shut the door. Since the property was so old, the house and the garage were separate buildings, and I led him up the path through the small garden at the rear of the house to the back door.

Everything inside was as we had left it, of course. I was being foolish to think that my family would have done anything to disturb the place. They might be disappointed and angry with me, but they would never do anything to damage my house.

Well, to put it more accurately, the *prima*'s house.

I flicked on the kitchen light, then the lights in the hallway just outside, and went to the closet downstairs and took off my coat. Connor followed me and did the same. After he'd hung up his coat, he looked around the newly decorated interior and nodded, apparently in approval. On our earlier tour of the house, we'd moved quickly, and I hadn't allowed Connor much time to give me any feedback.

"You've done a really good job with this place," he said. "Updated, but still respecting the lines and the character of the house."

His approval sent a flush to my cheeks. "Oh, well, I hired a decorator," I said deprecatingly.

"You hired a good one. And you still had to approve her selections, didn't you? It's not as if you just let her do anything she wanted."

"And how do you know that?"

"Because it still feels like you." He came to me then and took me in his arms, bent down to brush his lips against mine.

That kiss felt so good, warm, strong, tasting sweet and dark from the last glass of wine he'd drunk. I waited until he pulled away, then said, "I guess that's why I like your apartment so much. Because it feels like *you*."

"I know something else I want to feel," he murmured, his hands running up under my jacket, smoothing over the curve of my hips and up to my waist, then higher….

"Hmm," I replied, even as the heat flared in me again. It hadn't even been twenty-four hours, and I wanted him, wanted him like nothing else in my life. I reached up and ran my fingers over the bulge straining against his jeans. "Me, too."

In response, he bent and gathered me in his arms, lifting me as if I weighed nothing at all. I let out a little squeak of surprise and then giggled, burying my face in his neck, feeling him carry me up the stairs, take me to my room, and lay me on the bed. For a second he stepped away, but only to point at the wood piled up in the fireplace, setting it alight. The seasoned oak blazed up at once, banishing the chill of a cold December night.

"I like that," I said, bending down to unzip my boots and pull them off.

"So do I." He came back toward the bed and kicked off his own shoes, not bothering to unlace them. "I may even forgive you the claw-foot tub because of that fireplace."

"I'm glad my house has some redeeming qualities."

"Some," he agreed, bending down to undo my belt, and then the button and zipper of my jeans below it.

When I'd changed, I'd also put on some of the underwear from my stash here at the house, a satiny red pair of panties with black lace trim and a matching bra. Connor's eyes widened when he saw I wasn't wearing the practical but oh-so-boring cotton bikinis of the past few days. A little growl escaped his throat.

"I like that."

"There's more," I said, pushing up my T-shirt so he could see the bra underneath.

His green eyes warmed and seemed to darken. "I think there's only one thing better than seeing you in that."

"What's that?"

"Seeing you without it."

He reached out and grasped my T-shirt and pulled it off, then found the front clasp of the bra and unlatched it, warm, strong hands descending to cup my breasts. The need was building in me now, strong and insistent, and I let out a sigh as he lifted his hands from my chest just long enough to tug the underwear down and toss it to one side. Then his fingers were there, touching me, stroking me, and I let myself surrender to him, to his touch…to everything about him.

Somewhere deep inside I'd worried a little about making love with him here in Great-Aunt Ruby's old room, but her spirit was long gone, and, as Connor had said, I'd made the place mine. It felt right now, to pull him down onto the bed next to me, to touch him, feel his strength and heat, have him inside me, filling me again as I sank down on top of him, watching the heavy lashes brush against his cheeks as he closed his eyes in ecstasy.

And it felt even more right to have him hold me afterward, to lie in the strength of his encircling arms and know that he loved me, loved me enough to come to the heart of his enemies' territory, to risk my family's retaliation, just to show that when it came to the two of us, it was just as Sydney had said.

We weren't Wilcox and McAllister, but only Connor and Angela.

And that was as it should be.

CHAPTER ELEVEN

Cold Shoulders

WE DOZED OFF, THEN GROGGILY GOT UP ABOUT AN HOUR later and went in to brush our teeth, taking turns because the antiquated bathroom only had a small vanity with one sink. Then we fell asleep for real, snuggled up against each other, letting the dying fire lend its own warmth to the room. My wistful fantasies had come true; I finally did have Connor lying here next to me in the big king-size bed.

The next morning I was awoken by a metallic buzzing sound. Connor's phone. He'd left it on the nightstand, and apparently it was set to vibrate.

I reached out and picked it up without looking at the screen, and dropped it on his chest. "For you."

"Wha—oh." He sat up, grabbing the phone before it fell down in the depths of the rumpled bedclothes. "What time is it?"

"A little past eight," I replied after a quick glance at the clock on the mantel.

A sound of disapproval escaped his throat, although I thought it was directed more at whoever was contacting him so early in the morning. He brushed his finger across the screen to unlock it, then scowled.

"That good, huh?"

In response, he angled the phone so I could read the text displayed there. Just four words, in all caps.

ARE YOU FUCKING INSANE?

"I guess Damon finally figured out where you were," I commented. It was a lot easier to be blithe about one of Damon's rages when he was safely miles and miles away. "I thought you said he doesn't like using phones."

"He doesn't. But since this is pretty much the only way he can get hold of me right now…." A little light began dancing in his eyes as he started tapping in a reply.

I craned my head to see what he was writing, but the angle was wrong, and all I caught was a glare off the screen.

When he was done, Connor helpfully turned the phone so I could see what he had just typed in. *Crazy, yeah…crazy in love. Talk l8er.*

The "crazy in love" line sent a warm shiver down my spine. Even so, I grinned and asked, "So which part of that message is he going to hate more…the 'in love' part or the text-speak?"

An answering smile lit up Connor's face. "Hard to say. But I figured I'd throw both in, just to really piss him off."

I leaned over and kissed him. "Do you know how much I love you?"

"I have a vague idea, yeah."

"So what are you going to do about Damon?"

"Nothing."

Shooting him a dubious look, I said, "Nothing?"

His shoulders lifted, and I let myself admire the shift of the muscles under his smooth, warm-toned skin. "Well, it's not as if he's going to come down here and get into it with me. So he can stew in his juices until we get back to Flagstaff."

"And what then?"

"We'll deal with it then. But I'm thinking it's about time I told him to back off and butt out." He leaned across me and dropped his iPhone back on the nightstand.

This display of bravado surprised me. No, I didn't exactly think Connor was under Damon's thumb completely, but their previous interactions had seemed to indicate that Connor usually let his older brother get his way. Where this new confidence had come from, I wasn't entirely sure. I didn't want to take all the credit myself, but….

Mary Mullen had told me Connor was lost. At the time I'd wondered at her remark, but didn't have much opportunity to pursue it. Maybe it was simply that he'd lost his way, allowed his brother to control his life because he didn't have many other options. It was possible that being with me now had given him the chance he so desperately needed to separate himself from his brother's whims and ambitions, to make his own future.

I hoped so. He'd been through enough already. It was time for him to shine.

But first things first. I leaned over and gave him a kiss...on the cheek, because I could tell from the set of his jaw and the glint in his eyes that he was not in the mood for anything else. "Do you want to shower first, or should I? Because I know if we both try to get in that claw-foot tub at the same time, we're just asking for trouble."

———

He let me shower first, and then went in the bathroom when I was done. I didn't know if Damon had replied while I was out of the room, and I got the feeling I really shouldn't ask. So I didn't.

Instead, while Connor was showering I went downstairs and went to take stock of the refrigerator to see what I could make for breakfast. There was an untouched carton of eggs, and an unopened

package of applewood-smoked bacon. I recalled that
I'd planned to make Adam a big breakfast the day
after—well, the day after we were going to spend a
night together. A night that never happened, thanks
to Damon Wilcox.

I couldn't even be angry about that. Not anymore. Not when his little plot had brought me to
Connor.

But then I thought, *Adam*, and shook my head.
I really, really hoped that he wasn't around, that I
wouldn't have to see him. Cowardly, I know, but I
also knew that him seeing me with Connor would
only hurt him, and I didn't want that. I wanted some
time to pass so he could get a little distance, move
on, maybe—I hoped—meet somebody else, and
realize he shouldn't have to settle for someone who
didn't really love him, not in the way he deserved.

Shaking that off for now, I realized that everything I'd bought was still fresh enough to use. After
all, it hadn't even been a week yet. Or rather, I'd
bought these items exactly a week ago, just the day
before I'd been taken from this very house and my
entire life had changed.

For the better, although I certainly hadn't
looked at the situation in that way at the time. Now,
though....

I glanced upward, more or less in the direction
of the bathroom. In the background, I could hear

the faint metallic sound of water running through the pipes. If I even turned on the tap right now to start some coffee, I knew I'd hear Connor yelling a few seconds later, since the antiquated water heater couldn't handle the load. So much I'd planned to do here, so much that still needed to be done. Would it happen? I had no idea. I didn't know where Connor and I were going to end up permanently. It seemed unthinkable that I would abandon my clan, leave Jerome, but I didn't know if I was strong enough to live with their censure day in and day out.

Well, worry about that later, I told myself. *Baby steps. Like getting breakfast together first.*

That seemed logical enough. *Never make big decisions on an empty stomach,* my aunt had told me once, and although she apparently wasn't speaking to me right now, that didn't mean her advice wasn't sound.

The water turned off upstairs, which meant I could make myself some much-needed coffee. I slipped a hazelnut cream pod into the Keurig and then pulled out the ingredients to make a batch of biscuits. Mixing and sifting the flour and baking powder helped to take my mind off my problems, and so did the smell of bacon once I got that going. Nothing like bacon to take your mind off your woes.

Being male, Connor was drawn to the smell of that bacon like a moth to a flame. He came into the room a few minutes after the scent began to drift out of the kitchen and through the house. His nose twitched appreciatively.

"Bacon? Seriously? I was sure we would have to go out and then get glared at by every McAllister within a fifty-foot radius." His hair was still damp; obviously he'd just blotted it and hadn't bothered with much else. He was fully dressed, but I noticed he'd wandered down in his socks, leaving his shoes upstairs.

"I wouldn't subject you to that. Coffee? I know it's not your French press, but I've got some flavors that aren't too frilly. Italian roast, maybe?"

His gaze flickered toward the coffeemaker, and for a second I thought he might make a crack about pre-fab coffee. But then he nodded. "Sounds good."

I went and got it started for him, and went back over to the stove so I could flip the bacon. "I forgot to ask last night—you're not going to be sticking pins in voodoo dolls or something to make sure you can get a room at the Weatherford for Anthony and Sydney, are you?"

A grin. "Wow, you still have such a low opinion of me, don't you?"

"No, but…." Damn, had I offended him?

"It's okay," he said, relenting. "No voodoo dolls. But a Wilcox cousin owns the place, and he generally leaves a room vacant in case anyone in the family needs it for business or something."

That sounded fairly innocuous. "Okay." I hesitated, then asked, "How much of Flagstaff does your family control…really?"

The Keurig beeped, and Connor went over and poured his coffee into the mug I'd already set out for him. He settled down on one of the rickety chairs at the kitchen table before replying, "Not as much as you probably think, but…we've been there for more than a hundred years. Of course we own a lot of real estate in and around town, same as you McAllisters do here in Jerome."

Logical enough, I guessed. It was time to get the eggs started, so I decided to let it go for now. "How do you like them? Scrambled? Over easy?"

"Scrambled."

A boy after my own heart. Runny eggs were one of my irrational dislikes. I cracked half a dozen into a bowl, put in some milk, and beat them to a froth before pouring them into a skillet I'd had preheating.

"I could get used to this," he went on, watching me as I worked.

"To what? Me in the kitchen? I guess next it would be barefoot and pregnant, right?"

His expression went dark. "No, probably not that."

Shit. We'd danced around the issue, left it alone, hadn't addressed it after I'd assured him that the little charm I mentally uttered every time we had sex

would be enough to protect me. And it would—or
so I'd been told. Even so, I could still hear Margot
Emory's words echoing in the back of my mind.

*The wives of Jeremiah's line would never live to see
their children grow up.*

"Sorry," I began, but he shook his head.

"No, we should have talked about it before this.
It's out there, waiting. And I don't know what to do
about it."

"We'll figure it out," I said, trying to sound
reassuring, but I didn't believe my own words. The
Wilcox curse had been claiming its victims for the
last hundred and thirty years or so—who was I to
think that Connor and I could possibly come up with
some way of circumventing it?

"Damon hasn't had much luck with that,"
Connor remarked bitterly, and sipped his coffee.

"I know, but…." A sudden thought occurred to
me. "When I was told of the curse, the words were
'the wives of Jeremiah's line.' So what if we just stay,
I don't know, shacked up together and never make it
official?"

"You think that wasn't tried?"

"Was it?"

"Oh, yeah." He drank some more coffee, while
I hurried back to the stove and flipped the bacon,
then started pushing the eggs around in the skillet
so they wouldn't get too brown. "Jeremiah's son,

Jacob, he had a child with one of his cousins out of wedlock. She went insane and threw herself out of a second-story window."

Although the kitchen was warm, it felt like someone had just dragged an icicle down my back.

"And that son, Jonah, he thought maybe it was just a coincidence, and convinced his childhood sweetheart—a third cousin—that she should also be with him without the benefit of matrimony. She was knocked down by a runaway horse and killed a week after she moved in. So Jonah got himself a nice biddable second cousin, had a son with her—and then she died of scarlet fever a few months later."

"Stop it," I said. I wanted to put my hands over my ears, but I was busy with the food—and Aunt Rachel had trained me so well that I didn't even think about not tending to it.

"I wish I could," Connor said, eyes glittering. "But you need to know the truth. I love you, and it kills me that something terrible could happen to you. If we don't ever have a child, maybe—*maybe* you'll be safe."

I didn't want to think about that. While I certainly wasn't eager to have a baby anytime in the near future, I'd always thought one day I would have a family. It's just what the *prima* did—married her consort and had children and lived out her days as the matriarch of the clan. Acknowledging that such a future might not be viable for me was not something I wanted to face.

"Well, maybe it's just the whole *primus* thing," I said. "What about the children of the men who were of Jeremiah's line but were the younger brothers?"

"I don't know," Connor admitted, and his dark brows pulled together in a frown. "After Jeremiah—he did have family who came with him, three brothers and a sister, and their children—all of the *primuses* were only children. Until now...until me."

"Really?" I asked, startled. I had to turn away from him then, since, as with most meals, everything was ready at once, and I had to get the eggs dished up and the bacon draining and the biscuits out of the oven before they went from golden brown to just plain brown. Once everything was ready, and I'd taken the food over to the kitchen table, I went on, "So what does that mean?"

He shrugged. "No one knows for sure. I told you everyone thought it was strange that my mother lasted so long after Damon was born. They thought she'd be gone within the year, just like all the other *primus* wives had. But she seemed to be all right, and time went on, and then...then there was me. The miracle baby."

This last was said in such dry tones that I knew he thought the exact opposite, that he wasn't such a miracle after all. I would beg to differ, but I wasn't about to get into that argument right now.

"Well, then," I said, "maybe the curse doesn't apply to you. After all, you're of Jeremiah's line, but you're not the *primus*. It could be okay."

"Do you want to risk it?"

The question hung, heavy in the air. I swallowed. "Not right away. No, of course not. But I think it means there might be some hope."

"Hope." He was quiet for a moment, considering. "That would be nice. But my family history doesn't have too much hope in it."

No, I thought, *not much hope at all. Suicide and madness and untimely death. Not a very good basis for family planning.*

I didn't say any of that, of course. Instead, I reached out and touched his hand, squeezing his fingers gently, so he'd know I wasn't about to give up, that I wanted to be with him, no matter what.

Even if it kills you? I wondered.

I refused to answer the question.

———

We ate in silence after that, neither one of us wanting to pursue the subject any further. Maybe it was better to let it go for now. After all, even though we shared the consort bond, knew this thing between us was serious and not some fling to be put aside in a few days or weeks or even months, we still had plenty of time. I had just turned twenty-two, after all, and I'd always wanted to wait until I was closer to thirty before I started a family. That was a lot of years to figure out how to stave off the Wilcox curse.

After we were done with breakfast, and Connor had washed the plates and silverware, and put them in the dish drain— he insisted on doing that, even though I said it was no big deal—I said, "Can I ask you another question?"

His expression told me that he really didn't want me to, but he replied, evenly enough, "Sure."

The image of the young woman with the honey-blonde hair, the one I'd seen Damon put his arm around, flickered in my mind. "Why do the women in your clan even allow themselves to be with the *primus?* I mean, at the first hint that he might be interested, you'd think they'd head for the hills."

He finished wiping his hands on the dish towel and then hung it back from the hook where he'd found it. "Why do women in some off-shoot religions right here in America allow themselves to be married off to a man who already has five wives? Why did people drink the Kool-Aid at Jonestown? You can call it cultural conditioning or brainwashing or whatever you want—in my clan, it's considered an honor to be the wife of the *primus,* to bear his child, even though you won't be around to see that son grow up. And while you're in that position, even if it only lasts for six months or a year or two, you're the queen of the world."

"That's—sick," I replied, staring at him in disbelief. Something in the cold mask that had settled over his features as he gave his reply reminded me a little too much of his brother, and I shook my head to rid it of that image.

"You think so, and I think so, but…." He lifted his shoulders. "It's just the way it is."

I had to ask. "And your mother thought the same way?"

"I don't know. I was only three when she died, remember? We didn't exactly have a lot of mother-son heart-to-heart talks. And if she ever said anything to Damon, he never shared it with me."

No, he probably wouldn't. I could tell from the tight set of Connor's mouth and the shuttered look in his eyes that he really didn't want to discuss the topic any further. Fine, I'd let it go for now. I'd heard enough, actually—enough to be very glad that we McAllisters had a way for me to sidestep the curse for now. No baby, no untimely death. Simple math.

"Okay," I said. "You want to get out of here for a while? It looks like it's shaping up to be a nice day."

———

It was, too. When we left the house about ten minutes later, Connor still looking grim and preoccupied, I was glad of the bright sun overhead, the deep clear blue of the sky, the white puffs of clouds that moved with winds aloft, sending racing shadows over the hillsides. He didn't exactly smile, but as we walked, with the crisp, cold breeze pulling at our hair and the scarves wound around our necks, I could see the set of his shoulders begin to relax a little, even though he was walking through what was, for him, enemy territory.

Since it was the Friday of a holiday week, and so many people had the days between Christmas and New Year's off, Jerome was packed with tourists. I used to hate days like this, since everywhere I went was overrun, but now I was glad of the crowds, glad of the protective coloration they provided. They made it so much easier for Connor and me to blend in with them. I couldn't know for sure that members of my clan weren't watching us, but I didn't see anyone, and I took care to guide Connor toward the shops owned by civilians, and not McAllisters.

I began to relax. Big mistake.

The two of us were just leaving a shop that specialized in rocks and minerals and various Arizona-themed tchotkes when I heard Adam's voice.

"So it is true."

Connor and I halted, and then we both seemed to realize at the same time that we were blocking the doorway. Although I wished I could run back in the shop and hide in the storeroom, I knew that wasn't a very practical option. So we moved outside and paused a few steps away from the door, in front of one of the shop windows.

"Hi, Adam," I said, trying to sound casual and probably failing utterly. Beside me, Connor had gone tense, but he was silent, waiting for me to take the lead here. I didn't like it, but it made sense. This wasn't his fight.

I could tell Adam wanted to make it his, though. Scowling, he glanced from me to Connor, where his angry blue-gray stare lingered. "I didn't want to believe it," he said. "I *couldn't* believe that you'd actually stoop so low as to be with a *Wilcox.*"

Connor's jaw clenched at that, but he said nothing.

"Adam, he's my *consort,*" I replied.

"Right, like I'm supposed to believe that."

"Believe whatever you want. I know what the truth is."

That was definitely not what he wanted to hear. I could see the way his chest rose and fell under his sweatshirt, the way his cheekbones were flushed with anger. A family passed us, two kids in tow, and I could almost feel the woman's curious gaze settle on our tense little group. It was pretty clear that the three of us weren't exactly having a friendly conversation.

"Look," Connor put in, "this has been hard for everyone. We're just trying to figure it out as we go along, okay?"

"Hard?" Adam repeated. He looked like he wanted to push Connor over the nearest cliff—not that I thought he'd probably win any kind of physical contest between the two of them. Connor had about two inches on Adam, and was much more muscular.

As for a magical contest, well, I still didn't know the extent of Connor's talents, but unless Adam could use his weather magic to summon a storm cloud to throw a few lightning bolts Connor's way, I had a feeling he wouldn't prevail in a confrontation like that, either.

"You don't know what 'hard' is, Wilcox," Adam continued. "Hard is seeing the woman you love stolen out right from under you—only to find out she's gone over to the enemy side!"

"Whoa," I cut in. "I'm not on their side."

"Whose side are you on, then?"

"Mine." I reached out and took Connor's hand, wrapping my fingers around his gloved ones. "His. The rest of you—McAllisters and Wilcoxes and whoever else tries to interfere with that—can just fuck off. Let's go, Connor."

I pushed past Adam, and although I could tell he wanted to reach out and grab my arm, keep me from leaving, something in the warning glare I shot at him must have told him that he needed to back off, and now. Connor wisely kept silent, following me as I threaded my way through the crowds, marching back up the hill toward the house. Any desire I might have had to spend some time showing him around my hometown had been effectively killed by that encounter.

It wasn't until we were back inside the big Victorian at the top of the hill that Connor said anything. "You can't really blame him," he told me gently as I slammed the front door behind us.

"Yes, I can, and I am," I snapped, unwrapping the scarf from around my neck and unbuttoning my coat. "He wouldn't have acted that way if my consort had turned out to be Alex Trujillo or someone like that."

"Alex Trujillo, huh? Any reason you should mention him out of all the possible candidates you kissed?"

My face felt flushed, and it probably didn't have much to do with the cool and breezy air outside. "No, I'm just saying that if my consort had been one of the 'approved' candidates, then Adam wouldn't have had a problem with it."

"I'm not so sure about that." Connor took off his own scarf and coat, then hung them in the downstairs closet next to mine. "I don't know him, but it's pretty clear that Adam's in love with you. It can't be

easy to see the person you love with someone else—
even if that person isn't a big bad Wilcox. But since I
am, that makes it that much worse."

I didn't want to acknowledge the truth in his
words, but deep down, I knew he was right. Yes,
Adam would've dealt with it if I'd ended up with
Alex or someone else like him, but he wouldn't have
been happy. What he'd wanted was for me to never
meet my true consort, so I could end up with him
instead.

"Is it too early for a drink?" I inquired. "Because I
could really use one."

"Hey, it's always five o'clock somewhere,"
Connor replied lightly. "But I don't think that's really
going to solve your problem."

"I don't think anything is."

His eyes, watching me, were sympathetic. It
really had been stupid for me to come here, but I just
hadn't wanted to acknowledge how deep the preju-
dice against the Wilcoxes ran. For whatever reason,
it was more important to my family that my consort
was one of the enemy than I was one of them. That
I was their *prima*.

And that hurt worst of all, because the *prima* was
supposed to be everything—clan leader and touch-
stone, the person they looked up to, the one who
provided strength and protection and guidance. Or
that was how it had seemed to me when Great-Aunt

Ruby was the head of our clan. But she wasn't some untried and untested girl, and her consort had been someone universally liked and respected.

The hurt and betrayal must have been clear in my face, because suddenly I was in Connor's arms, and he was holding me close, my face against his chest so I could hear his strong, slow heartbeat and feel the slight scratch of his wool sweater against my cheek. There, encircled in that embrace, I knew I was safe and loved and wanted—the complete opposite of how my family had made me feel.

A knock came at the door, and I let out a sigh. "Let's ignore it."

"Are you sure? Maybe it's Adam, coming to apologize."

"I doubt that. He's just as stiff-necked and stubborn as I am."

Connor chuckled, and brushed a kiss against the top of my head. "Hey, it's your house. I'll ignore it if you want me to do."

The knock sounded again, louder this time. I waited, hoping whoever it was would go away. Then I heard Tobias's voice. "Angela? Are you home?"

Damn. Adam I could have ignored, because I was angry with him, and probably ditto for my aunt, because that wound was even more raw. But Tobias?

"I'd better go see what he wants," I said, and disentangled myself from Connor's arms.

He nodded, and followed me out to the foyer, then took a quick peek through one of the side windows. "Oh, great—it's the guy who looks like he could rip my arms and legs off."

"Shh. I told you he's a big teddy bear." Trying to adjust my expression so my recent angst wouldn't be too obvious, I opened the door.

Tobias gave me a diffident smile. "Hi, Angela. Are you busy?"

"No. I mean—we were just sort of hanging out. Come on in."

I stepped out of the way so he could enter, and I noticed Connor backing off a pace or two. Despite everything that was going on, I couldn't help smiling a little. Figuring I might as well get it over with, I said, "Tobias, this is Connor Wilcox. Connor, this is Tobias Mills. He's my aunt's—" I broke off and tilted my head to the side. "How do you two refer to yourselves, anyway?"

"'Very good friends' will do," he replied, dark eyes twinkling at me. "I'd say it was nice to meet you, Connor, but I have a feeling you wouldn't believe me."

Connor's eyebrows went up. "Well, I—"

"Never mind," Tobias cut in. "Angela, do you mind if we talk a little?" His gaze shifted to Connor and then back to me. "Alone?"

"No problem," Connor said at once. "I can go upstairs to the library. I left a book up there anyway. Nice to meet you, Tobias." He approached me, squeezed my hand, and gave me a quick kiss on the cheek. "It'll be fine," he whispered, and headed up the steps to the second floor.

I wasn't so sure about that, but I made myself turn to Tobias and said, "Let's go back to the family room. Can I get you a cup of coffee or anything?"

"No, I'm fine."

So much for that delaying tactic. I led him toward the rear of the house, toward the cozy space that was now the TV room and my preferred hangout, since the living room still felt a little too grand and formal, even after all the redecorating I'd done.

There were logs stacked in the fireplace, but I didn't bother to set them alight. I didn't want to make the room too comfortable. I only wanted Tobias to have his say and then leave so I could get the hell out of here. Maybe I was being a coward, and maybe I was crazy for thinking I'd be more welcome back in Flagstaff, but that was the way it sure felt.

"Just one thing, Tobias," I said, as he settled himself on the leather sofa. "I'm not in the mood for a lecture, so if that's why you've come here—"

"It isn't." The laugh lines around his eyes looked deeper than I remembered. He seemed tired, which wasn't normal for him. He was always hearty, energetic, up for anything. "So Connor Wilcox really is your consort."

"For the hundredth time, yes, and if you think it's something I planned—"

"He seems like a nice young man."

That comment stopped me in my tracks. "He—what?"

"He seems like a nice young man." Tobias scrubbed his hand over his goatee and paused, seeming to consider. "Never thought I'd say something like that, but it's true. And it's what I'll go back and tell Rachel, although I doubt she wants to hear it. You've shocked everyone with this, Angela, and it's going to take some time for them to come to terms with it. But I just wanted to let you know that they'll come around eventually."

"And how do you know this?" Tobias wasn't an elder, so I didn't see how he could be so sure.

"Because I know them. The McAllisters need their *prima*. They're not going to cast her out simply because her consort is none of their choosing. They'll all come to acceptance in their own way. Why, Rachel—"

"Yes, what about Rachel?" I demanded. "Because yesterday she was looking at me like something she wanted to scrape off her shoe."

"She's sorry about that, Angela. She said as much to me. She said she was shocked and scared and didn't know what to think. She's already regretting how she behaved toward you."

"So why couldn't she come and tell me that herself?"

He gave me a calm, level look. "Now, Angela, you know your aunt isn't very good at apologies."

That was true. It took a lot to get her to lose her temper, but when she did, it was well and truly lost...and afterward she generally wanted to act as if the explosion had never happened. "Does she know you're here?"

"No, and she'll probably kick my ass when she finds out. But that's not important. What's important is that you just give us a little time. Everything will work out in the end."

I wanted to believe that. I really did. But my relatives weren't the only ones who needed some space. "I'll give you as much time as you need," I replied, "because I'm going back to Flagstaff."

A frown, one he quickly erased. "Do you really think you'll be safe there?"

"I'm safe with Connor."

"That isn't what I asked."

"What do you want me to say, Tobias?" I crossed my arms and met his worried gaze. "I'm not going to deny that Damon Wilcox is a slippery bastard, and I don't trust him at all and never will, but I also know he won't do anything to me. I've bonded to his brother, and there's nothing he can do about that. And staying here…." The words disappeared somewhere between Tobias and myself, erasing themselves before I could finish the thought. "It's not going to work. Not right now, anyway. You tell Aunt Rachel what you need to tell her, and the whole clan, if you want. I'm not going away forever. But it hurts to be here right now, hurts to have people looking at me like I'm some kind of leper. So, as you said, let time heal things for a bit. If you need me, you know where to find me."

He cleared his throat. "Well, actually, I don't."

"Then call. I have my phone now. But I want—I just want to be with Connor for a while."

My words didn't seem to have reassured him very much, but he gave a reluctant nod. "All right. You're the *prima,* and you'll do what you feel is necessary. But don't—don't be away so long that you forget who you are."

 He left after that, murmuring a quiet goodbye, and I saw him to the door, then shut it behind him.

Forget who I was? How could I do that, when every resentful glance told me that a McAllister *prima* shouldn't have betrayed her clan the way I had?

Taking a breath, I went upstairs to tell Connor I wanted to head back to Flagstaff.

CHAPTER TWELVE

Resolutions

CLOUDS HAD BEGUN TO GATHER WHILE WE DROVE NORTH, AND as we pulled into the parking space behind Connor's building, a few fat white flakes started to fall. Good. I loved being in his apartment with the fire going and the weather closing in outside. It could be just the two of us in our own little bubble of warmth and solitude.

Nice illusion. It wasn't really true, though.

We'd been in the place maybe ten minutes before a harsh knocking came at the door. I'd heard that pounding before.

I looked over at Connor. He was standing by the fireplace, ready to set it alight, while I'd just come down from returning some things to the upstairs bathroom.

"I suppose it's no good to ignore him, is it?" I asked. "I mean, he'll just blast the door open."

"Probably," he agreed. His expression showed more resignation than anything else. "I'll get it, though."

No arguments here. I nodded and stepped out of the way, back toward the living room, as Connor opened the door.

"Hey, Damon," he said, as Damon brushed past him and stood glowering in the tiny entryway.

"'Hey, Damon' my ass," was his reply as he scowled first at Connor, then at me.

In that moment, I was very glad I'd removed myself to a safe distance. Although I didn't think Damon would really do anything to either one of us, he was still pretty fearsome when he was in a mood—which seemed to be most of the time.

He continued, "What, did you think I wouldn't notice your little jaunt to Jerome?"

"No," Connor replied wearily. "I figured you'd be spying on us one way or another. But we're back now, so what difference does it make?"

"Yes, you're back." That black-eyed stare transferred itself to me. "Back fairly quickly, too, I might add. What, did you not get the open-armed welcome you were expecting?"

Although I willed myself not to react, I must have flinched.

A cruel smile touched his mouth. "Ah, so they did reject you and your consort. What did you expect?"

I found my voice. "I didn't expect anything," I lied. "I only wanted them to know I was okay. Now they know, so I didn't see the point hanging around when there was so much more here in Flagstaff that I wanted to have Connor to show me."

That sounded plausible, although I wasn't sure Damon would buy it. But Connor added, "Yeah, I want to take her up to the Snow Bowl, and maybe out to Winslow to the Turquoise Room. And some of her friends are coming up here for New Year's. She's been cooped up in Jerome for most of her life, so it makes more sense for us to be here."

Throughout this little speech, Damon listened with one eyebrow cocked in an expression eerily similar to one I'd seen on his brother's face several times. When Connor was finished, Damon said, "You don't really expect me to believe that, do you?"

Connor shrugged. "It's the truth. I was just about to call Joseph to get Angela's friends set up at the Weatherford. Do you want to wait and listen while I do that?"

"Don't be ridiculous." He shifted his attention from Connor to me. "You might as well admit that your clan has rejected you. Your place is here now, with us. It's time for you to really join your powers to the Wilcox clan."

This was what I'd been fearing all along, that sooner or later Damon would try to force the issue.

After all, it was one of the main reasons he'd wanted to take me for his own. Yes, as a possible way of breaking the curse, but having the strength of a *prima* in addition to a *primus* would make the Wilcoxes stronger than any clan in the region.

Since I knew I was valuable to him, even as his brother's consort and not his own, I realized he couldn't do anything to hurt me. That realization gave me the courage to reply, "My powers are my own, Damon. I'll use them as I see fit, and not just because you think they're your due because I've bonded to a Wilcox."

His mouth thinned to a tight line. Then he seemed to force in a breath. "That's…very shortsighted of you."

"Is it?" I turned away from him, went to the fire. Just a touch, just a little push from those newly kindled powers of mine, and the logs blazed up and began to crackle. "You know, Damon, you should really stop trying to rule the world. You're going to give yourself a heart attack."

Connor didn't gasp—he was too in control of himself to do that—but somehow the room felt as if it had lost some of its oxygen. Damon's face darkened with fury.

"You're very sure of yourself, aren't you?" he said. "I'm afraid your confidence may be misplaced."

Without bothering to say another word, he stalked to the door and went out, slamming it behind him.

For a moment neither Connor nor I said anything. Then I remarked, "You know, he really needs to take some anger-management classes. He slams doors more than anyone I've ever seen. Good thing you don't have anyone living below you, or they'd probably be calling the cops."

"Angela—" Connor began, his tone a warning. Then he stopped himself. "He's really not someone you want pissed off at you."

"Maybe not, but since he seems perpetually pissed off, I can't take all the credit."

Instead of answering, Conor crossed the room and pulled me into his arms, held me close. I was fine with that; this was exactly where I'd wanted to be, here in front of the fire, with my consort as the snow fell outside. Everything else could wait.

———

It turned out that he really had meant what he'd told Damon—Connor took me up to the Snow Bowl, the recreation area outside Flagstaff, where we tromped around in the snow, got caught in the crossfire of a massive snowball fight between several groups of kids who looked to be in fifth or sixth grade, and slid around in saucers until we were exhausted and laughing and wet. He tried to convince me to try skiing, but as I wasn't really in the mood to break any bones, I demurred.

And another day we roamed around downtown Flagstaff, eating and drinking at his favorite places, window shopping and doing some real shopping, too, since my wardrobe was in serious need of a boost. We did drive out to Winslow, which didn't have too much going on, except a fabulous meal at the Turquoise Room in the historic hotel there. Then it was back to Flagstaff, with a promised return trip to see the Meteor Crater sometime after New Year's.

It was fun playing tourist for once, rather than being the person who had to wait on tourists all the time. Certainly there was a lot more to do and see than I'd expected. I did notice that Connor didn't seem to make any contact with members of his family, and wondered if he was trying to keep me away from them. Certainly Damon appeared to have decamped for the time being, and I would be lying if I didn't say I was relieved.

Still, I couldn't help wondering in the back of my mind whether he really had given up on me, or whether he was just off concocting some new plot, maybe one involving the "alternative magic" he'd mentioned to Connor. About all I could do was hope that he'd abandon any plans he might be formulating once he didn't have so much time on his hands;

classes started back up at Northern Pines in less than a week.

I hadn't seen anything of Mary Mullen since we'd gotten back, but that didn't necessarily mean anything. One thing I'd learned from dealing with Maisie—and the other ghosts in Jerome—was that they came and went according to their own timetables. Unless I called to them specifically, many times weeks and sometimes months would go by without hearing from them. Time just wasn't the same for a ghost as it was for us mortals, even if we did happen to be witches.

The morning of New Year's Eve, I rolled over in bed and stared up at the ceiling, thinking. Connor had been able to secure the hotel room for Sydney and Anthony without any problem, and they were going to come up late in the afternoon and get settled in. Then we planned to go out for a late-ish dinner and start making the rounds downtown.

This all seemed perfectly innocuous, but I couldn't help wondering if Damon had been biding his time, waiting so he could swoop down at the worst possible moment. I tried to tell myself that was silly, that he wouldn't do anything on a night when the town was swarming with revelers. Even so, unease still nagged at me.

"You're frowning a lot for a girl with a big party day in front of her," Connor remarked, turning on his side to watch me.

"Sorry. I'm just—I don't know. I can't stop thinking about your brother."

"Should I be jealous?" Connor inquired, and I reached over and smacked him on the shoulder.

"Don't even joke about that. Just…no." I pushed myself up to a sitting position, holding the sheets against me. I'd fallen asleep right after the previous night's lovemaking session, and my clothes were still scattered all over the floor. "It just seems as if he backed off way too quickly. He's not really going to give up that easily, is he?"

Connor's expression, which had been relaxed and still a little drowsy, darkened. He sat up as well. "I don't know. The thing is, he knows he can't *force* you to do anything. And how much *can* you do, anyway?" I raised an eyebrow, and he hastened to add, "No insult, Ange, but besides talking to ghosts, I haven't seen you actually *do* all that much."

I didn't bother to tell him that was how I'd been raised, that flashy shows of power were the quickest way to invite unwanted attention. "And what about you, mister? I've seen you light a fire or two, and I know you were able to change your eye color, but somehow I have a feeling there's a little bit more to it than that."

"You really want to know?"

"Yeah, I do."

He drew in a deep breath. "Okay." And suddenly it wasn't Connor looking at me, but his cousin Lucas.

Even though I knew it had to be only magic, I couldn't help giving out a little squeak and clutching the sheets to me even more closely, making sure my breasts were completely covered. It sure looked like Lucas, dark eyes and the Wilcox high cheekbones and long, strong nose. I noticed there were the beginnings of some iron gray at his temples.

"That's, um...impressive," I managed.

The illusion disappeared, and Connor was staring back at me. "Thanks."

"So can you look like anybody?"

"No, they have to be my approximate height and weight. I couldn't take on your appearance, for example. But Lucas, or my brother, or any man around my size, yeah."

That seemed a lot more useful to me than talking to ghosts. "I'm surprised you don't use it more."

"I don't like it. Feels like lying to me." He shook his head, then pushed back the covers and got out of bed so he could retrieve his underwear.

I had to admit I'd rather be looking at his backside than Lucas's...or Damon's. Shudder.

"And it takes a lot of effort," he added, pulling on some jeans over the boxer-briefs. "Holding a full-body illusion like that? I can do it for maybe an hour, max."

"But just the eye color?" I asked, recalling how convincing those brown eyes had been when I first met him. "That's easier?"

"Much easier. I can do that all day without breaking a sweat." He reached for the sweatshirt he'd tossed over a chair the night before, then added, "Okay, I've shown you mine. You show me yours."

"Very funny."

"I mean it."

To stall him, I bent over the side of the bed and grabbed my own discarded underwear, then slipped it on. Since we were probably just going to scrounge breakfast downstairs after this, I didn't worry about my bra, but instead pulled on my long-sleeved T-shirt from the day before. "It's not that simple."

"How so?"

Ever since Connor and I had been together, I'd felt the *prima*'s energy surging through my veins, bright and strong, but I didn't know exactly what I was supposed to do with it. Maybe nothing more than my little display earlier, when I'd lit the logs in the fireplace. Maybe the real power, the *true* power, was waiting until I needed it, whenever that might be.

"It's nothing obvious," I replied, trying to figure out the best way to describe it. "That's not how it works with a *prima*. I mean, I'm not going to go around blasting doors and invading people's dreams and all the fancy stuff your brother does. It's more like"—I scrunched up my nose, searching for the words—"I guess it's something like ground water, deep under the desert floor. It's there, but until you drill down and hit it, it's not obvious. That's a *prima's* power, Connor. It's there against the time when it's needed."

He'd been listening to me, his head tilted slightly to one side as he considered my words. After a pause, he asked, "And talking to ghosts?"

"That's different. That's just my gift—me, Angela McAllister. It doesn't really have anything to do with being *prima*. At least, none that I can tell, beyond the talent being strong enough that it made me good *prima* material."

"It's interesting," he said. "I mean, it's very different from how the power goes from *primus* to *primus*. That's always been father to son, at least in our clan."

"Are there any other clans with a *primus*? Margot Emory said—I mean, I was told that the Wilcoxes are the only ones."

"Not that I know of. There must have been once, but it seems as if we Wilcoxes are the only ones clinging to the bad old days."

He frowned, and I went around the bed so I could give him a quick hug. "You're not all clinging to it. You seem like you're trying to change things."

"I do?" he replied, surprise clear in his features.

"Well, you're not doing every little thing Damon tells you to, and you seemed willing enough to make peace with my clan, even if they're not meeting you halfway. So I definitely don't think you're stuck in your family's past."

A hand lifted to brush back my hair and push it behind my ear. "You have a generous soul, Angela."

It was such an out-of-character thing for him to say that I couldn't help raising my eyebrows.

"You do. I wish things were different, that there wasn't this cloud hanging over us. You deserve better than that."

There was such a note of melancholy in his tone that I felt my breath seize in my chest. No, we really didn't deserve this. I'd always thought all that "sins of the fathers" crap was just that—crap—and never more so than now. Connor certainly shouldn't have to suffer just because his great-great-great-whatever-grandfather had been a first-class son of a bitch. Damon I wasn't so sure about. As far as I could tell, he'd pretty much earned whatever he got.

"Well," I said, attempting to sound casual, "I guess the best we can hope for is that Damon will hook up with some fourth or fifth cousin who's willing to be queen for a day." Again I thought of the young woman I'd seen with Damon at the pot-luck, and wondered if that was exactly what he had planned. "If he has a son, then you're safely out of it."

"Not exactly. I'm still of Jeremiah's line."

Crap. Trying to untangle all this was like trying to unwind all the fine chains at the bottom of my jewelry box—no matter what you did, you found another knot to slow you down. "But it would get him off your back a little, wouldn't it? At least if he had an heir, he wouldn't care so much whether you did or not."

"Probably. But it's sort of awful to wish for someone else to suffer that kind of fate, isn't it?"

I knew that, of course. Even so, I replied, "I did say 'willing,' you know."

"Yeah, you did. I just don't want to think about it right now." He kissed the top of my head, then let go of me and stepped away. "For now I just want to think about getting some food inside me. And coffee. That must be why my brain still feels so fuzzy."

A good excuse, but I guessed his real reason was that he didn't want to discuss the subject anymore. I couldn't blame him; it was almost New Year's. A fresh start, and not the sort of day that we needed to drag a bunch of baggage into. Whatever the true solution to the situation might turn out to be, I didn't think we were going to discover it today.

So I followed him downstairs, and hoped I could push everything aside and just enjoy my time with him and my friends. At least we'd already made plans that would fill it up pretty well—a movie after lunch, then come home to change and have Syd and Anthony meet us after that. We'd probably share a bottle of wine here first, have some cheese, that sort of thing, and go out to eat afterward. Things should be busy enough that I wouldn't have any time to worry about Damon Wilcox or the curse that hung over his family like the proverbial sword of Damocles.

That was the plan, anyway.

———

Sydney and Anthony were late coming over—"it took us more time than we thought to get settled," she told me breathlessly over the phone, which I thought was probably Syd-speak for *we decided to test out the hotel bed first.* No matter, since Connor had made our dinner reservations for eight-thirty. When my friends did finally appear, she looked more or less calm and composed, but I caught a faint pinkish blotch on her neck that I guessed was her attempt to cover up a fresh hickey. I tried not to smile; I'd resorted to the same subterfuge on numerous occasions over the past week.

"Awesome belt," she said, nodding as she gave my outfit the once-over.

Flagstaff was just as casual as Jerome, so something sparkly for New Year's wasn't really appropriate.

I wore a black long-sleeved wrap T-shirt and some new skinny jeans tucked into my riding boots, along with the concho belt Connor had given me and some turquoise pieces I'd owned since high school. The ensemble had met his approval as well—he said my butt looked very "grabbable"—but I wasn't going to repeat that particular comment to Sydney.

"Thanks," I replied. "Connor gave it to me for my birthday."

Her eyes widened. Sydney had a pretty good idea of the market value of things, and I could practically see her adding up the numbers in her head as she gave the belt another once-over while Anthony went with Connor into the kitchen. Another approving nod, and she mouthed *keeper* at me even as the guys came into the living room with the wine and some glasses.

Anthony had brought a bottle from the tasting room where he worked, and so the conversation just sort of naturally drifted to wine and winemaking and all the opportunities opening up in the Verde Valley. Things were booming, according to him, and he was hoping to hit the ground running once he was done with getting his viticulture certification in June.

"Well," Connor said easily, swirling the wine in his glass in a contemplative way, "if you hear about any good opportunities for investment—land opening up, someone with some vines who wants to sell their property—let me know. Maybe we could work something out. I don't know much about wine growing, but I always thought it would be an interesting business to be in. And if I had an expert running things...."

Anthony didn't need any more of an opening than that. "I'll definitely keep my eyes open. More property changes hands than you might think. People dream about owning a vineyard but don't realize how much work it actually takes. But if you're serious—"

"I am," Connor said.

I raised an eyebrow at him, and he just gave me a half-smile. This was the first I'd heard of any ambitions in that direction. Then again, Connor did like and appreciate wine, and knew a good deal about it. And Goddess knows that he didn't seem to be lacking for cash. Maybe he thought that now the Verde Valley wasn't completely off-limits to him, he could pursue something he hadn't had a chance to before. I certainly wasn't going to protest. Owning a winery sounded like a pretty great idea to me.

Besides, any indication of long-range planning for the future meant there was hope, that maybe we'd find a way through our current mess and have an actual life together.

Sydney had been uncharacteristically quiet during most of this conversation, but after we were done with the wine and were bundling up to head out to dinner, she whispered, "What, is Connor *rich*, too?"

I nodded, winding a scarf around my throat.

"Some people have all the luck," she muttered, and finished buttoning up her coat.

If you only knew, I thought. Not that I didn't love being with Connor. I did—I loved both him and being with him, which was not always easy to pull off, no matter what the books and movies might have to say on the subject. But I wouldn't wish our particular baggage on anyone, let alone my best friend. I'd rather Connor were poor and curse-free than rolling in cash. From what I could tell, their wealth hadn't made the Wilcoxes particularly happy.

I pushed those thoughts out of my mind, though, as we headed outside and over to the next street where the restaurant was located. The sidewalks were already crowded with people, making the icy night feel warmer than it really should. It had warmed up for a day or two, just enough to melt a lot of the snow down in the city proper, but temperatures still dropped into the single digits overnight.

The restaurant was packed, but since we had reservations, we only had to wait about five minutes for a table to be ready. I looked around as we were seated, but I didn't see anyone I recognized from the Wilcox holiday potluck. Not that that meant much; about the only two I could probably pick out of a lineup were Lucas and Marie, and while Lucas had seemed like the cheery sort who might brave downtown Flagstaff on New Year's, I couldn't say the same thing for Marie. Maybe the Wilcoxes had a New Year's get-together of their own. If they did, I wasn't sorry to be missing it.

After that, though, I tried not to think about Connor's family, or what they might be doing at this particular moment. It was enough to peruse the menu, to discuss the options—the restaurant offered Spanish food, but with some southwestern touches—and talk about places we'd eaten and the sort of things we liked. Sedona was actually common ground for all four of us, since we'd all been there at various times, and we made a pact to meet there in the near future and brave the lines at Elote.

Dinner took a while because the restaurant was so crowded. It was almost ten by the time we headed back out, and it seemed as if even more people were flocking to the downtown area.

"They do realize we have almost two hours to go until midnight, right?" I inquired plaintively after someone almost ran over my foot with a stroller. Who the heck brings a stroller to a New Year's Eve celebration anyway?

Connor looked as if he was trying hard not to laugh. "Actually, they do two pinecone drops—one at ten to match up with the ball drop in New York, and then another one at midnight our time. A lot of people with kids come to the ten o'clock one."

"Then let's get our asses into a bar," Sydney remarked. "Because I don't care about New York, but I do care about getting run over by soccer moms."

He grinned and led us a couple of streets over to a dark little bar that definitely was twenty-one and over, and not a stroller in sight. Neither were any empty seats in evidence, but we squeezed in at one end of the bar and ordered another bottle of wine. It wasn't exactly a wine sort of place, but they scrounged up some merlot for us.

"Don't say it," Anthony warned Sydney as her eyes started to dance.

"Say what?" she said innocently.

"'I'm not drinking any fucking merlot!'" he and I announced in unison, and Connor burst out laughing.

"They obviously know you too well."

She looked like she wanted to pout, but as she was already a little tipsy, she couldn't quite muster the energy to make it look convincing. Instead, she shook her head and said, "Fine. At this point, it probably doesn't matter all that much."

Which it didn't. We drank and talked and laughed, and eventually it was getting close enough to midnight that we decided we'd better close out our tab and head over to the Weatherford. It seemed as if just about everyone else in downtown Flagstaff had the same idea, so we had to sort of push our way through the crowd to get close enough to see what was going on. Luckily, both Connor and Anthony were tall, so they walked ahead of Sydney and me until they reached a good spot. Then we settled in ahead of them, letting them provide a kind of barrier behind us.

The pinecone was lit up, glittering as it hung from a crossbar beneath the hotel's roof. Although the night was very clear, it almost looked as if a sort of mist had settled over the intersection with all the breath puffing upward from everyone into the frigid air.

"Five minutes to go," Connor whispered in my ear.

For some reason, I shivered. Not from the cold— I'd bundled up pretty well—but because I couldn't ignore the importance of this night, this moment. Being together on New Year's meant we were looking forward to the coming months, that we were making a commitment to some sort of future together, even if right now we didn't know exactly what that future might be.

Beside me, Sydney looked flushed and happy, and I wondered if she were having thoughts along the same lines. Sure, she'd spent New Year's with guys she was dating, since she was not the type to sit home alone on the biggest party night of the year, but being here with Anthony had to mean something different. She'd never dated anyone this long before, and certainly wasn't showing any signs of wanting to end things.

"One minute!" someone called out using a megaphone.

The crowd stilled somewhat, everyone preparing for the big moment.

"Thirty seconds!"

I felt Connor's gloved hand take mine, fingers entwining. Warmth went through me at his touch, and suddenly I wasn't cold at all.

"Ten, nine, eight…"

Now everyone was chanting the numbers, counting down.

"Three, two, one," I said aloud with everyone else.

"Happy New Year!" we all cried, and Connor was turning me around and kissing me, and I caught a glimpse of Syd and Anthony hugging and kissing each other as well. Then people began singing "Auld Lang Syne," Connor, too, and I was surprised to hear what a nice baritone he had.

Tears stung my eyes, but they weren't sad tears. No, I was just happy to be here, happy to be with him, no matter what might happen next. My Aunt Rachel used to shake her head over the fuss about

New Year's, saying it was the solstice and Yule that were truly important, that New Year's was just an arbitrary date, but I had to disagree with her on that. It did mean something. It was a new beginning of its own, a way to mark a transition from one period in your life to another.

I knew I was shifting from the Angela I had been, the one who did everything that was expected of her, to someone more in control of her destiny. Not to say that control was complete, far from it, but I was still making my own decisions instead of allowing them to be made for me.

Goddess willing, I would make the right ones.

CHAPTER THIRTEEN

The Turn of the Wheel

AFTER MIDNIGHT, WE WENT UP TO SYD AND ANTHONY'S room at the Weatherford for champagne. Well, it wasn't precisely a room, more a suite on the top floor of the hotel, complete with sitting area and a tiny kitchen. No wonder they'd wanted to give the place a workout before coming to meet Connor and me. The bed definitely looked as if it had been made up hastily—no hospital corners there—but I decided not to mention it.

The champagne put the final alcoholic haze on the evening, and even Connor's gait wasn't completely steady as he led me back to the apartment afterward and more or less pushed me up the stairs.

"I'm fine," I protested, flailing weakly at him.

"If by 'fine' you mean drunk, then yeah," he replied with a grin. "But it's okay. I'm pretty wasted myself. This is why it's great we didn't have to drive."

"Definitely," I said.

By then we were inside. He shut the door and started to pull me toward the stairs.

"No," I said. "I want to do it down here. On the rug in front of the fireplace. I don't even care if it's scratchy."

"The fireplace?"

"The rug, silly."

He shook his head but offered no argument, only took me by the hand to the living room, then paused to get the fire going. While he did that, I unbuttoned my overcoat and unwrapped the scarf from around my throat, and flung them on the sofa. My boots I pulled off and pushed out of the way under the coffee table.

I began to undo the buckle of my belt, but he came over and stopped me.

"No," he murmured. "I want to undress you."

Something in the quiet intensity of his gaze kept me from making a flippant remark, made me stand silent as he undid the buckle and then the button and zipper of my jeans beneath. He drew them down slowly, being careful to leave my underwear in place. I'd hoped the evening would conclude this way, so I'd put on a new pair I'd just bought, emerald green satin with black lace trim, and a bra to match. As he pushed up my top, he caught sight of the bra, and sucked in a breath.

"When did you get that?"

"The other day, when we went to the mall. You had to use the bathroom, so I sneaked into Victoria's Secret since it was only two shops down from the restrooms."

"Resourceful," he said, eyes gleaming.

"I try to be."

No chance to talk after that, because he pulled off my top and dropped it on the floor, his mouth going to my neck and trailing hot, tickling kisses from throat to collarbone to the swell of my breast, just before he pushed the bra to one side, his mouth closing on my nipple.

I whimpered, and then we were sinking down to the rug, my hands eager on his belt buckle, wanting his jeans and underwear out of the way, wanting nothing more than bare flesh against bare flesh. The fire flickered and snapped in the background, but we didn't need its warmth.

We had one another.

He was so ready for me, as ready as I was for him. I touched him, marveling at the rock-hard flesh under the silky skin. There had been times when we'd made love for hours, exploring one another's bodies, stroking and licking and touching, but this wasn't one of them. I wanted him in me, needed that joining more than anything else, as if by coming together in such a way we could sanctify the evening, seal the pact we had made to face the future together.

Although I said nothing, he seemed to understand what I wanted. His fingers found my core, stroked gently, and then he was pushing inside me, rocking with me as I wrapped my legs around him, driving him deeper, wanting him in the very center of my soul.

As always, we climaxed within a second of one another. Maybe it was because of the consort bond, or something else, something even more primal. All that mattered was the shivering heat, the explosion, the wordless convulsion as Connor and Angela disappeared for that single endless second, becoming something else.

Becoming one.

Afterward he carried me upstairs, tucked me gently in bed, then slipped in next to me, his warmth dispelling the chill from the icy sheets. I pushed up against him, cradling my head on his chest, and fell asleep that way, secure in his strength, secure in his love.

In that moment, it was enough.

———

As if the world truly had turned a page after New Year's, the days seemed to pass more quickly than ever. Soon enough, the university was back in session, and we had no further contact from Damon. After a week went by, and then another, I began to believe that he truly must have abandoned his schemes, had resigned himself to the idea that the McAllister *prima* would never allow him to use her powers for his own ends. And since Connor had gotten confirmation through the family grapevine that Damon was making overtures to Jessica Lowe, the young woman from the potluck, I figured I was safe. I couldn't help feeling sorry for her, but if she was a Wilcox, then she knew what she was getting into.

My feeling of relief only increased when I got my monthly visitor a few days after New Year's. Not that getting my period was that much fun, but at least it meant the charm was working, meant that I didn't have to worry about the curse descending on me. Well, the Wilcox curse anyway.

Connor asked if I would like to get back to making my jewelry, and offered one of the upstairs bedrooms in the apartment next door for me to use as my studio. That sounded like an excellent idea—after thinking it over for a while, I'd decided to withdraw from my online coursework for a while, and I couldn't just sit around and watch TV all day. Connor ordered some furniture and equipment for me, had the room painted almost the same cheerful turquoise as my old bedroom back at my aunt's apartment.

The supplies, though, I had Sydney bring up. I didn't want to face the Jerome contingent quite yet, and since my jewelry-making tools and loose stones and other items all fit easily into a few small boxes, she was all too happy to get everything together for me and drive up with Anthony on a Saturday when we could all go out on the town. She seemed to be getting quite a taste for Flagstaff nightlife. Not that I could really blame her. Maybe in the grand scheme of things Flagstaff wasn't a big city, but compared to Cottonwood it was practically a metropolis.

All through this placid domesticity, though, I had this niggling sensation in the back of my mind, a feeling that things couldn't go on like this indefinitely. I wasn't sure why, because it seemed as if Connor and I were being left alone to live our lives. I tried to tell myself that it was silly, that my unease was probably due to guilt over not returning to Jerome and nothing more, but I couldn't quite seem to convince myself of that. And as far as I knew, I had absolutely zero precognition, so it couldn't be some hazy vision of the future trying to work its way into my mind.

Even so, I managed to shove the feeling away as January began to move into February. Imbolc, the ritual start of spring, came and went with little fanfare; the Wilcoxes didn't follow the old calendar and holidays the same way the McAllisters did, save the major quarterly observances of the solstice and the equinox. But it was on Imbolc when the homesickness came over me the worst, thinking of how we would be calling on Blessed Brigid, celebrating her with fire and feast. In Flagstaff, February 2nd was Groundhog Day, and that was about it.

But I pushed the melancholy aside, reminding myself that I was here with Connor, and that was the most important thing. As time passed, either my family would become reconciled to the relationship, or they wouldn't. I couldn't put my life on hold simply because they were too narrow-minded to understand that Connor was the only man I'd ever truly want or need.

A few days after Imbolc, he was just putting the finishing touches on the autumn aspen painting I'd first seen back in December, looking at it with narrowed eyes as he put a dab of color here, a touch of shadow there. I came downstairs from my own studio, fingers tired from wrapping thin copper wire around some new pieces of Kingman turquoise I'd acquired a few weeks earlier.

"So what are you going to do with that one?" I asked.

"Stack it up against a wall somewhere, I suppose," he replied with a shrug. "Or maybe replace one of the paintings in the apartment. It would go pretty well over the fireplace, actually."

Coming closer, I admired the sure, strong brush strokes, the way he'd managed to evoke the slanting quality of the autumn light. "Or you could, you know, put it in the gallery."

His face went still. "You know I don't sell my stuff."

"Well, why not give it a try?"

"Because putting my art in the gallery just because it's my gallery isn't a good enough reason. It's like…selling your kid's finger-paintings or something."

"Um, if I had a kid whose finger-painting was this good, I'd sure as hell be selling it." I wanted to put my arms around him, if only to get that dead expression off his face, but since he was still holding a brush with wet paint on it, I decided that wasn't such a good idea. "You're selling my jewelry, aren't you?"

"Well, that's different. People really like it. That's why I have you working your fingers to the bone, getting together enough stock for Valentine's Day."

That was true. Oh, I wanted to be working, and it was gratifying to see the way my pieces sold so quickly, but the pace at which I'd been churning out earrings and pendants and talismans was a lot more intense than back in Jerome, where the demand hadn't been as high. "You are a slave driver," I agreed with a smile. "And I also think you have a weirdly distorted idea of how people are going to receive your work. Why not put a couple in there, see what happens?"

His expression was still dubious. "I don't know."

"How the hell did you manage to get an MFA if you have so little confidence in your work?"

"I did, once. But...."

He let the words trail off, but I had a good idea what he meant. Yes, when he was surrounded by people who encouraged him, he felt good about his art. When he came back to Flagstaff, though, he was stomped on by Damon, who had some weird notion that being an artist wasn't good enough for a Wilcox. Whatever. Damon seemed to be out of the picture for now, so I certainly didn't care what he thought... and neither should Connor.

"Then this should be a real confidence booster. And if they don't sell, if they sit neglected in a corner for more than a week, then I swear I'll never bring it up again. Deal?"

For a minute he didn't say anything, just stared at the painting, brows lowered. His fingers tightened around the brush he held. Then, slowly, "Deal. I'll pick two or three and get them installed tomorrow. I needed to do some rearranging anyway, since one artist who was supposed to get me several pieces just emailed this morning and said she was running behind schedule. This can fill in the gap."

"Good," was all I said, but inwardly I was rejoicing. Maybe once he got some outside confirmation of how good he really was, he'd stop this nonsense about only painting for himself. Not that I wanted him to do anything that didn't make him happy, but he was going to paint no matter what. It was a compulsion. He could go a few days without picking up a brush if he had to. However, he'd get moody if too much time passed without working on something. The gallery wasn't so busy that he had to spend all day there, especially now the holidays were past, so most of the time he could paint four or five hours a day. We were going to end up drowning in canvases if he didn't start selling some of them.

The next morning he took three of his paintings down to the gallery with him—one of a windswept tree on the Grand Canyon's rim, one a rather brooding winter scene with a dark pine forest, patches of snow gleaming on the ground, and another that looked like it might be someplace in Sedona, maybe in Oak Creek Canyon, with autumn-hued trees hanging over a narrow stream and red rock canyons looming above.

"Don't expect too much," he told me. "Even pieces from in-demand artists can take a while to move. It's not like buying a postcard or something."

"I know that," I replied. "I dropped about ten grand a few months ago on work for the Jerome house."

His eyes widened a little. "So who's the rich one around here?"

"We both are, I guess, which makes things nice and even. Just promise that you're going to put a fair market price on these."

"Oh, I was thinking maybe fifty bucks for the big one," he began, and I swatted him on the arm.

"Don't you dare!"

A flashing grin, and he bent down to kiss me before tucking the two smaller paintings under his left arm and picking up the remaining one, of Oak Creek Canyon, with his free hand.

"Can you get the door for me?" he asked.

I hurried over and opened it for him, then watched him go, smiling as I shut the door. Once I was alone, though, the smile faded. What if I was wrong? What if people didn't respond to his paintings the same way I did? Being good was no guarantee of success.

Since it was a fairly quiet time of year, his assistant Joelle more or less ran the gallery, so he didn't stay down there after he'd gotten the paintings installed. He came back up and started working on a new one, now that the aspen picture was drying. It was fascinating to watch his process at this stage, the way he arranged a bunch of photos of the scene he wanted to paint on a tack board to one side, then started sketching in the outlines of the projected painting on the canvas. More trees, these ones like flaming torches in a high alpine meadow.

I lingered to one side, watching him, wondering if he was going to tell me to leave, but he didn't. Maybe he'd forgotten I was there. In a way I didn't mind, because it gave me a chance to really study him, watch the fine profile outlined by the light pouring in through the big windows off to one side, the way his heavy dark hair kept falling forward as he worked and how he kept shoving it out of the way with an impatient hand. His hands were beautiful, too, lean and strong, the fingers long and sensitive. I recalled how those fingers felt, touching me, and a little sigh escaped my throat.

He turned then and looked at me. "This must be sort of dull for you."

"No, I like watching you work, if it doesn't bother you."

"It doesn't bother me at all. I'm just surprised you're not working on your own stuff."

"I will. My fingers are a little sore." Which was true. Setting stones and bending wire for six or seven hours a day took far more of a toll than doing the same thing for two or three hours a couple of times a week.

"Mmm...I'll have to do something about that." He set down his pencil and came over to me, lifted my fingers to his mouth and kissed them gently, one at a time.

Delicious shivers worked their way up and down my spine. "I think maybe you need to take a break, too."

"Great idea." He took my hand and started to lead me toward the door so we could go over to the apartment, but then his phone, stuck in his jeans pocket, started to ring. Ignoring it, he pulled me out to the landing.

"Aren't you going to get that?"

"Not important. It can go to voicemail."

I wasn't about to argue, not with the heat coiling in my belly, needing release. It wouldn't be the first time we shared a little afternoon delight, and obviously he didn't think it was going to break his concentration too much. Maybe it would even help.

His phone went quiet, then started up again. We looked at each other.

"Go ahead and answer it," I told him. "If they're calling back this quickly, they must have a reason."

"Or it could be telemarketers," he argued.

"I've never once heard you have to deal with a telemarketer. I figured maybe you'd put some kind of Wilcox whammy on your phone so only people you want to talk to get through."

"Very funny," he said, but he did pull the cell out of his pocket and look at the display, then frown a little as he lifted the phone to his ear. "Joelle? Is there a problem?"

Silence as he listened to what she had to say.

"What? No, that can't—" He stopped; apparently Joelle had cut him off. "Okay, well, yeah, I can be down there in a few minutes. Just hang on." Shaking his head, he ended the call and shoved his phone back in his pocket.

"What is it?" I asked. "Something wrong?"

"No." Incongruously, he began to smile. "Something right. Really right. Joelle said a man came in and asked about my paintings, said he was really impressed."

"That's awesome!" I exclaimed, and reached out and pulled him to me.

"There's more. Apparently he owns one of the biggest galleries in Sedona, and he wants to do a show of my work. He's down there, waiting to talk to me."

"Then what are you waiting for? Go!" I let go of him, laughing at his obvious befuddlement. "I'll still be here when you get back...promise," I added with a wink.

That seemed to spur him to action. He hurried down the stairs, and I watched him go, smiling and thinking how well our lives seemed to go when we didn't have to worry about Damon sticking his nose into them.

Everything seemed to go on fast-forward after that. The owner of the Sedona gallery, one Eli Michaels, came upstairs to see the rest of Connor's paintings, both in the studio and in the apartment. Thank the Goddess that both places were reasonably clean, and that I was more or less presentable, since Connor and I tended to go out for lunch a good deal and I tried to make sure I was ready to go at a moment's notice. To tell the truth, I was pretty sure Eli barely noticed I was there; he was far more interested in looking over all those canvases.

"Impressive," was his evaluation. "I'd like to do a show at the end of the month, if you can be ready for that. We need to get your work out there as soon as possible."

Connor sort of stammered out a "sure," sounding very unlike his usual confident self.

"Excellent," said Eli. "I'll be in touch. If it's not asking too much, I'd prefer that you take down the pieces in your own gallery. I'd like this to be a proper debut."

"No problem."

"Very good. I'll let myself out."

And that was that. Connor and I looked at each other, and I let out a little squeal and flung myself at him. We celebrated properly, upstairs in the big king-size bed, and then went out for a decadent dinner at the Cottage Restaurant, where I had what was probably one of the best meals I'd ever eaten in my life. Then of course I had to call Sydney and tell her the good news, promising her that as soon as I had a firm date for the art opening, I'd let her know.

When I hung up, though, I realized that I should have been calling my aunt to tell her about it—if things were different. If we hadn't avoided speaking to each other for the last month and a half.

I also realized that Connor hadn't called anyone at all. "Shouldn't you at least let Damon know? He might surprise you and actually be proud."

"I doubt it," Connor replied, his expression grim. "I'll let Lucas know. He'll spread the word."

That seemed to be that. I could tell he didn't want me to press the issue, so I decided to let it alone for now. Once we did have the actual date and time from Eli Michaels—February 27th—I emailed Aunt Rachel and told her the news. She could ignore it if she chose. The decision lay with her. At least the opening would be in Sedona, in neutral territory. I didn't think anything in the world could have induced her to set foot in Flagstaff, except maybe a phone call from me saying it had all been a terrible mistake and that I needed her to pick me up right now. That might do the trick.

But since that wasn't going to happen, it seemed a meeting in Sedona was my best bet for seeing her any time soon. Not that I was going to hold my breath.

The rest of February whizzed by, punctuated by a lovely Valentine's Day where Connor and I both took the day off and went up to the Snow Bowl and had lunch in the snow, then came back to town and spent the afternoon making love before going out for another amazing dinner. The fateful Thursday arrived, and we drove down to Sedona, twisting our way through Oak Creek Canyon. It had flurried a little the night before, but the narrow highway was clear, moonlight gleaming on the snow between the trees.

I honestly didn't know what to expect from that evening. Sure, I'd been to art openings in Jerome, but they were friendly, folksy affairs for the most part. This was a very different sort of thing, the kind of event announced with glossy postcards sent all over Sedona and Flagstaff, the kind where I actually went out and bought a new outfit, a slinky black wrap dress and boots with actual heels. Connor fussed and worried and ended up wearing his usual dark sweater over jeans and boots, but it worked for him. Besides, no one expects the artist to show up wearing a suit.

The gallery was almost intimidatingly elegant, with its muted lighting and glossy wooden floors. It was huge, too, so big that Connor's exhibit only took up one large room—and he was displaying a lot of paintings, fifty in all. Despite the size of the space, people already crowded the exhibit hall.

I blinked, realizing I recognized a good number of the attendees from the Wilcox holiday potluck. For some reason, I really hadn't expected that. Neither had Connor, apparently; he looked at them in surprise, even as Lucas approached us with a grin, plastic flute of champagne clutched in one hand.

"This is amazing," he said. "Can't believe you've been hiding this from us all these years!"

Connor managed a watery smile. "Well, I did get my degree in studio art."

"True, but I suppose I never really thought about it. I mean, my degree's in anthropology, but it doesn't mean I use it." He transferred his attention me. "And I'm guessing you're the one who coaxed him out of his shell?"

"Well…." I didn't want to tell Lucas just how much poking and prodding had been involved. That was between Connor and me. The important thing was that he had finally gotten his art out there for the world to see.

But somehow Lucas seemed to guess, because his brows lifted, and he shot a sly glance at Connor. "That's about what I thought. As they say, behind every great man is a woman. Good job, Angela."

Then he looked past us, surprise flitting over his features. "Looks like your brother actually did decide to show up. I wasn't sure."

"Great," Connor muttered.

"I'll head him off at the pass," Lucas said, and clapped Connor on the shoulder before moving off toward the entrance to the exhibit hall.

I shifted my position slightly so I could see where he was heading. Sure enough, there was Damon, looking elegant in a black jacket over a dark gray dress shirt and jeans. At his side was the young woman I first saw at the holiday potluck. Now that I could get a better look at her, I saw that she had the graceful bone structure most of the Wilcoxes seemed to share, but her hair and eyes were much lighter.

"That's Jessica, right?" I whispered to Connor.

His gaze tracked to where I was looking, and then slid back toward me. "Yes."

"She's pretty."

"I suppose so. Damon isn't the type to attach himself to unattractive women."

Which didn't surprise me much. "And she's another cousin?"

"Yeah. Her great-great-whatever grandmother was Jeremiah Wilcox's younger sister. Jessica's always had a crush on Damon—I know some of the cousins she went to high school with used to tease her about it."

That seemed strange to me, that she'd be pining after someone so much older than she was, but attraction was a weird thing. So maybe she really didn't mind being the sacrificial lamb, so to speak.

Then Connor tensed, murmuring, "Wow."

I'd been covertly watching Damon and Jessica move farther into the hall, then get intercepted by Lucas, who was smiling and pointing at the closest painting with an enthusiasm I could see even from twenty feet away. He was definitely the most un-Wilcox-like Wilcox imaginable, and I wondered at his friendship with Damon, since they seemed so diametrically opposed in their temperaments. But I looked to see what had attracted Connor's attention, and realized my Aunt Rachel and Tobias had just entered the gallery.

They both appeared more than a little ill at ease, which, considering they were surrounded by Wilcoxes, was fairly understandable. Behind them came Margot Emory and Henry Lynch, who also looked as if they'd like to be just about anywhere else.

"Holy crap," I said. "I didn't think they were really going to show."

"We'd better go say hi, then," Connor replied.

I didn't question why he wanted to go greet my family members when he hadn't made a move to do the same with his own brother. But as Damon appeared more or less occupied at the moment, it seemed prudent to leave him alone and focus our attention on the McAllister contingent.

Connor took my hand, and we moved toward the entrance to the exhibit space. I managed to get a smile more or less fixed on my face, although my heart had begun to pound and my stomach felt as if it had a flock of sparrows rather than butterflies zooming around in it. Silly, really. I was going to say hi to my aunt and Tobias and two other people I'd known all my life. This wasn't the same as facing all those Wilcoxes for the first time.

Even so, I had to take a breath as we approached Aunt Rachel. Tobias smiled at us, but her expression was hard to read—strained, yes, but underneath the tension was something else as she gazed around her. Surprise, maybe? It was entirely possible that she hadn't expected much from Connor's art, had inwardly thought he must have bought his way into having an exhibition.

"Hi, Rachel, Tobias," I said, sounding almost normal. "I'm really glad you could make it—all of you."

Henry nodded, although Margot only acknowledged me with the barest lift of her eyebrows.

Probably she'd come along only to provide support for Rachel and Tobias, and not because she cared about seeing Connor's art.

For the first time, my aunt seemed to really look at Connor—at *him*, not at the brother of the Wilcox *primus*. "This is really quite amazing," she said. "I had no idea you were such an accomplished artist."

Of course you didn't, I thought, *because you couldn't be bothered to learn anything about him, except that he was a Wilcox.*

"Thank you," he replied. "I'm—that is, Angela and I are both really glad you could make it."

"Yes, it's quite a cozy scene," came Damon's voice, and I could actually feel the muscles at the back of my neck tense up.

I wasn't the only one, either; Connor's jaw tightened, and both Margot and Henry stepped forward to flank Aunt Rachel and Tobias.

"Oh, now," Damon went on, "surely there's no need for you to all be bristling at me like that, is there? We're all on neutral ground, after all." But even as he spoke the words, I saw Connor's cousin Marie and a few others whose names I couldn't recall converging on our little group. Lucas, however, was staying at the far end of the gallery, chatting up an attractive woman with striking pale hair, clearly a civilian.

Great. The last thing I needed was for all our family members to reenact the rumble scene from

West Side Story right in the middle of one of Sedona's ritziest art galleries. I felt Connor's fingers tighten around mine, and I cast about frantically for something innocuous to say that would defuse the tension. Nothing came to mind, however.

"Now, now," I heard a woman say. "Look at all of you, snarling at one another like two wolf packs fighting over the same bone."

Her voice was vaguely familiar, and I half-turned to see Maya de la Paz approaching alone, although when I looked past her, I saw standing a few feet away some of the tall young men from her clan I recognized from bodyguard duty back in Phoenix. Alex, however, was not among them.

"P-prima?" I stammered, and she smiled at me.

"Hello, Angela. I must say you are looking very well. As for the rest of you"—her gaze moved from the quartet of McAllisters to the Wilcoxes—"this is an art exhibit. There is plenty to look at, and free champagne. Don't call any more attention to yourselves than you already have."

For a moment, no one moved. Then Damon let out a clearly forced laugh, and snaked his arm around Jessica's slender waist. "Come on, darling. Let's take a look at Connor's daubs, shall we?"

They moved off, but not before he shot a truly venomous glance in Maya's direction. She appeared singularly unimpressed.

"We'll look around, too," Tobias said, and took my aunt's hand in his. They headed toward the nearest painting, and after a brief hesitation, Henry and Margot followed them.

"Thanks, Maya," Connor said.

"It is nothing. I wasn't sure what would happen, with McAllisters and Wilcoxes in such close proximity, so I thought it best to make the trip up." Her dark eyes glinted as she smiled up at Connor; she was tiny, so her head didn't even reach his shoulder. Not that it mattered. What Maya de la Paz lacked in height, she more than made up in *cojones*. "Besides, I wanted to see Connor's work. I wondered if he was ever going to put that degree of his to use."

His expression turned sheepish, but I overlooked that, wondering at the familiar way she addressed him, and how she knew he'd been an art major. It wasn't the sort of thing I had expected her to know.

Those questions must have been clear on my face, because Maya let out a chuckle and said, "And now you want to know how I could know Connor at all, when his clan and mine are not exactly what one would call close."

"Hardly," he said with a grimace and a quick glance toward his brother, now safely on the other side of the exhibit space.

"It's simple enough, though, isn't it?" she went on. "Connor wished to get his degree at ASU, which has a very good art program, but since ASU is in my clan's territory, he had to come to me to get permission when it was time for him to transfer from Northern Pines in his junior year. I'll admit I wasn't sure at first, but it was clear to me soon enough that he is nothing like his brother. So I gave him the dispensation, and he lived down in the Phoenix area quietly enough for four years, which is more than I can say for some of the younger generation in my clan."

At that remark, Connor looked as if he wanted to sink into the floor. I rescued him by saying, "That was very generous of you, Maya—and I'm very glad you could make it here tonight."

"I was curious," she admitted. "But your work is wonderful, Connor, so I'm glad you've decided to get it out there so others can see it."

"Thank you," he said. His wasn't the sort of complexion given to easy blushes, but I could see a brief stain of color along his cheekbones before it faded. "It was mostly Angela's doing, but—"

"She might have convinced you, but it was your hand that held the brush." Her gaze was warm, as if holding both of us within it. "I will admit that when your aunt first contacted me, Angela, I was sure that Damon's actions were going to bring us all to the sort of clan warfare that hasn't been seen for more than a hundred years. But when I learned you were with Connor, I told Rachel that all would be well, that he was not typical of his clan."

So that was why I'd heard nothing else after Maya had supposedly told Damon that "it wasn't over." Well, actually, it was—once she got the true lay of the land and realized I was not with the *primus,* but his brother, a man she obviously liked and possibly had some affection for. "I appreciate that—we both do."

"Yes," Connor added at once, although I could tell he was squirming a little inwardly at the "not typical of his clan" remark.

"Well," she said, "I wish to look more closely at these paintings of yours, Connor, so I will leave you now. I think we will not have any more disruptions this evening."

No, I sort of doubted that. Even Damon wasn't the type to make a scene, not here anyway, so I thought the rest of the evening should go more or less smoothly.

Which it did, with various Wilcoxes coming up to congratulate him on the show, and even Aunt Rachel and Tobias approaching us once we were safely alone and praising his work. And, in an exchange that made me want to laugh, Lucas sidled up to me, nodded toward Margot, and asked who that "exquisite creature" was. Somehow managing to keep a straight face, I told him she was one of the

McAllister clan elders and probably wouldn't be all that receptive to any advances from a Wilcox.

"But is she single?" he persisted.

Somehow I managed to talk him down, and he went off to get another glass of champagne. Connor and I did get a chuckle out of the whole thing, because I couldn't imagine anyone less likely to have romantic success with Margot Emory than Lucas Wilcox.

By the end of the night, more than half the pieces on display had discreet little "sold" labels attached to their description cards. I didn't even want to calculate how much Connor had just made in one evening, but I knew it had to be a lot.

The only sour note in the evening came from, of course, Damon. He'd made a perfunctory pass of the paintings, didn't even acknowledge Connor at all, and left early with Jessica in tow, murmuring something about ducking around the corner for a real drink. As he left, though, he shot me a look of such venom that I couldn't help recoiling, although I knew I was perfectly safe here.

Despite that, I couldn't help wondering why on earth he should be so angry with me. I'd kept a low profile the entire night, allowing Connor to bask in the praise of family members and strangers alike. I certainly couldn't think of a single thing I'd said or done to provoke such ire.

Well, nothing except convince his brother to put his art on display when Damon always hated the idea...nothing except allow Connor to step out a little further from the primus's shadow. When I thought of it that way, then I supposed I could see why Damon might be so angry. He didn't want his brother independent; he wanted him under his thumb, the same place he'd wanted me. That we were both proving to be so difficult to manage had to be a thorn in his side.

What he would do about it—if anything—I had no idea.

CHAPTER FOURTEEN

The Shadow of the Wolf

SINCE THE SHOW WAS SUCH A SUCCESS, CONNOR THREW himself into his work even more than he already had, painting sometimes eight or ten hours a day while Joelle ran the gallery. I wasn't quite so dedicated, but I kept plugging away at my jewelry. If nothing else, it gave me something to do.

Maybe I should have felt neglected, but it was so good to see Connor happy and painting that I really didn't mind all that much. And although I couldn't persuade Aunt Rachel to come up to Flagstaff—that would have been asking way too much—I did borrow Connor's FJ once or twice to drive to Sedona so she and I could meet for lunch. For some reason, I didn't want to go back to Jerome without him. It would've felt like a capitulation, like I knew they still didn't accept him. In my mind, I'd resolved that I would only return to

Jerome with my consort at my side, and only when I knew they would take him in, if not with open arms, at least with the acknowledgment that he was their *prima*'s chosen life mate.

So March arrived, still bitingly cold. It was far too early for the trees to start budding in Jerome, let alone Flagstaff, but something in the shift of the angle of the light told me spring wasn't too far off. I'd spent two months here, two months more than I had ever expected I would. Strange to think of that, and even stranger to realize that I enjoyed it here, enjoyed the new sights and sounds and people. I'd even made friends with a couple of the female Wilcox cousins, two girls who were around my age and all too ready to gossip whenever the occasion arose—which meant basically every time we got together.

"Aunt Janelle is just going nuts," Carla Wilcox told me over coffee one bitingly cold morning. A freezing fog had descended on the town, and I was surprised she'd braved the icy roads to meet me at a coffee shop a few doors down from the apartment Connor and I shared.

"Seriously," Mason Tillman put in. She and Carla were cousins of some kind, but I'd given up trying to sort them all out. She was a senior at Northern Pines and had a loft apartment here downtown, so she'd walked to the coffee shop, too.

Aunt Janelle was Jessica Lowe's mother, apparently. It sounded as if she wasn't all that resigned to the Wilcox curse descending on her daughter's head, no matter what Jessica herself might think about it.

"So what is she doing about it?" I asked, then took a sip of my chai latte.

Carla rolled her eyes and let out an exaggerated sigh. "There isn't much she *can* do. I mean, Damon's the *primus,* so she's sure not going to go up against him, and Jessica has been mooning over Damon for, like, forever, so she won't listen."

"She told her mother that she'd rather have a year with Damon than fifty years with someone else," Mason added.

Ugh. Why couldn't Jessica have a crush on Channing Tatum like a normal twenty-something?

"It's just creepy," Carla said. "I mean, not that I think *he's* creepy, of course, but he's almost eleven years older than she is, and she's never been interested in anyone else. She totally flipped out when he got married to that civilian woman, and then when she died, Jessica was actually happy, which, I'm sorry, is just *wrong.*"

Yes, it was. I guess I was just surprised that a couple of Wilcoxes would think that as well. Obviously they were not quite the great monolith of evil I'd been raised to think they were. I liked Carla and Mason, and I thought Sydney would like them, too.

My opinion of Damon was just as low as it had ever been, and I couldn't really warm up to Marie, either, but these two girls and Lucas and a few others were far nicer than I'd ever imagined any Wilcox could be. They were so open, too—Carla telling me the first time we talked that her talent was what she referred to as the "mother of all bumps of direction."

"Seriously," she'd said. "It's part of the reason I decided cultural anthro would be a good major. I never get lost, like, *ever*. I could probably get dropped in the wilds of Peru somewhere and find the nearest highway and hike out, no problem."

At the time, I'd reflected that it seemed as if everyone had a better talent than I did. I was even falling down in the ghost-talking department. Mary Mullen seemed to have taken a powder forever, as far as I could tell. Maybe all the headboard-thumping had driven her right on to the next plane of existence.

I swirled the stir stick in my chai, watching pale brown traceries appear in the foam. "Jessica would have to be in high school when Damon's wife died, wouldn't she?" I asked, attempting to do the math in my head.

"Yes," Mason replied. "And seriously, I tried to tell her that crushing on someone that much older when she wasn't even legal yet was gross, but she wouldn't listen. Wouldn't even date anyone else, which was crazy, because she was always pretty and had so many guys who wanted to ask her out. But no, she said she knew in her heart that she was meant to be with Damon, and that was that."

No wonder she'd latched on to him the second he'd decided to go trolling for a baby mama, since that whole plan for kidnapping me hadn't worked out so well. "Then I guess there isn't much anyone can do about it," I said. "And whatever she was thinking in high school, she's certainly an adult now, so I guess it's none of our business."

Carla frowned. "I suppose. But if we don't talk about *them,* who will we talk about? Everyone else is so *normal.*"

Oh, if only my aunt were around to hear that pronouncement. She'd probably fall over in shock at the mere notion of referring to a Wilcox as "normal." "Well, I have a question, actually," I ventured, finally gathering the courage to ask about the thing that had been bothering me for weeks.

"Ooh, what?" Mason asked.

"What's the deal with your cousin Marie? I swear, I've probably only exchanged twenty words with the woman, if that, but I keep getting the impression that she really doesn't like me very much." There, I'd said it. Marie's vague hostility still puzzled me, but when I'd tried to broach the subject to Connor, he'd just told me I was imagining things. I still didn't know Carla and Mason all that well, but one thing I did know was that they didn't have much of a filter. If they were thinking something, they were basically saying it.

The two of them exchanged a glance. "Honestly?" Carla said after a brief pause. "I don't really know. She's never been all that friendly to *anyone*. I mean, she and Damon are sort of close, or as close as either one of them can be, since neither of them is exactly the friendly type, but I think that's partly because he's the *primus* and she's our seer, so they have to work together on—well, on stuff," she finished lamely.

It was pretty clear that she'd been thinking of my kidnapping and then realized that probably wasn't the best example of "working together" to bring up around me. I decided to let it go. Done was done, and in the end, everything had turned out for the best. I was willing to forgive a lot when it came to my ending up with Connor.

"Yeah, maybe it's because she is the seer, or because her mother was Navajo, but she never seemed to really be that friendly with anyone," Mason added.

"Really?" I asked. That is, I'd noticed that Marie appeared to be far more obviously Native American than anyone else in the family, whose Navajo blood was many generations back, but I couldn't quite figure out how that had worked. "Isn't that sort of unusual? I mean, I just figured that the local Navajo didn't have that great an opinion of the Wilcoxes— no offense," I added quickly, as I saw the two girls exchange a glance.

"Oh, no worries," Mason said. "That's ancient history. And yeah, it did seem a little strange to us, but who knows what happened with Marie's parents. Her father was my grandfather's oldest brother, but he died before I was born. And her mother went back to live on the tribal lands after Cousin Marie graduated from high school, so I don't think any of us ever even met her."

"But Marie stayed?"

"Yeah," Carla replied, swirling the foam on the top of her cafe latte.

"And she never got married or anything?"

"Not that we know of. I heard somewhere that she was engaged once, but it didn't work out."

"They broke up?"

"No," Mason said slowly, drawing out the syllable as if she were racking her brain at the same time, trying to recall the particulars. "I think he just… disappeared or something. Like, here one day and gone the next. Or at least that's what I overheard at a family party once. I forget who was telling the story. Maybe your mom, Carla?"

"Makes sense," Carla remarked after sipping her latte. "My mom loves to gossip about *everyone*."

Like mother, like daughter, I thought, suppressing a grin. I wasn't sure how much use any of this information was going to be to me, but gaining some extra knowledge never hurt. At the very least, I now knew that Marie's hostility wasn't necessarily directed at me, but more just a part of her personality.

As the three of us finished up and made our goodbyes, however, I couldn't help wondering about that long-ago fiancé of hers. What really *had* happened to him?

I knew better than to ask Connor, though. He was so embroiled in his painting that he probably wouldn't much appreciate me dredging up ancient family history. Which was fine. Our future together was far more important than whatever had happened to Marie before I was even born.

———

A few days later we were sitting in the living room, watching the morning news as we ate toast and eggs and sipped coffee. One good thing about Connor's painting mania—he didn't tend to get started until after nine in the morning at the earliest, so at least we could have a leisurely start to our day. We didn't always turn on the news, but he was thinking about doing some *plein air* painting soon and wanted to catch the weather report. Apparently the Wilcoxes didn't have anyone with true weather sensitivity, something the McAllisters definitely had up on them. On the other hand, we didn't have a healer, nor a true seer, so the balance sheet still wasn't all that even.

All of the Arizona news came out of Phoenix, which had always made the weather reports pretty much useless to me back home in Jerome. Flagstaff, however, was a big enough city that it did actually get a mention from the Phoenix newscasters, although in general it seemed as if they tended to ignore what was going on in the northern half of the state.

Not today, however. I'd just settled back on the couch with a fresh cup of coffee when the news returned after a commercial break. The female newscaster fixed her version of an appropriately concerned expression on her face and said, "Authorities have reported discovering the body of a female Northern Pines University student early this morning. Details are still sketchy, but the local police have informed us that there doesn't appear to be any evidence of foul play and that the young woman appears to have been the victim of an animal attack, although such attacks are very rare. The victim's name is being withheld pending notification of the family, and the police and local wildlife officials are saying this is most likely an isolated occurrence. However, until the animal involved can be identified, they urge residents near the university to be on their guard. In other news—"

I picked up the remote and hit the "mute" button. "An animal attack? Is that common around here?"

Connor frowned. "Did you miss the part where they said these kinds of attacks are rare?"

"No, but—"

"Probably a bear. It doesn't happen very often, but this time of year I've heard they can be pretty hungry and cranky. We'll probably never know what happened, since it sounds as if the girl was alone when she was attacked, but it's not the sort of thing you need to worry about." He paused, watching me closely, and his expression softened. "It's awful, I know, but I've seen a few bears while I was out hiking, and they really don't tend to be that aggressive."

"Okay," I said, but I wasn't sure if I meant it. Something was pricking at the back of my mind, telling me this didn't feel right at all. In general my instincts were pretty good, although I didn't know if that was some kind of witchy sixth sense or what Sydney liked to refer to as "her gut." In the end, it probably didn't matter all that much.

"Can you turn the sound back on? The weather report is about to start."

"Sure." I picked up the remote and unmuted the TV, then listened with half an ear as the weatherman talked about building high pressure and an extended dry spell, with wind warnings in effect for the next twenty-four hours. Not that unusual; we often got strong winds in northern Arizona at the shift of the seasons. The equinox was only two weeks away.

If it really had been a bear attack, I wasn't all that thrilled about Connor going out and painting in the middle of nowhere armed with only an easel and a brush. As it turned out, though, his destination was Oak Creek Canyon, not anywhere near Flagstaff. That made me a little more relaxed about the situation, especially after he said he wanted me to come along so we could hike around West Fork, get lunch at the Indian Gardens trading post. It sounded like a fun outing.

"I can't guarantee it'll be bear-free," Connor said. "I mean, it's the wilderness. But if I were a bear, someplace that gets visited by that many tourists is probably the last place I'd want to hang out."

"What about all those pic-a-nic baskets?" I inquired with a grin.

"It's Oak Creek, not Jellystone. I think we'll be okay."

I had to agree with that. Still, though, my spidey-sense kept tingling...and not in a good way.

Two days later I was sitting at the same café where I'd met Mason and Carla the previous week.

Connor had gone to meet with Eli Michaels at his gallery in Sedona, a business meeting I obviously hadn't been invited to. Not that I minded too much; I didn't want Connor to think we had to be joined at the hip twenty-four/seven. And it probably was a good thing for me to get out on my own every once in a while, although going approximately four doors down from our apartment couldn't really be classified as being adventurous.

Someone had left a copy of that morning's newspaper lying on one of the chairs at the table I'd selected. I picked up the paper, figuring I'd give it a quick glance-through. Connor and I had bought an iPad Mini the previous week during a splurge at Best Buy, but I didn't feel like digging it out of my purse.

I set down my coffee, then picked up the newspaper and smoothed it out before me. The top part of the front page was dedicated to bond issues and street improvements—necessary, I supposed, but not the sort of thing I really wanted to waste my time reading. But then I saw another, smaller headline in the lower right-hand corner of the page: "Coroner Determines Cause of Student's Death."

It had been a few days since that first report on the TV, and I hadn't seen any follow-up to it. Then again, Connor and I didn't watch much news, or anything else on broadcast television. If we wanted to relax in the evening, we watched Netflix or HBO or something. Not that I'd been dwelling on it, but the report of the girl's death had felt like a hanging thread, something that needed closure.

Picking up my coffee and blowing on it gently, I scanned the article.

According to the preliminary coroner's report, Theresa Irene Ivey, age 20, died of blood loss caused by extreme trauma in the form of wild animal bites to the jugular.

I shivered. In other words, something tore her throat out.

Analysis of the bite marks shows that the animal in question appears to be a gray wolf. Fish and game officials are puzzled, as gray wolves are not native to the area. "We're attempting to save the Mexican wolf from extinction," Harold Willis, a wildlife expert explained, "but those wolves roam a small area in the Blue Range, hundreds of miles from Flagstaff. They are not a threat, and in any case, it was not a Mexican wolf involved in the recent attack."

Authorities speculate that perhaps someone in the area was illegally keeping a gray wolf as a pet, and it escaped and attacked Ms. Ivey. However, no one has come forward to report a missing wolf, and inquiries have turned up no leads. The investigation is ongoing, and people are urged to be cautious but not worried. The animal that attacked Ms. Ivey did not have rabies, and authorities are unsure as to why she was the victim, as the attack occurred near her apartment, in a populated area.

Anyone who sees a wolf is encouraged to dial 9-1-1.
Under no circumstances is anyone to approach the animal.

There was also a small photo of the victim. When my gaze shifted to study it, I sucked in a breath, cold descending on me, even though the café was actually almost too warm.

Theresa Ivey looked like me.

All right, not exactly. Her chin was more pointed than mine, her features actually not all that similar, once you began to study them one by one, but still, she had long wavy dark hair and fair skin and eyes that could have been blue or green or gray—the black and white photo obviously couldn't show that level of detail. But if you were looking from a distance, or out of the corner of your eye, well, then, you could say we looked a lot alike.

Just a coincidence, I tried to tell myself. After all, Flagstaff wasn't tiny Jerome. In a population of more than 60,000 people, there were bound to be a good number of college-age women who were more or less my same physical type.

For some reason, that didn't make me feel all that much better.

Although my stomach was roiling enough that drinking a cup of coffee suddenly didn't sound like such a great idea, I made myself take a few more sips just so I wouldn't be entirely wasteful. Then I folded up the newspaper and tucked it under my arm. I wanted Connor to see this.

———

"All right, it's kind of strange," he admitted after reading the article and studying the photo. "Especially the wolf part. There are no wolves for hundreds of miles—haven't been for years and years. But the victim? I think you're trying to see patterns that aren't there."

"Isn't that what witches do?" I asked, then added quickly, as his brows began to knit together, "That is, see patterns that are *hidden* to most people. What's the point of having powers if they can't help us do things regular people can't?"

He let out a sigh, then pushed the paper aside and laid his hand on top of mine. We were sitting on the couch next to one another; he smelled slightly of linseed oil and turpentine, but I didn't mind all that much. It was just good to be there next to him, to feel the reassuring strength of his body next to me. Although I could tell he didn't think the resemblance was anything but a coincidence, his tone was gentle as he said, "I don't know…I think you could be reaching here. Like the article said, it was probably somebody's pet wolf that got loose somehow and, I don't know, went after her because she had food on her or something. They don't mention it, but it has to be something like that. Wild animals don't attack without reason."

No, generally they didn't. Again that sense of unease washed over me, the feeling that some threat hovered on the horizon, out of sight but still danger-ous, like the scent of smoke that precedes a fast-mov-ing brushfire. But I knew if I said anything else I'd sound as if I were trying to invent something that wasn't there. I didn't know *what* was wrong, only that something was. And until I could figure it out, there wasn't much point in pressing the issue.

———

Three days later, another body was found, this time right on campus at the edge of one of the park-ing lots. The bite wounds were identical to the ones on Theresa Ivey.

"Everyone is really freaking out," Carla said, and she and Mason exchanged a worried glance. They were both seniors at Northern Pines. "No one's sup-posed to walk alone, especially not at night."

They'd come over to hang out and talk, and we were in the living room, enjoying the warmth of a newly laid fire. Who cared if it was almost the Ides of March—the temperature had stayed below freezing for the past two days. Connor was over in his stu-dio, painting, so he certainly didn't mind me having Carla and Mason over. In fact, although he hadn't said it out loud, I got the feeling he was glad that I'd made friends at all, if maybe a little surprised that I'd warmed up to two of the Wilcoxes the way I had with the cousins.

"Did you—did you know either one of them?" I asked.

Carla nodded. "I knew Alison, the second girl. She was in my social statistics class. Not that we were friends or anything, but we traded notes a couple of times. I think she worked part-time as a waitress at one of the breweries downtown here. I can't remember which one, though." Her face clouded, and then her gaze sharpened as she looked at me.

"What?" But somehow I had a feeling that I knew what she was about to say.

"No, it's nothing." Leaning forward, she picked up her neglected cup of chai and wrapped her hands around it, as if she needed it to ward off a chill, even though the room was plenty warm.

Mason was giving her cousin the same quizzical look I knew I wore on my face. "It's something—you wouldn't look that way if it wasn't. So spill."

A hesitation, and then Carla's fingers tightened on the heavy brown mug she was holding. "It's just—you wouldn't know this, because they haven't released any photos of Alison, but she looked a lot like Theresa, the first girl who was killed. I mean, not like sisters or anything, but the same coloring and height."

Cold was working its way down my spine, too, and neither the cozy room nor the cup of hot tea I held were doing much to help.

She continued, "And I remembered how when I first saw you at the potluck in Christmas, I thought you reminded me of someone, and then when I went back after winter break, I realized it was Alison from my stats class. I didn't really think about it after that because I was busy, and, well, people are always reminding you of someone, right? But after the attacks started, and I realized both of the girls who were killed looked sort of like you, Angela...." Trailing off, she lifted her shoulders. "I don't know. It's nothing, right? Or is it some kind of messed-up serial killer, with, I don't know, Wolverine claws or something? They always have a *type,* right?"

For a long moment no one said anything. Mason, apparently realizing I wasn't going to answer her cousin's question, said derisively, "They were *bite* marks, not claw marks, so there goes your serial-killer theory. It's just a weird coincidence. I mean, yeah, both girls had dark hair. So do I. Does that make me a target for the next wolf attack?"

"Nobody's going to be a *target,* because that's not how wolves think," Carla snapped, obviously irritated that Mason had shot down her serial-killer theory so quickly. "I mean, they must have attacked because they were hungry and the girls had food or something. It had nothing to do with what they *looked* like."

"How do you know?" Mason shot back. "None of the reports said anything about *food*. They would have mentioned it if that was really what happened. And they'd be telling everyone not to carry food with them when they walk around campus. It's just common *sense*."

Carla didn't appear to have an answer for that. Her mouth opened and then shut, as if she'd thought of a rebuttal, only to realize it wasn't going to help her case any.

"It's strange," I agreed, since I figured I'd better contribute something. "I don't think it means anything, though." Well, that was what I told them. I thought it did mean something, although what, I couldn't really begin to guess. "There are lots of dark-haired girls who attend Northern Pines. I'm not going to run a statistical analysis or anything, but I have a feeling it would be a lot stranger if they were both redheads or something like that."

"True," Carla agreed. "I know we all are looking for a pattern because that's what people do. Doesn't mean there is one."

I forced myself to nod. Did two data points really constitute a pattern? Carla's statistics professor would probably have a few choice words on the subject.

In the meantime, I'd just have to hope that those two data points—also known as Theresa and Alison—wouldn't expand into something far, far worse.

CHAPTER FIFTEEN

Yee Naaldlooshii

THE NEXT DAY, THE BODY OF ANOTHER YOUNG WOMAN WAS found, and the day after that, yet another. Classes at Northern Pines were canceled, according to Mason, who called me to say she and Carla and some of their friends were taking an impromptu vacation to Tucson.

"The campus was crawling with fish and game people, police, sheriffs, maybe even the FBI," she told me. "I would've stayed away even if they hadn't canceled classes indefinitely, but at least this way everyone's going to have a short semester, so I won't have to play makeup with my classes. Besides, it's eighty-five degrees down in Tucson. I'm *so* ready to bust out some sandals."

"And you got permission?" I asked. After all, Tucson was de la Paz territory. Maya had been extremely friendly the last time we met, but I wasn't sure how she'd feel about a mass invasion of Wilcoxes.

"Oh, sure. Lucas handled it. Not sure why, since Damon should've been the one to make the call, but he's been under the weather lately."

"Really?" I interjected, thinking that sounded odd. Somehow I couldn't imagine any virus being brave enough to take up residence in Damon Wilcox's body.

"Yeah," she replied. "I guess he hadn't been in to teach for a couple of days even before everything got shut down. Anyway, I gotta go. You stay safe!"

I murmured that I would, and ended the call, my mind churning. Connor had been forced to agree with me that something strange was going on after images of the murdered young women were plastered all over the the news and stared up from the front page of every newspaper in town. All of them between twenty and twenty-three, all with long, dark, wavy hair, all fair-skinned, all slender. The tallest five-foot-seven, the shortest five-foot-four. In dim lighting, or if viewed by someone with bad vision, they probably would have looked almost identical.

"As long as you stick close to home, you'll be fine," he'd told me after I'd shoved that day's paper in the trash, not wanting to have another face a little too much like mine staring at me from beneath a lurid headline. "The attacks were all on campus, or near campus housing…a lot of which backs up to open land. But here, downtown? No way would a wild animal come anywhere near this place."

That made sense, but I still tried not to go out by myself except in broad daylight. Too bad, because I'd started to explore Flagstaff on my own, driving around in Connor's FJ and enjoying the sense of freedom it gave me, even as he stayed indoors and painted like a madman. Another gallery show was planned for late April, and because he'd sold so many paintings already, he had a lot of work to do to rebuild his inventory.

After Mason's latest revelations, my brain started working at the mystery. So Damon had been feeling ill lately? It could mean nothing…

…or it could mean everything.

No, that was ridiculous. I couldn't deny that Damon was a master of dark and unknown magic, magic he'd manipulated to do things no one else could. And he'd certainly made himself scarce lately, but that didn't mean much, other than him not wanting to see how happy Connor and I were together. True, Damon had apparently hooked up with Jessica. However, I had the distinct impression that was all about getting an heir, and had very little to do with true love or attraction. At least, not on his side. Jessica was clearly crazy (and I do mean *crazy*) about him.

But even stacking up every damning thing I knew about Damon still didn't seem enough to make the leap from unscrupulous warlock and dabbler in dark magic to bloodthirsty and murderous wolf...were-wolf...whatever. That was silly. Werewolves weren't real. Neither were vampires or chupacabras or zombies. Witches, yes, of course. We were just people, though—people with some unusual gifts, true, but even the blackest warlock I've ever heard of had never gone rampaging around, killing college students just for shits and giggles. For one thing, it was the sort of behavior that attracted far too much attention. I couldn't deny that murder had been done in the name of magic and power, and probably would again someday. But not wholesale murder. Not like this.

And I knew I didn't dare say anything of my crazy suspicions to Connor, because he would definitely think that my dislike of Damon had gotten the better of me at last.

"That's some frown you're wearing," Connor said, breaking my reverie as he came into our apartment from the studio across the hall.

Somehow I managed to keep myself from startling. "Is it? Sorry, just thinking. Mason called and said she and Carla are heading down to Tucson for some sun and to get away from it all. The campus is closed until further notice, apparently."

He leaned down over the back of the couch and pressed his lips against my neck. Despite my worry, a delicious shiver passed over me at his touch. I reached up and behind me, pulling him closer, shifting so that now we were face to face, kissing, mouths opening to taste one another again.

"Taking a break?" I murmured after he pulled away slightly so he could draw in a breath.

"I am now."

I didn't need any further encouragement. Slipping off the couch, I stood and went over to him, put my arms around him, let him gather me up and take me to the stairs, then up to the bedroom we now shared. So good to forget everything except the warm scent of his skin, the strength of his hands as he caressed me, the unbelievable sense of completion as he filled me again, our bodies moving together in perfect rhythm.

Afterward, I lay in his arms and listened to the deep, regular sound of his heart beating, felt the slow rise and fall of his chest beneath my cheek. It was so good to be here, safe in the circle of his arms. I wished it could always be like this, just the two of us with no outside worries or complications. Unfortunately, I knew that wasn't the way the world worked.

———

At first the closing of the campus seemed to have stopped the attacks. A day went by, then two, then three, and the whole town seemed to breathe a collective sigh of relief. Whatever had caused the hideous rampage seemed to be over.

Until the body was found near a carport at an apartment complex a mile from the university. Same savage bites to the throat, same general description for the victim: early twenties, dark-haired, slender.

And I got a call from my Aunt Rachel, who was so spooked by what she'd read in the local paper that she even told me that Connor and I should leave Flagstaff for a while and come to Jerome.

"It would be good to see you, and I can't stop worrying—that is, I was already worried, with you surrounded by Wilcoxes, and now with these horrible attacks—"

"The Wilcoxes really aren't a problem," I cut in. "They've been very kind to me."

"Oh, really?" Disbelief fairly dripped from her tone. "*All* of them?"

It was pretty obvious who she'd meant with that "all of them" remark. "Okay, Damon is not exactly the sweetest guy I've ever met, but there are some cousins who're my age and have been really nice. They're just people, Rachel. Not the boogeyman, not the big bad."

"They're brainwashing you."

Of all the—"No, not really. Maybe it's easier for you to think that than to realize this feud is silly and has gone on long enough."

A long pause. Then she said coldly, "Angela, I love you, but you don't know what you're talking about. You've let yourself ignore their history because you care for Connor, and as far as I can tell, he does seem like a nice enough young man. It's unfortunate he was born into that family. But all his good qualities have blinded you to who and what they are."

I realized then it wouldn't matter what I said. She'd long ago formed her opinion of the Wilcox clan, built on stories of their iniquities, stories that had been passed down from generation to generation. Talk about brainwashing. "Whatever. I'm not the one who's blind here. Anyway, I think we're just fine where we are. None of the attacks have taken place anywhere near our apartment, and I'm careful. I've stopped going out alone. So I'll be okay until the authorities get it handled."

"Angela—"

"It was nice talking to you, Rachel." I hung up without waiting for a reply. It was rude, but I didn't want to hear any more of her diatribes about the Wilcoxes.

But her words had gotten me thinking again, thoughts going down pathways I'd tried to avoid. I'd asked Connor a few days earlier if he'd heard anything from Damon, and he'd said, his tone almost abrupt, that no, he hadn't, but it wasn't a big deal because they often went as much as a week at a time without talking if there wasn't anything that Damon deemed worthy enough of conversation. What Connor had left unsaid was that Damon probably didn't have much use for him anymore, that the little brother who'd once worshipfully done pretty much anything Damon asked was gone, replaced by someone who'd found his own purpose in life, and the sort of love the *primus* couldn't begin to comprehend.

Maybe it really wasn't a big deal. For all I knew, Jessica was keeping him trapped in the house so they could work full-time at making their perfect little Wilcox heir. Ugh. There was a visual I really didn't need.

So I went across the landing to the studio and let myself in. The air was thick with the scent of linseed oil and turpentine. Once the weather warmed up, Connor would be able to open the windows and let the fresh air carry those smells away, but it was still far too cold for that.

His back was to me as he worked away on a large canvas, part of a triptych showing a panoramic canyon scene. There were at least ten reference photos clipped to the easel, all of which showed a blazing blue sky above rock formations so grand they had to be from the canyon of the same name. The photos must have been taken the summer before, and I suddenly ached for the return of warmer weather, of sandals and hot winds scented with dry grass, of a time that didn't feel weighted down by perpetual winter. Well, the equinox was only three days off now. It would still be a long time before truly comfortable temperatures returned to Flagstaff, but they were on their way.

I was going to wait until Connor hit a stopping point before I said anything, but one of the floorboards creaked under my feet, and he turned at once. The slightest frown creased his forehead before he smoothed it away, then set down his paintbrush and came toward me.

"Everything okay?" he asked.

It was a valid question; generally I left him alone until he was done painting and was ready to come back over to the apartment. I didn't like to disturb him when he worked, knowing how important it was for him to finally give free rein to his talents, to finally have the chance to be known for the gifted artist he truly was.

"Maybe. Yes. No."

He grinned, green eyes dancing. "I don't think it can be all three at once, sweetheart."

My insides wanted to melt at his casual use of the endearment, but I knew if I didn't broach the subject soon, I'd never have the nerve. Actually, I wasn't sure if I had the guts to say it now, not with those green eyes I loved so much watching me, open and with no idea of what I was about to ask.

"Connor, I—" Damn it, I should be tougher than this. I was the McAllister *prima. In name only,* I thought bitterly, and tried to push the notion aside. That was yet another situation which would have to be resolved in the near future. This problem—*possible problem*, I reminded myself—with Damon had to be addressed first. Was I willing to let more innocent girls die just because I was too cowardly to have this conversation with Connor?

He came to me then, pulling me against him and holding me close. One hand stroked my hair, and I caught a faint drift of the sage and chamomile soap he used to clean up when he was done painting for the day. "What is it? You know you can tell me anything."

Could I, really? I knew he loved me, and I loved him, but even with that, even with the consort bond, there was so much we didn't know about one another. And Damon had been the only person close to him for so many years. Connor truly wouldn't be alive if it weren't for his brother's intervention, and for all my personal dislike of the *primus,* I couldn't ignore how important that one fact was, how the saving of a life created an enormously strong bond as well, even beyond the one they already shared as brothers.

And if I turned out to be wrong…if these sneaking doubts and suspicions were only that, and not the instincts of a *prima* at work…would Connor forgive me for thinking these things of his brother?

I didn't want to think about that. He'd only been in my life for a few short months, but even so I couldn't imagine losing him. No, that would never happen. The bond between a *prima* and her consort was unbreakable, even when stretched to the limit.

The words came forth in a rush, as if I knew I had to say them now before I talked myself out of uttering them. "I have a very bad feeling, Connor. You haven't heard from Damon, and Mason said he'd been ill and hadn't taught for a few days just before the attacks started. And with all those girls resembling one another…resembling *me*…you just can't say that's a coincidence anymore. I know you said he'd moved on, had focused his energies elsewhere, but I'm not sure I believe that. I think he's still angry that his plan didn't work, that he was unable to join his powers with mine, that he couldn't use me to break the curse. I don't know exactly what's going on. I just feel that somehow he's behind it."

Through this whole speech, Connor listened silently. When I was done, he let go of me and stepped back a pace. Even that small separation was enough to cause my heart to miss a beat, telling me the words I'd just spoken were exactly the wrong ones.

Eyes narrowing, he said, "Do you have any idea how ridiculous that sounds, Angela? You have no proof. None at all. Just a few random facts that barely even connect. So what if Damon was sick and missed a few days of work? He's the *primus*, but he's still a regular man. There's a bad flu going around. Did you stop to think it might just be that?"

"No, but—"

"And I already told you that we're not in constant contact, so not hearing from him for a while doesn't mean all that much, either."

"But what about all those girls?" I burst out. "Have you ever heard of a wild animal that attacks only a certain physical type? It's not possible!"

He didn't exactly look away from me, but I could see the way his gaze shifted, the way he wouldn't quite meet my eyes. "There has to be some rational explanation—"

"Then tell me what it is, because I sure as hell haven't been able to come up with one." I went to him then, took both his hands. At least he didn't try to pull away, although normally he would have twined his fingers through mine. Instead, his hands just sort of sat in mine, limp and cool. Fine. I tightened my grip on his fingers. "Look, Connor, I would love for you to prove me wrong. *Please* prove me wrong. Just—I don't know—call him."

"And what if he doesn't answer? He hates phones anyway, and if he's not feeling well—"

"Then let's go out to his house. Make something up as a reason...we wanted to welcome Jessica to the family or something."

His expression told me that was a silly idea. "Jessica's already in the family, remember? Distantly, but still. They'll know we're snooping."

"So what? If I'm wrong, I promise I'll never suspect Damon of anything again. Isn't it worth looking a little foolish to clear this whole thing up?"

For a few seconds he remained silent, clearly thinking it over. At last he let out a breath and gave a reluctant nod. "Okay, if only because it means you'll finally let this thing go. Then we can get back to normal."

Normal. I wasn't so sure about that. How could anything be normal when young women were dying horribly? But at least if Damon was cleared of suspicion, it would mean this whole horrible killing spree was just some bizarre quirk of nature, with no darker motivation behind it.

"Thank you," I said simply, and I meant it. Connor might not believe me, but at least he was willing to indulge me.

He pulled his car keys out of his pocket. "Let's go."

———

The ride out to Damon's house was a tense, silent one. I watched the bleak late-winter landscape with its dead, dry grass and small patches of ice pass by outside the car window and tried not to think about what would be worse—having the *primus* laugh at me for entertaining such foolish suspicions, or having those suspicions confirmed.

Connor drove without looking at me, his eyes fixed on the road ahead. Goddess only knows what he must have been thinking. That I was wasting his time, that if I really cared about him, I would have taken him at his word?

I couldn't say, because he sure wasn't talking, and I didn't have the courage to ask.

About twenty minutes after leaving the apartment, we pulled into the long driveway and stopped in front of the garage. Parked in front of one of the garage doors was one of those odd-looking Nissan Juke compact SUVs. I raised an eyebrow at Connor, and he shrugged.

"Must be Jessica's."

Right. I'd forgotten that, according to Carla, Jessica had pretty much moved in with Damon. Or that was what everyone had decided, as she'd packed up some of her things and announced to her mother that she was spending "a few days" at the *primus*'s house. No one had seen her since, but if they were shacked up trying to make the next Wilcox heir, that wasn't so strange.

Except that he'd supposedly been too sick to go to work.

Dead, dry pine needles were scattered across the expansive driveway and the front doorstep as well. Again, not that strange, since we'd had some bad winds a few nights earlier. But they made the place look neglected, abandoned.

Now who's seeing things that aren't there? I scolded myself.

Connor was frowning, though. "The gardeners should've been here to clear all this away. Damon has them out twice a week because the property is so big."

"Maybe the windstorm came through right after they were here, and they're coming tomorrow or something."

"Maybe," he said, but his tone was dubious. But he seemed to shrug and stepped up to the door, then rang the doorbell.

I could hear it echo hollowly through the house, but there was no answer. We stood there in silence— ten seconds, fifteen, twenty. I could practically see Connor counting off how long it was okay to wait before he pressed the little glowing button in its fancy dark bronze mounting again. Another push of his gloved finger against the bell, another wait.

Of course, it was entirely possible that Damon and Jessica had gone out, were taking advantage of his forced vacation because of the campus being shut down to take a day trip somewhere or go out to eat or shop or whatever. It was hard for me to wrap my brain around Damon doing anything so common-place, but he'd maintained the façade of being an upstanding member of Flagstaff society for his entire adult life, and so I knew he most likely must do those kinds of things from time to time.

But even though that seemed the most plausible explanation, I couldn't accept it. Something was wrong here, a dark, pulsing sensation of evil at the heart of the imposing house. Stepping past Connor, I drew off my glove and laid a hand against the doorframe.

"What are you doing?" he asked.

I couldn't really answer, because I didn't know for sure. The *prima* fire in my belly, usually coiled and quiet and quiescent, suddenly flared within me, and I felt it more strongly now, waves of malice, of ill intent. And somewhere within it, the foul coppery stink of blood.

Retching, I lifted my hand and backed away. Connor went to me at once, catching me as I stumbled on the step that led down to the driveway. "Angela! What is it?"

"Something awful," I gasped. "I felt it. I don't know what's in there, but please, Connor—I think we should go."

"Go?" he demanded. "We just got here!"

"I know that. But I think—I think we shouldn't face whatever it is by ourselves."

His hands tightened on mine. "If Damon's in trouble, if he needs our help—"

What could I say to that? Looking into Connor's face, I realized he would never walk away if he thought his brother was in any kind of trouble. Unfortunately, from what I'd just felt, it seemed more that Damon himself was the source of the black energy I'd sensed. But I doubted I could convince Connor of that. All I could do was be on my guard.

"Okay," I said reluctantly. "But we need to be careful—and we need to be ready to run."

He nodded, although he gave me a strange look, as if wondering whether this was all simply more of my overactive imagination. "All right."

So we went back to the front door. Connor laid his hand on the heavy bronze handle, clearly preparing to unlock the door using magic. Then his eyes widened.

"It's already open," he murmured.

The muscles at the back of my neck tightened further. Every instinct in me was screaming to run, to get out of there as fast as my feet would carry me, but somehow I managed to stand my ground, wait as Connor pushed the door inward.

A wave of stale, warm air greeted us, bringing with it the acrid scent I'd somehow sensed mentally before I even smelled it with my nose. Blood, metallic and strong, and beneath that the cloying odor of decay.

It was dim inside, all the blinds and curtains closed. Connor reached out and flicked the light switch in the entryway, turning on the pendant lamp that hung from the high ceiling.

"Holy shit," he breathed, even as I raised a hand to my mouth to keep myself from gagging.

The place looked like a whirlwind had struck it. Furniture toppled over, lamps and vases smashed. But that wasn't the worst. Lying on the floor, arms stretched toward the entryway as if she had been desperately trying to escape, was Jessica Lowe. At least, I assumed it was her—I thought I recognized the spill of long honey-colored hair. Mercifully, she now lay face down.

Even from where I stood, I could see the blood spattered across the wooden floor, the dark spray on the walls. The shirt she wore was shredded, claw marks showing clearly on her pale flesh.

"We need to go," I whispered, laying a hand on Connor's arm and beginning to tug him back toward the door. "We have to call the police."

"No. Not the police. Not yet," he whispered back. He didn't try to free his arm from my grasp, but he did use his other hand to pull his cell phone out of his jacket pocket.

"What are you talking about? Something killed her!"

"I know that. But think about it, Angela. Think about how much attention this will bring on all of us. We can't afford that kind of scrutiny."

As much as I hated what he was saying, I knew he was right. The McAllisters obeyed the same rule—do what you must, but never risk bringing unwanted attention on the clan. It was the only way we'd survived undetected for so long.

I nodded mutely, my body tense, somehow knowing the threat was still here, although the house was completely still. Flesh crawling, I wondered if who—or what—had killed Jessica was watching us as we stood in the entryway. At least we could be out the front door in a few steps if necessary.

Had Jessica thought the same thing?

I shivered, and watched as Connor selected someone from his contacts list and waited while the call connected. "Lucas?" he said. "I need you to come out to Damon's house now. We've—well, we've got a situation. And bring Marie with you." A pause as he listened to Lucas's response. "I don't know. Just get here as quickly as you can." He ended the call and turned toward me. "I think we'd better wait out in the car. Just to be safe."

That sounded like an excellent plan to me. I had just opened my mouth to reply when I heard a hideous growl, and a dark blur of a shape launched itself at me.

No time to think, no time to do anything except call on the power within me to flare up and outward, a flash of golden glowing light bursting away from me and knocking my attacker back a good three yards. It got to its feet, growling, and as I stared at it, a sick, choking feeling rose in my throat.

Yes, it was a wolf, a huge thing with gray matted fur and sharp bloodstained teeth showing between its snarling gums. But those were not the eyes of a wolf staring at me. No, they were black, utterly black, so dark you couldn't see the pupils.

Damon Wilcox's eyes.

All this went through my mind in the endless space between one heartbeat and the next. Before I could even blink, Connor had leapt in front of me, shielding me with his body. He stared down at the wolf, horror clear in every tense line of his frame.

His words, when they came, broke my heart.

"Don't hurt her, Damon. Please. I love her."

A low guttural growl, and the wolf—Damon— crouched lower. I stiffened, gathering my own strength to strike, should the need arise, should he leap for us, teeth bared to tear yet another throat. Then it made the oddest whimpering noise as it stared up at Connor. A shudder went through it, almost as if some part of its mind was trying to get it to move backward while its wolfish instincts were telling it to attack.

Stained teeth flashing, it leapt forward again. Once more I moved purely on instinct, somehow knowing that Connor had neither the magic nor the will to confront his brother. My hands went up, even as I focused the energy and flung it forward, this time using it as a weapon rather than a barrier.

A horrible yiping howl, and the Damon-wolf went flying backward, hitting one of the overturned tables. I heard a terrible *crack*, and thought maybe I had broken its ribs. But no, it got to its feet and shook its head, and I saw that the force of the impact had split one of the table legs in half. The wolf growled, and I raised my hands again. Beside me, Connor was taking in deep, gasping breaths, his body halfway blocking me still, as if he wanted to act as my protector but knew I was far more suited to this fight than he.

Once more I had that sensation of time stretching out, of a second seeming to take hours to pass. I heard my own ragged breathing, the low snarling growl emanating from the wolf's throat. Those black pupil-less eyes met mine, and in them I saw a terrible hunger, a need that would never be slaked. Although the house was stuffily warm, my body went ice cold. Could I push the creature back a third time if it attacked again?

But after that one long, hideous pause, the Damon-wolf let out a sound halfway between a bark and a snarl, and slunk away, a dark incongruous shape against the gleaming wood floors and expensive rugs. Broken glass crunched under its paws, and then it was gone.

Neither Connor nor I moved. We only stood there, huddled together, bodies tense, sure it would come back at any moment. Then, from far off, I heard a drawn-out baying that could only have come from the creature. Somehow it had gotten outside, had moved off.

And then, much closer, the rushing sound of tires in the driveway. The *thunk* of one car door shutting, then another, and a few seconds later Lucas Wilcox's tall form filled the doorway. Behind him I could see Marie, expression impassive as always, although I caught the slightest widening of her eyes as she took in the destruction around us, the limp form of Jessica Lowe's body on the floor.

Lucas, however, was not nearly as reserved. "Fucking hell!" he exclaimed almost the second he walked into the entryway. His gaze fell to Jessica, and I saw his mouth tighten, and the glitter of sorrow in his dark eyes. "Poor kid," he added softly. To my surprise, he went and knelt next to her, laid a hand on her head, then seemed to murmur some words, although I couldn't make out what they were. Then he pushed himself to his feet, expression grim. "What happened?"

I opened my mouth to reply, since Connor seemed more or less stunned, still grappling with the realization that his brother had succumbed to an evil he couldn't begin to contemplate. However, Marie forestalled me, saying,

"Damon sought power where he should not. I warned him, told him not to stray down paths he couldn't begin to comprehend. But he ignored me, and has become the *yee naaldlooshii*."

"The *what?*" Connor demanded, seeming to come out of his stupor.

Her eyes were a warm brown, striking against her black hair. They appeared calm, seemingly untouched by the horrors around us. "A shapechanger—what some call a skin-walker."

"Oh, come on," Lucas said, shaking his head. "That's just a legend. You're not suggesting—"

"She doesn't have to suggest," I broke in. "Connor and I both saw it. A huge gray wolf…but with Damon's eyes."

Beside me, Connor shuddered, but he didn't say anything to contradict me. Somewhere inside, he might have wished he could deny what we had seen. Luckily, he was not the type to challenge the evidence of his own eyes.

"Yes," Marie said. "It is usually the eyes that give it away."

Lucas looked baffled, scared, and angry all at the same time. "I'm sure there's a perfectly logical explanation—"

Marie turned her cool gaze on him. "There is one, and it is that our *primus* has given in to a great evil. His was always a questing soul, and this time it sought power in the very worst place it possibly could."

"So what do we do?" Connor asked, voice tight. "How do we help him, make him get better?"

"You cannot help him." Her tone was implacable, impersonal as a judge handing down a sentence. "Once a man has destroyed the humanity within himself in exchange for these powers, there is no redemption. All we can do is stop him before he takes any more innocent lives." At last she glanced down at Jessica's prone body, expelling the smallest of breaths as she did so. Even as Connor shook his head in denial, she went on, "Would you hesitate to kill a rabid dog? That is what your brother has become, Connor.

"The only thing we can do is put him out of his misery."

CHAPTER SIXTEEN

Doppelgänger

I DROVE US BACK TO TOWN, SINCE CONNOR WAS IN NO SHAPE to get behind the wheel. Lucas and Marie stayed behind at Damon's house, calling for reinforcements to get the place cleaned up by any means necessary, magical or otherwise. Apparently they planned to have Jessica's body moved to a location near one of the previous wolf attacks, to leave her there and have the authorities think she was just another victim, one who hadn't been discovered as quickly as the others. It wasn't so very far from the truth.

As Connor and I prepared to leave, though, I saw a flicker out of the corner of my eye, and realized it was Jessica, standing in the middle of the hallway and watching as Lucas and Marie began tidying up as best they could. Well, the one thing most of the ghosts of my acquaintance had in common was sudden, violent death. It shouldn't have surprised me that Jessica remained in Damon's house, her soul shackled to this world by the very obsession that had led to her death.

I wished I could speak to her, but she disappeared the second I turned toward her and our eyes met. Time for that later, maybe, although the thought of having to return to that house anytime soon made my flesh crawl. And I said nothing to Connor as I took the FJ's keys from him and got into the driver's seat. He had enough to deal with right now without being informed that his brother's house was now haunted.

We were about halfway home when he finally spoke. "You're not saying it."

"Saying what?" I asked, although I thought I knew.

"'I told you so.'"

"What good would that do?" I lifted one hand from the steering wheel, reached down to lay it on top of his where it rested on his knee. At least he didn't try to move it away…but neither did he try to touch me in return, only sat there, not responding at all. A nervous quiver went through my stomach, but I told myself he was just in shock, trying to process everything we'd just seen and heard. "I'm so very sorry, Connor."

"Are you?" he asked, staring straight out the window at the buildings and cars passing by. "I mean, you never liked Damon."

Well, he didn't give me much reason to, I thought. I would never say such a thing to Connor, though. Not now. He loved his brother, and even if I couldn't fully understand that love, I had to respect it. "I didn't agree with his methods," I said carefully. "But I would have been willing to meet him halfway, for your sake."

A brief, curt nod, and Connor shifted in his seat, pulling his hand from beneath mine. I didn't try to prevent him from doing so. The last thing he needed right now was me clinging to him. I was here, and I'd listen to anything he had to say, but I wouldn't force myself on him. Somehow I knew that would only make things worse.

We pulled into the alley behind our building, and I parked the SUV. At least I was more or less used to driving the FJ by that point, so there wasn't any fudging or having to back up and try again, which had happened once or twice as I was familiarizing myself with the vehicle and the cramped parking space I had to squeeze it into.

Connor got out and I followed him, trailing behind as he unlocked the rear door to the building and let us in. We walked upstairs in silence, and still said nothing as we entered the apartment.

In the back of my mind, I'd sort of been hoping that he might find some kind of equilibrium once we were back home and in familiar surroundings, but if anything, being in the apartment only seemed to worsen his mood. He unbuttoned his coat and flung it over the back of a chair rather than hanging it up properly. Not a big deal, of course, but I knew Connor, knew that he was usually careful about such things.

As I was taking off my own coat and putting it away, his gaze fell on a couple of paintings that he'd stacked up against the wall in the hallway. He'd brought them over from the studio the day before, wanting to see them from different angles and in different lighting. Now, though, his brow darkened as he stared at them, and before I could do or say anything, he'd driven his booted foot right through one of them.

"It's all bullshit!" he growled, kicking away the ruined painting. "All of it! What the fuck was I doing, sitting here and making a bunch of fucking *paintings* when my brother needed me?"

Aghast, I could only stare at the wreckage of what a few seconds ago had been a summer-toned landscape of warm grass and tall, cool pines. "Connor—"

I could tell he was about to do the same thing to the second painting. Without thinking, I reached out with my mind, whisked it out of harm's way, sent it winging across the room until it settled safely against the wall under the windows.

"You're getting pretty good at that, aren't you?" he snapped. "Where did all this come from, anyway? Last thing I heard, about all you were good for was talking to ghosts."

The rasp of his voice as he said those hateful words was so similar to Damon's that I wanted to put my hands up to my ears so I wouldn't have to hear it anymore. But that would be a childish gesture, and ultimately futile. I drew in a breath, then said, "It's like I told you before—the *prima*'s power is there against the time when it's needed."

For the longest moment, he didn't reply, only glared at me, and I couldn't help wondering what his next attack would be, what burst of anger I would have to deflect. But something in him seemed to crumple, and all of a sudden his shoulders drooped. He raised his hand to his hair, ran his fingers through it as if somehow that would clear the fog of anger from his mind.

"I'm sorry," he said at last.

Relief pulsed through me, and I went to him then, pulling him against me and wrapping my arms around him. He clung to me, and I whispered, "It's okay. It's okay."

Except I really didn't think it would be.

———

I made us grilled cheese and tomato soup for dinner—ultimate comfort food—and we went to bed early. No lovemaking that night, but I held him close, tried to reassure him with my presence until he finally fell asleep in my arms. He'd had one terse phone call from Lucas saying that the house had been cleaned up and Jessica "taken care of," which meant her body must have been left somewhere to be found.

Maybe once upon a time the Wilcoxes could've made a person evaporate in a puff of smoke or whatever, but these days everyone had too much of an electronic trail. Sure, people did disappear from time to time; of course they did. In Jessica's case, though, there would have been a lot of questions asked. She was from a prominent and well-connected family, and she'd been seen in public with Damon. It wasn't a risk the clan members were willing to take. After so many other young women had been killed, her death in exactly the same manner wouldn't cause nearly as much uproar as a mysterious disappearance might.

Horrible that her poor body was just dumped somewhere, though. I didn't want to think about that, nor her pale face watching me from the shadows of Damon's entry hall. There had to be some way to get her to move on, to relinquish her hold on this plane of existence. That had never been my power, though. I could talk to ghosts, but they had to be the ones to decide it was time to move on. It had happened once or twice in Jerome, so I knew it was possible. I just had never been the one to help them make that transition.

Cleaning up the scene of the crime, however, didn't help much with the ultimate problem of what to do about Damon. I'd vaguely heard the term "skin-walker" before, but hadn't paid much attention to it, thinking it must be only a legend. What was happening here in Flagstaff was real, though, and I had to trust that Marie knew what she was talking about. Anyway, I had the evidence of my own eyes to prove that Damon had succumbed to some sort of horrible dark spell. Was the killing of the young women purposeful, to fulfill a black and needy magic, or was it the wolf striking out with no control, killing those who looked like the girl who'd thwarted his attempt to grasp even more power?

Lying there in the dark as Connor slept fitfully against my shoulder, I had the horrible thought that maybe it would've been better if Damon's plan had worked, that he'd somehow managed to bond with me even though he was not my consort. At least that way only one life would have been ruined, not seven. *Eight,* I amended mentally, adding Jessica to the list of the wolf's victims.

No. The word resonated from somewhere deep within me, not sounding like myself at all. Then I would never have been with Connor, never felt the rightness of bonding with the one man in the world who was meant to be mine. All this was terrible, and I couldn't see my way through to a happy ending, and yet I knew there had to be one, had to be some way for us to find our way past the darkness to one another.

With that thought to soothe my fears, I fell asleep at last as well, my warmth blending with Connor's and wrapping around both of us, sheltering us, keeping us safe.

For now.

———

He was subdued the next morning, but calm, as if the sleep into which he'd escaped had helped him to put some distance between himself and the terrible events of the day before. That calm was shaken a little when the morning news reported the discovery of an eighth victim. The reporters made special note of the fact that this young woman did not match the descriptions of the others, and no one was sure exactly what that meant.

They'd never figure it out, of course. All the policemen and sheriffs and fish and game officials in the world wouldn't be able to hunt down this wolf. No, that task must fall on us.

Would you hesitate to kill a rabid dog? Marie had asked. Most people would say no...but the question became a little more complex when the rabid dog in question was something that used to be a man. And not just any man, but the *primus* of the Wilcoxes, a dangerous warlock who already had more power at his disposal than anyone else around.

Except you, I thought, and stirred my coffee uneasily. Connor and I were sitting in the living room, the TV on, although neither of us was paying much attention to it. He was staring out the window, at the blue sky peeking in between the blinds, as if wondering how the sun could be so bright and the sky so clear when the world had been turned upside down. His world, anyway.

I had wondered in the past why it was that a *prima* of my clan could hold back the power of the Wilcoxes when, to all outward appearances, they were so much stronger than we McAllisters. Now that the magic had been fully awoken within me, I thought I began to understand. It was a power called on only when needed, but no less potent because of that.

Damon Wilcox was the *primus*...and therefore only a *prima* could hope to defeat him.

The toast and eggs I'd just eaten churned uneasily in my stomach. Knowing you must do something didn't make it any easier to take, especially when that something involved confronting a magically enhanced supernatural being who also happened to be your brother-in-law in everything but name.

Connor's phone buzzed. He must have set it to vibrate the night before. I glanced over at him, expecting to see him lean over to pick it up, but he ignored it, gaze still fixed on the sky outside.

After a few more buzzes, it went silent. A second or two ticked by, and then it began buzzing again.

"Goddammit," he said, and finally retrieved it. His eyes narrowed as he scanned the display, then lifted it to his ear. "What?"

His brusque tone seemed to indicate it must be someone in the family. I certainly couldn't imagine him talking that way to Joelle, or any of his civilian friends. I knotted my hands in my lap and waited, hoping it was merely Lucas calling to give another progress report.

But then Connor said, "We'll be over in an hour. See you then." He ended the call, and tossed the phone back on the coffee table.

I winced as it smacked against the glass surface, but luckily neither of them seemed about to shatter. After waiting a second or two and realizing he wasn't about to volunteer any information, I asked, "Who was that?"

"Marie. She wants us to come over."

Great. Although I knew it was necessary to meet with her, since she seemed to have a better grasp of the situation than anyone else, I wasn't really looking forward to it. Something about her set my teeth on edge.

Worse, though, was the realization that Connor had just told her we'd be there in an hour, and we were both sitting on the couch in assorted pajama bottoms and T-shirts and sweatshirts. No way I'd have time to wash my hair.

I stood up. "Well, I'd better shower, then."

Before yesterday, such a statement would have led to him offering to join me at least half the time. Now he gave the barest of nods and said, "Okay."

Since I knew better than to push it, I only nodded as well and went upstairs.

———

Marie didn't live all that far away; we ended up walking, since her house was located on the northeast side of the downtown section. The homes here were mostly older, maybe not quite as old as the buildings in Jerome, but still probably constructed in the early years of the last century. I imagined it must be beautiful in the summer or in the fall as the leaves on all the tall old trees turned, but now they were still bare and forlorn. Spring came late to Flagstaff.

I'd somehow managed to keep myself from indulging in idle chitchat to fill up the terrible silence between us. With Connor so on edge, I didn't want to do or say anything to set him off. As we walked,

I couldn't help brooding over what Marie wanted to say to us. Give us tips on how to kill a skin-walker?

Her house was a pretty two-story Craftsman painted a warm barn red. Funny, but somehow I hadn't imagined her living in a place like this. Stark adobe seemed more her style.

We paused on the front porch, and she opened the door almost as soon as Connor rang the bell. Had she been staring out the window, waiting for us?

As always, she looked serene enough, but I saw the slightest narrowing of her eyes as she greeted her cousin and invited us in. The furnishings were simple—a brown couch and matching chair, although both had colorful pillows with southwestern patterns to liven them up a bit. Navajo weavings hung on the walls, although the floors were bare wood.

"Sit down," she said, pointing to the sofa.

It seemed more a command than a request. But I didn't protest, just took a seat on the couch. After a brief hesitation, Connor did the same.

Usually this was around the time when someone would offer coffee or tea, or at least water, but Marie didn't seem too inclined to play hostess. Instead, she crossed her arms and stared down at us. "This will not get better," she said. "This is not something we can ignore. The *yee naaldlooshii* will continue to kill until it is stopped."

"His name is Damon." Connor's voice was quiet, but I could hear the edge to his tone.

"Once, perhaps." Marie looked from him to me, where her gaze rested. "To become the yee naald-looshii is to lose one's humanity. And Damon is in an even worse case than those who have taken this darkest road before him, because he did not approach it with the proper respect. In arrogance, he reached out for a power he did not understand, one he underestimated, thinking it lesser than the magic that has lived in this family's blood for uncounted generations. There is no going back from such a thing."

"There must be," Connor protested. "I refuse to believe that there is no way to bring him back to himself."

For the first time her expression softened, and I realized she did care for Connor a good deal, even if hers was not the type of personality to reveal such a thing willingly. "For your sake, I wish it were possible. But it isn't. The only release for Damon is in death. Perhaps then his soul can finally find some peace."

I could feel Connor tense next to me, saw the way his fingers tightened on his knees. "You're wrong."

Surprisingly, she laughed. "How easily you say that, Connor. But I'm not. You think this is an easy thing for me, to say that the primus of this clan must be killed? It's going to be terrible for all of us. He has no son, no child to inherit his gift. So you know what that means."

Connor's fingers went white-knuckled. "No."

"Something else you don't want to hear? Well, I'll say it anyway. You're the last of Jeremiah's line. The power must pass to you. There is no other way."

This pronouncement made my own blood go ice cold. For some reason I hadn't allowed my mind to take this leap, to realize what the final consequence of killing Damon would be. Yes, there were many, many Wilcoxes, but they were all descendants of Jeremiah's brothers and his one sister. It was different in my own clan, where the *prima* could be any girl of a given generation. But for the Wilcox clan, the *primus* must be Jeremiah's direct descendant.

Mouth dry, I said, "Aren't we getting a little ahead of ourselves? Maybe we should focus on how we're going to track down and...neutralize...Damon before we start worrying about who his heir is."

"'Neutralize,'" Connor remarked. "That's one way to put it. What, are you suddenly working for the CIA or something?"

"Do you want me to say it outright?" I retorted. I hated all of this—hated the brittle stillness that had come between us, hated that Damon had put us in this position in the first place.

Hated that killing him would result in Connor being the new Wilcox *primus*. I didn't even want to think what that might mean for our relationship.

He didn't respond, only stared off into a corner, not meeting Marie's or my eyes.

"Killing a skin-walker is no easy thing," she said. "Even a witch would have a hard time doing such a thing, but you, Angela, you are not just any witch, are you? A *prima* has the strength to confront the *yee naaldlooshii*."

She seemed confident enough of that fact. I wished I could say the same. Yes, back at Damon's house I had driven off the wolf-creature, but I certainly hadn't hurt it. I somehow knew that if I had been alone, it would have torn my throat out just as it had done to all those girls who looked like me. It had backed away, because Connor was there. That tiny shred of mercy told me there was still a bit of Damon inside the skin-walker, even if most of its humanity had been lost.

"Assuming I do have that strength," I began, making it clear from my tone that I wasn't sure I had her same confidence on that point, "how do we even find him? I mean, there are probably a hundred government officials of varying types out looking for the killer wolf, and they're not having much luck. And I somehow doubt he's going to go back to his house."

"No, he won't," Marie replied. "We have some family members there keeping watch just in case, but you're right—I doubt he will return there now that his secret has been discovered. My belief is that he will take to the wild. We will have to lure him out."

"And how exactly are we supposed to do that?" Connor asked. His tone was openly skeptical. I had the feeling he would try to throw up as many road-blocks to her plan as possible—anything to keep the current situation from progressing to its logical conclusion.

Her gaze shifted to me and settled there. I tried not to react, to hold myself still, but I didn't know how successful I was. Not very enjoyable, being pinned in place by such an unwavering stare.

Still watching me, she said, "The same way you attempt to catch any wild animal.

"With bait."

—

Her plan was simple. Damon, even in his current state, still seemed to be fixated on me, on having the McAllister *prima* in his power. So the easiest thing to do would be to put me in harm's way, so to speak, and bring him to me that way.

"No way," Connor said at once. "You're not doing that to Angela. Haven't enough people been hurt already?"

"And more will be hurt if we don't stop your brother." Marie gave me a chilly look of appraisal. "Can you do it, Angela?"

I thought of all the pictures of the dead girls I had seen. No, the papers hadn't published any crime scene photos. They'd actually shown some restraint in that. But those faces flashed through my mind, each one a life and a future cut short. Could I really allow the killings to keep happening, just because I was currently scared shitless?

Voice firmer than I'd hoped, I said, "I'll do what has to be done. But it can't really be as easy as just standing in the middle of the woods somewhere and shouting 'come and get me.'"

A thin-lipped smile. "No, it's not that easy. And that's why we need your help, Connor."

At that he stood up, fists clenched at his sides. "Are you kidding me? You want me to help lure my brother somewhere so you can murder him?"

"How can you murder something that isn't human?" she asked calmly, unruffled in the face of his anger. "As I said yesterday, this is more like putting down a rabid dog before that animal can cause any more misery or harm."

At first Connor didn't reply, but only stood there, color flaring along his high cheekbones as he stared at a spot on the wall, refusing to look at his cousin. I waited quietly, knowing he'd have to wrestle through this himself. Goddess knows I would hate to be placed in a similar situation. I had no siblings, so I couldn't quite understand that kind of bond, but what if Marie had been asking me to do the same thing to Sydney, or my Aunt Rachel?

A little shudder went through me at that thought, and I wished I could put my arms around Connor, tell him how much I loved him and how I knew no one should ever be put in such a position. But because Marie was standing there watching us, and because I could sense he wanted no interference from me, nothing that would keep him from making this decision on his own, I kept still, and waited.

Time ticked by, unbearably slow. At last Connor shifted and met Marie's patient gaze. "What do I have to do?"

She didn't quite let out a breath, but I saw the tense set of her shoulders ease slightly. So she hadn't been as sure of him as she wanted us to believe. "As Angela pointed out, we'll have to do a little more than have her simply offer herself up to him. He is still canny, watchful. There are very few people he trusts. And you are no longer one of them, Connor, because he knows you love this girl, and have put her before him. Since the solstice, he no longer trusts me, either, because he thought I should have warned him that there was a possibility Angela would bond with a Wilcox other than the *primus*. But the one person he still trusts implicitly is Lucas."

It clicked into place then—Connor's features shifting to those of Lucas. That gift of illusion, of taking on someone else's form. It was the one thing that might draw in the Damon-wolf. Might.

"So I pretend to be Lucas, offering up Angela as a sort of gift?"

"Exactly. It would make sense, because the one thing Lucas hates more than anything else is disruption. Angela was the catalyst that made Damon turn to the magic of the *yee naaldlooshii*. So it doesn't require that great a leap to have Lucas think that by turning her over to the *primus,* somehow he'll get his old friend back. Everything returned to the status quo."

Connor ran a hand through his hair, clearly turning the idea over in his mind. "Maybe. That is, I know in real life Lucas would never do such a thing, but Damon would…and he does have a tendency to believe that everyone thinks the same way he does."

Marie did not exactly reply, but she did give the barest of nods. "So you will do it?"

"I—" A long pause, so long that I wondered if he was going to reply at all, or throw his hands up and walk out then and there. After all, this was the moment when he would have to commit to her plan, as much as every cell in his body must be protesting it. At last he murmured, "Yes."

"Good. I am still analyzing the pattern of his attacks and trying to determine the most logical place where he will strike next. And perhaps a vision will come to me, but I can't will that to happen. If it's meant to be, I'll have a clear seeing." Her shoulders lifted. I could tell she didn't much like admitting even that slight deficiency. Tone brisk, she added, "For now, go home. I hope I'll have a location for you tomorrow."

"Okay," I said, and finally reached out to take Connor's hand in mine. He didn't resist, and I felt a tiny flicker of hope. Maybe he had begun to resign himself to the situation. "You know where to find us."

We left then, and walked back through Marie's quiet neighborhood to the busier streets of downtown. By then it was almost noon, and people were hurrying to lunch, or maybe to do some shopping.

My appetite had deserted me, and I guessed Connor felt the same way.

After we were back in the apartment, I asked, "Why Lucas?"

He shot me a mystified look. "You heard what Marie said. He and my brother have always been friends."

"No, I know that. I'm just wondering why. Lucas seems like such a nice person—"

"And my brother isn't," Connor finished for me.

Oh, shit. "That's not what I meant—"

"It isn't?" He smiled thinly, and again the resemblance between the two brothers struck me, although most of the time it wasn't that obvious. "Well, Lucas has an interesting gift. Luck."

"Luck?"

"Not about everything. He's never been married, always says he hasn't met the right one yet. I know he's had a lot of girlfriends, both civilians and not, but it never works out. Not that he doesn't keep trying."

"Like trying to pick up my cousin Margot?"

Despite everything, he flashed a quick grin at me. "Never thought I'd say I was glad to see a McAllister being so standoffish. She never even gave him a chance to get close, and thank God for that. We'd already had enough scenes that evening."

That was true. It was hard for me to even imagine someone thinking of Margot in that way, but I had to remind myself that being a clan elder was all about power, not age. She was probably a little younger than Lucas. "You were saying about his luck?"

Connor shrugged and went into the kitchen, then extracted two bottles of water from the fridge and handed one to me. I smiled my thanks at him; it was cold, but very dry, and all that talking had irritated my throat. "But with money, finances? He has a sense. He just knows. The Wilcoxes have always done well for themselves, but the last thirty years more than ever. When things went sour with the last stock market crash, he'd told everyone in the family to move their investments into safer things like T-bills a month before it happened. I was in college, but I remember friends dropping out because their families had just lost everything and couldn't afford to keep paying tuition. But we Wilcoxes? We sailed through it like nothing happened."

"That is a pretty handy gift," I admitted. "Better than talking to ghosts, that's for sure."

"Yeah, you could say that. So you can see why my brother would want to keep Lucas around. And also, with Lucas there's no agenda. As you said, he seems like a nice person—because he *is* one. When you're always looking over your shoulder the way my brother is, having someone like Lucas around makes a lot of sense. He's always been very loyal to Damon. You and I know that he's too good a person to really turn you into some kind of burnt offering, but Damon doesn't. He'll believe that his friend is doing his best to help him out." A grimace twisted Connor's mouth, and he added, "If Damon is even capable of rational thought anymore. I can't imagine that he would knowingly have killed any of those girls. Especially Jessica. He might not have loved her, but he would have been protective of her."

I shivered. Yes, I could see that. Jessica was willing to sacrifice herself to provide a Wilcox heir, and Damon would respect that, would take pains to make sure she was safe. The skin-walker spell truly had to have driven him out of his mind for him to kill her.

"So," Connor continued, "logically I know Marie's plan makes sense. And I know why we have to do it, but...."

The hopelessness in his voice broke my heart. I set my bottle of water down on the kitchen table, then went and put my arms around him. "I'm sorry, Connor," I said, and I meant it. No one should have to go through this torture. Not even Damon Wilcox.

It seemed that Connor heard the sincerity in my tone, or maybe he simply felt it vibrating through our bond. Whatever it was, this time his arms went to encircle me as well, and he crushed me against him, clinging to me the way a man might cling to a life raft in a storm-tossed ocean. I stood there and offered whatever wordless comfort I could.

In that moment, it was the only thing I could do for him.

CHAPTER SEVENTEEN

Equinox

IT WAS NOT QUITE NINE THE NEXT MORNING WHEN CONNOR'S phone rang. We'd both gotten up early, our sleep restless even after making frenzied love sometime after midnight, when he'd woken me and pulled me to him, clearly needing the reassurance of my flesh against his. Of course I didn't protest; I needed his touch just as much as he needed mine.

We were tired and preoccupied, but at least we'd already showered and dressed. No TV this morning; we were sitting at the dining room table and nursing another round of coffee when the call came through.

The hesitation before he reached for the phone was obvious, but after the third ring he picked up, handling the phone as if it had been infected with some sort of highly contagious virus. "Marie," he said. A pause as he listened for a moment. Then he asked, "Are you sure?" Another pause. "Okay, we'll be out there as soon as we can. I'll need to get Lucas's car from him."

I stared at Connor, mystified, as he ended the call and set the phone back down on the tabletop. Finally I asked, "What was that about the car?"

"Marie said they'd guessed wrong—Damon... the wolf...whatever...anyway, he did come back to the house last night. He's still there now. So we need to go."

"And you need to take Lucas's car so the illusion will be complete."

A mirthless smile. "Something like that."

"How did she know? A vision?"

He nodded. "Yes. She said she meditated on the problem last night, and as she lay down to go to sleep, she saw the wolf come back to the house, sniff around the perimeter, and then go inside."

Frowning, I asked, "Wasn't it locked up?"

A lift of his shoulders. "The clean-up crew made sure every door and window was locked. But I guess locks are no big deal for a skin-walker."

Somehow I managed to repress a shiver. Facing down a large, angry wolf was bad enough. One with magical powers? I didn't want to think about it. "Well, that's...convenient, I guess. I mean, at least we don't have to go wandering around in the woods, trying to find him." *And it's not so strange after all*, I thought. *Wolves do tend to return to their lairs.* "So now we have to go get Lucas's car, then drive out there?"

"Yeah. Not sure how I'm going to explain that."

"He's not in on the plan?"

Connor shot me an unreadable look. "No. I don't know for sure that he would try to stop us...but I don't know that he wouldn't, either. So I'll have to figure out some sort of excuse for needing his car."

I didn't envy him that task. But, as it turned out, that part wasn't so difficult. Connor called Lucas and said he'd screwed up and forgotten that he had a meeting with the gallery owner down in Sedona, and Angela had a doctor's appointment that she couldn't cancel, and if Lucas could help him out?

Of course Lucas agreed, and Connor said we'd be over right away to get the car.

"Doctor's appointment?" I asked, arching an eyebrow at him as we went down to get in the FJ.

"First thing I could think of. Besides, I know everyone's wondering when you're going to get pregnant. A doctor's appointment just sort of feeds into that, you know?"

I nodded, although I couldn't help but feel grimly amused at the subterfuge. Connor and I knew there was no chance of a pregnancy, thanks to the charm I used every time we were intimate, but his family wouldn't have any clue about that.

A late storm had dropped some snow the night before, but it had already begun to melt. Still, the roads were slick and treacherous, and I wasn't looking forward to driving Connor's SUV back to the apartment after he picked up Lucas's car. Hard to believe it was almost spring.

No, wait. Things had been so insane lately that I hadn't been paying much attention to the actual date, although earlier that week downtown Flagstaff had been even livelier than usual, since it was Saint Patrick's Day. But today was the twentieth. The vernal equinox, sometimes called Ostara. Not quite there, as that moment of perfect balance between shadow and light was due to arrive later this morning.

It was a day of power. Not the same strength as the solstice, but I tried to take heart in that. Perhaps I could harness the power of balance in my confrontation with Damon. After all, what he had done was a perversion of nature, of the order of things. It wasn't that huge a leap to think that maybe the universe would lend me a hand in restoring the balance to what it should be.

We pulled up in front of a house not quite as large as Damon's, but still pretty impressive, wood and stone, sitting on a lot that had to be almost an acre. The other homes in the neighborhood were equally large and well-kept. If there were any poor Wilcoxes, I had yet to meet one.

Connor got out and came around to the passenger side, then helped me down to the ground, holding my hand firmly as we negotiated our way up the icy front walk. Or maybe he was holding on to me for reassurance, just as much as providing a steady hand so I wouldn't slip.

It took a moment for Lucas to answer the door after we rang the bell. I knew he'd been expecting us, but the house was big enough that I thought it could possibly take him a good chunk of time to get to the front door, depending on where he'd started from. When he did finally open it, though, he smiled at us, cheery as ever.

I had a feeling he wouldn't be quite so cheery if he knew the real reason why we were there.

But since he didn't, he gave us a hearty greeting, invited us in. Even though the place was just a little smaller than Damon's house, something about it felt cheerier, more intimate. The colors were warmer—honey oak floors, walls a soft parchment color. And he had a fire going, sending the sweet scent of wood smoke through the building.

"Thanks so much for this, Lucas—" I began, but he just waved me off.

"No worries. It's not like you're leaving me stranded. I've got the Beemer SUV as a backup if I need to go out."

I raised an eyebrow at Connor, wondering what the hell Lucas's primary car was if the Beemer was merely a "backup." He didn't respond, though, and only said to Lucas, "No, we do appreciate it. With everything going on…."

The cheerful expression quickly faded from Lucas's face. "I know. But we all have to keep up appearances, and that means not missing any appointments, right?"

"Right," Connor agreed, although I thought I saw him wince slightly, and knew he must be thinking about a certain dark appointment we needed to keep out at Damon's house.

"Well, here you go," Lucas said, and held out a key with a leather fob to Connor. He took it, holding it as if he wasn't sure what to do with it. "I'll go open up the garage for you. Heading to Sedona, huh? Oak Creek Canyon might be slippery."

"Oh, I'm going to take the 17, even if it's going the long way around. I figured that would be safer."

Lucas nodded, appearing a little relieved. I couldn't blame him; that road was twisty and treacherous on a good day. On a morning like this, where you'd be more likely than not to come upon sudden patches of ice? Not the sort of place I'd want someone driving my borrowed car, that's for sure.

"Well, we need to get going—" Connor began.

"Oh, sure. Come on. And Angela, you can just let yourself out the front door."

"Thanks, Lucas," I said again, no less awkwardly, and waited as Connor gave me the key to the FJ. After that I headed back out to the SUV, walking gingerly on the icy flagstones of the front path, and sighed in relief as I let myself in and slid behind the steering wheel. Since it was cold and I wanted to get the heater going, I went ahead and put the key in the ignition and started up the engine.

A flash of red in the rearview mirror told me Connor was backing out of the driveway and about to start heading toward downtown. I squinted at the car he was driving, and my mouth fell open slightly. It was—well, I didn't know what it was, since sports cars weren't something you saw a lot of in Jerome. There was slightly more flash in Flagstaff, but more along the lines of Damon's Range Rover or the Audi SUV that one obnoxious client of Connor's had driven. Whatever the sports car might be, I was just glad Connor was the one driving it, not me.

I headed back into town, feeling my stomach clench as a pale sun slowly rose higher in the sky. It was easy to distract myself with thoughts of cars. That way I wouldn't have to think about what was coming next. How on earth could I possibly survive another confrontation with Damon...with what Damon had become?

But I couldn't completely lose it, because I had to stay focused on getting back to the apartment in one piece. I'd already passed one fender-bender at the intersection of Butler and Route 66 where someone obviously lost control and slipped into the intersection, getting sideswiped by a pickup that couldn't quite maneuver out of the way in time. Luckily—or not, depending on how you looked at it—I made it to the alley without incident, then pulled into our designated parking space. Connor hadn't told me to do that, but I figured it made the most sense, since we'd be leaving right away in Lucas's car.

I was just getting out of the FJ when Connor emerged from the building's back door. He must have parked on the street in front and come through the access hallway on the ground floor. In one hand he held his phone, but he slipped it into his pocket as he saw me.

"That was Marie. Damon's still at the house, so we need to go."

The lump that had been steadily growing in my stomach seemed to balloon to twice its size. "I don't know if I can do this."

"You have to." His green eyes bored into mine. "If I can, then so can you. Besides, there's no one else. If we don't—"

"Then more people will die. I get it." I gulped in a breath of icy air, and although it bit at the back of my throat, it also seemed to brace me, give me the strength I needed to get moving. "Okay. Okay. Let's go."

He led me back through the building, through the hallway that always smelled like an odd mixture of dust, beeswax, and mildew, and out to the street. The red car was sitting at the curb, looking very out of place against the dirty snow piled on the sidewalk.

"What the hell is this thing, anyway?" I asked, after he'd opened the door for me and then gone around to get in the driver's seat.

""This 'thing,' Angela, is a Porsche Cayman."

"I'm surprised he gave it to you to drive instead of the BMW." Not that it really mattered, but discussing the car seemed safer than just about anything else.

"I think he wanted me to impress Eli."

I supposed that made some sense. "It doesn't seem very practical for Flagstaff," I said, almost primly, as he edged out onto the street and then pointed us back toward Route 66.

"Probably not, but Lucas likes his toys. You should see his stereo."

Midlife crisis? I wondered. Not that I thought Lucas was quite old enough for one of those. He was a couple of years older than Damon, but not yet forty. "I can imagine."

Connor even smiled a little, but it disappeared as we began heading northwest toward Damon's house. "Might as well do it now," he murmured.

"What—?" I began, turning toward him.

But then his features began to shift, not a great deal, as Lucas had the same long nose and high cheekbones as most of the Wilcox men, but still, in a few seconds, the man sitting next to me wasn't Connor anymore, but his cousin, right down to the laugh lines in the tanned skin around his eyes and those first faint patches of gray at his temples.

I swallowed. "That's...still kind of amazing. And disconcerting."

He shrugged. When he spoke, even his voice sounded different. It had the slight lilt to it that I'd noticed in Lucas's inflection, as if nothing could suppress his inner *joie de vivre*. "I'd say you'd get used to it, but really, I hope I don't have to use this power often enough for you to get to that stage. I hate it."

"It feels like lying," I thought. Connor's words to me only a few short weeks ago. And how much worse now, when he was using it to perpetrate the worst lie of his life, the one that would fool Damon into thinking this man was coming as a friend?

Breathe in, let it out. I did this again, and again. My aunt had taught me this technique to center myself, to keep my energies clear and unflagging. Despite my efforts, a sudden worry surfaced, and I shifted uneasily on the leather seat. "What if—what if Damon still figures out it's not Lucas? What if you, I don't know, don't smell right or something?"

"It's a possibility. But the way Marie explained it, he's taken on the shape of a wolf, but he's not *actually* a wolf. His senses aren't the same. Sharpened, yeah. Better than a regular man's, but still not close to those of a real wolf."

I had to hope she was right. Or this could turn out very, very badly.

For us, that is. After all, if everything went according to plan, it was going to be a very bad day indeed for Damon Wilcox.

———

For all its low-slung sportiness, the Porsche handled the snow-slick roads out to the property very well, and I began to revise my initial estimate of its impracticality. The problem was, since Connor didn't have to drive all that slowly, we got there a lot faster than I would have liked.

He downshifted as we approached the driveway, hand white-knuckled on the gearshift. "Angela, I don't think I can do this."

I'd halfway expected this reaction. How could I not, when we were about to go in Damon's house and, in Marie's words, "put him out of his misery"?

I licked my dry lips, then said, "All you have to do is get me in there. I'll do everything else."

"And what will *you* do? Do you even know how to fight him?"

"No. I mean, I don't know now. But I will when the time comes."

"That's...crazy. That's no plan."

I shifted in my seat, staring at the face of Lucas Wilcox, and hoping to see something of the man I loved beneath those features. Of course I couldn't; the glamour was perfect. It had to be, for this to work. "Connor, all of this is crazy. The only thing I know for sure is that I love you, and I wish with all my heart that we didn't have to be here doing this. But I also know we're the only hope of stopping Damon. Stopping the killing."

As those words left my mouth, Connor twitched, as if recalling again why we were doing this. It wasn't simply that Damon had dabbled in forbidden magic. That could have been overlooked, if it had caused no lasting harm...or at least no harm to anyone except himself. But, as much as he might love his brother, Connor couldn't allow any more innocent blood to be shed. Whatever the cost, he knew that had to stop, here and now.

A grim nod, and he pulled into the driveway. As he parked in front of the center garage door and took the key from the ignition, I could almost see the shift in his demeanor, the way the cloud of doubt lifted from his brow, and suddenly he really was Lucas Wilcox, cheerful and untroubled.

"You ready for this?" he asked.

I couldn't trust myself to do anything more than nod.

"Then let's put on a show."

He got out of the car and came around to the passenger side, then grasped me by the arm and pulled me out. My feet slipped a little on a patch of ice in the shadow of the eaves, and his grip tightened.

"You're hurting me," I said.

"Just don't want you to fall down," he said sunnily, and dragged me to the front door.

The illusion was so perfect that even I felt a flicker of cold doubt, wondered for half a second whether this had all been some elaborate plan to deliver me to Damon once and for all. No. That was crazy. This was just Connor acting as he thought Lucas might if he really had gone off the deep end and had decided to help out his old friend by delivering me all wrapped up in a bow.

As before, the front door was unlocked. Connor pushed me through it, hand still like a band of steel around my upper arm. Playacting or not, that was going to leave a bruise.

Then again, I had far worse things to worry about.

A low snarl greeted us, and we both stopped dead on the Persian rug in the entryway. The clean-up crew had done a good job. You couldn't tell that a young woman had died violently here only two days ago.

The Damon-wolf was sitting on the threshold between the entry and the living room, unnatural black eyes glaring at us, teeth bared in a snarl.

Connor held up a hand and said, "Look what I've brought you, Damon. Think of her as a present. She's the one you were really trying to get, right?"

A slight head tilt, and the smallest suggestion of a whine, as if the creature was trying to process what Connor had just said.

"This isn't going to work!" I cried, going along as best I could. "When Connor finds out what you've done—"

"Well, he won't, because this is just Damon's and my little secret, isn't it?"

Another whine, and the wolf began to pad toward us. I held my breath, not daring to move. But as the creature drew closer, I saw it halt, then sniff the air. Its teeth bared, and a low growl began to emanate from its throat.

Oh, shit. Ohshitohshitohshit...

That was about the only coherent thought my brain could form. Because somehow it must have realized this was not Lucas, that the scent beneath the guise of his friend was that of someone Damon knew even better.

His brother.

Even though I'd been expecting the attack, its speed took us both by surprise. The creature was in midair, mouth open, before I could even begin to react. Connor, acting on instinct, thrust himself between the wolf and me, arm up to protect his throat.

The teeth latched onto his arm. Thank the Goddess that he was wearing a heavy leather coat, or that bite would have sunk straight to the bone. But it was still enough to knock him staggering, crying out in pain as he fell against me and we both collapsed to the floor, the weight of the creature—greater than I would have thought an actual wolf's would be—driving us backward, slipping along the tile floor.

Although I hadn't been touched by the Damon-wolf, I still let out a grunt of pain, feeling elbow and knee smack into the hard surface. But nothing seemed to be broken, and I couldn't worry about bumps and bruises now.

Blessed Brigid, give me the strength of a warrior now, I thought. The glowing energy within me seemed to flare up brighter than the sun, and I pushed out with it, concentrating all its force on the unnatural creature snarling and biting at Connor's face—now returned to its normal guise, the glamour ruined from shock and pain—as he held up his arm to shield himself, the leather jacket shredded beyond any hope of protecting him further.

An unseen force lifted the wolf and flung it away, aiming it so it plowed directly into the wall. It gave out a little grunt, then pushed itself back to its feet before charging at us once again.

I pushed out again with the power within me, but somehow the wolf seemed to be pushing back as well, resisting the power that was attempting to force it away. Fear surged up within me. *I'm not strong enough—*

And it leaped, teeth closing around my calf just above the hiking boot I wore. Red-hot pain seared through me, and I staggered backward, blinking away tears of agony, even as Connor burst out, "Damon, no!"

Focus, I told myself. *There is no pain. There is only the power.*

Somehow that allowed me to regain my balance. Once again I gathered up the brilliant *prima* strength surging within me and thrust it outward at the wolf, shoving it back so it couldn't get close enough to do any real harm.

"Please, Damon," Connor said, moving gingerly to a sitting position, then pushing himself up to his feet. Blood was dripping from his nose, and now I could see that more blood stained the torn leather of his jacket. "Please. You don't want to do this. Come back to us."

The wolf seemed to hesitate, black eyes watching us carefully. I didn't move, didn't dare breathe. Maybe this could work. Maybe Connor could somehow reach out to the shred of his brother still buried deep within the creature. After all, we'd taken Marie's assertion at face value when she said the only way to stop Damon now was by killing him. For all I knew, she had her own agenda at work, her own reasons for wanting the *primus* out of the way.

I could feel the world shift, feel the planet poised in that perfect tipping place between dark and light, neither one nor the other taking precedence. The power throbbed within me, but waited as well, as if it was holding its breath along with the rest of us.

Then Damon sprang. I saw the shock and horror on Connor's features even as I gathered up the strength I needed to drive the creature back, the power glowing within me like the white-hot center of a star. And as I did so, I felt the wrongness pulsing from the wolf, sensed how anything that might once have been Damon Wilcox had been warped and twisted to serve its need for chaos and death.

How can you save someone when there's nothing left to save?

As I flung the power outward again, it seemed as if the very earth itself lent its strength to my attack, that sense of balance asserting itself to destroy this thing that had perverted every law of nature. The light arcing out from me was no longer golden, but pure, searing white, the kind of light that will sterilize everything it touches.

The wolf let out an unearthly shriek and dropped to the floor. From the unnatural angle at which it lay, I could tell that its neck had been snapped. It whined, and as Connor and I both watched in shock, the shape of the wolf lying on the tile seemed to melt away, leaving the body of a man behind.

"Oh, God," Connor groaned, and went to him at once, dropping on his knees so he knelt by his brother's head. "Damon, can you hear me?"

No movement at first, but then the long black eyelashes fluttered against his pale cheeks. Only enough for him to open his eyes a fraction, to focus on his brother. "Connor...sorry."

"Don't try to talk." Wincing, Connor reached into his pocket to pull out his phone. "Stay still. I'm going to call 911."

"Don't...bother." Damon's eyes shut. Without opening them, he murmured, "This is why I wanted you, Angela. So...strong...."

A shudder went through him, and he seemed to go even more limp, if that were possible. Not sure whether I should approach or should stay out of the way, I hesitated, watching as Connor sucked in a breath.

"No...please, no."

From the corner of my eye, I saw movement, and realized Jessica's ghost had moved toward us, looking almost expectant, as if she'd been waiting here for the moment when Damon would meet her in death. There was even a faint smile on her lips.

Damon somehow managed to reach out and touch Connor's hand. "It's yours now. Take care of the clan."

And as Connor began to shake his head, words of denial rising to his lips, Damon's eyelids opened one last time. An expression of pure joy passed over his features, and he gasped, "Felicia!"

Then he truly went still, and Connor bent over him, shoulders shaking, a horrible wracking movement, as if he couldn't allow any tears to fall but at the same time couldn't contain the agony of grief surging through him.

And I looked up to see Jessica shake her head, tears glittering on her cheeks. Then she melted into nothing.

———

After that—well, I'd like to say that I'd forgotten large parts of it, but no, Marie came in only a few minutes later. Apparently she'd driven out after us and parked some distance away, waiting to see what would happen. When she spotted me helping an obviously distraught Connor into the borrowed Porsche, she took that as the signal to come in and start the mopping-up operations.

True, she was very efficient, and thank the Goddess for that. She told me to take Connor home, and that they'd manage everything. Numb, I did as I was told, some irrational part of me worrying that I was going to crash Lucas's car on the way back into town, and wouldn't that just be the cherry on the cake of everyone's day.

Crazy what your mind dwells on when it doesn't want to focus on the really important things.

But we arrived intact. Well, physically anyway. I helped Connor up the stairs after parking the Porsche on the street. Somehow or another we'd have to get the car back to Lucas, but that was sort of low on my list of priorities at the moment.

Connor slumped onto the couch, not looking at me, or at anything in particular. Not that I could really blame him for being shell-shocked; he'd just lost his brother and become the new *primus* of the Wilcox clan in the space of a heartbeat.

What that meant for us, I had no idea.

I couldn't dwell on that, though. Instead, I went and fetched him some water, which at least he did take from me, and then got a fire going in the hearth. False cheeriness, but better than the cold emptiness of the space between the two of us, a space that hadn't been there even an hour ago.

Of course I knew why. I'd killed his brother. Never mind that I'd had no choice, that if I hadn't done so he would've killed me and probably Connor as well in his blind animal rage.

He hadn't been an animal there at the end, though.

Tears began to sting my eyes, and I blinked them away. I had a feeling Connor wouldn't much appreciate me grieving over the man I'd killed. And how could I ever explain that they weren't tears of grief, but of relief and joy? I'd seen that same expression of utter elation on Aunt Ruby's face when she passed. I knew what it meant—despite everything he'd done, Damon Wilcox had not met damnation as he left this world, but the woman he loved, waiting for him.

It turned out to be convenient that he'd died in his home. Marie and her crew moved him upstairs to his bedroom, settled him there, and removed every trace of a struggle. Then she called the paramedics, saying she'd come to visit her cousin, who hadn't been feeling well, and found him dead in his own bed.

There were questions, but in the end, since there was no sign of foul play, the medical examiners ruled it a natural death, probably from an aneurysm. The wounds Damon's skin-walker form had suffered did not transfer to his human body, so there was nothing for the coroner to find. The Wilcoxes were allowed to grieve, to have the public memorial service that someone of Damon's stature in the community required.

I was surprised to see so many civilians there, so many weeping students—female, of course—so many sad-faced faculty members. Truly, it was quite the send-off. I wished I could ask Connor about it, ask him if Damon had really been that popular. My entire knowledge of him was based solely on what he had done as primus of the Wilcoxes, not as the public man he'd been.

But I didn't dare broach such a subject, because in the three days since Damon's death, Connor had barely spoken to me, except about practical things like planning the funeral. Something inside me was quiet and cold and still, frightened, knowing things were horribly wrong and not knowing what in the world I could do about it.

Of all people, Lucas was the one to give me some comfort. I'd thought he'd be furious over our subterfuge, but when I approached him at the reception after the service, he only gave a philosophical shrug and said, "There are some things you can't come back from, Angela. Damon crossed a line. He endangered all of us." For a second I thought I saw a flicker of real anger cross his features, but then he laid a comforting hand on my shoulder. "You did what you had to do. Don't ever forget that."

I'd only nodded, not trusting myself to speak. Although I never thought I'd find myself grateful for Marie, I had to admit that she'd done a good job of smoothing things over with the rest of the clan, of trying to make them understand that I'd done them all a service. Whether they truly believed that, I didn't know, but at least I wasn't getting death threats.

Then again, that probably wasn't very likely. After all, I was the consort of the new *primus*. Or was he my consort? I had no idea, couldn't begin to guess how his change in status would alter our relationship. Maybe I would've liked to have found out, to have the two of us come together while seeking some solace, some comfort, but Connor hadn't touched me. True, he hadn't gone so far as to ask me to move back into the guest room. It was enough that he lay huddled on his side of the bed, not reaching out to me, not cuddling together as we'd done so many times before.

Time, give it time, I told myself, trying to ignore the creeping chill within me. But maybe there were some wounds time just couldn't heal.

It wasn't that late when we got back from the reception, just a little before seven. A weird time, because usually around then I would have either started making something for dinner, or we would've decided where we wanted to eat if we were going out. I certainly didn't have much of an appetite, and

Connor had even less. The past few days he'd barely eaten anything.

We entered the apartment, and I set my purse down on the dining room table. Connor had been looking stiff and uncomfortable in his suit jacket all afternoon, so I wasn't surprised to see him shrug out of it and drape it over the back of a chair.

I started to limp toward the living room; the Wilcox healer had done a good job on me, but I still had some lingering muscle damage from Damon's attack. I had the vague idea that maybe I'd put on some music or turn on the TV. Anything to cover up the silence. But I hadn't gone two steps before Connor said, "This isn't going to work, Angela."

My heart started to thump painfully in my chest, but I forced myself to sound calm as I replied, "What isn't?"

"This. Us."

I inhaled, then turned to face him. He was still standing next to the dining room table, one hand resting on top of his jacket where it hung over the back of the chair. The puffiness from his bloody nose was gone, but there were bruised-looking shadows under his eyes. Even so, he was so beautiful it hurt me to look at him.

Or maybe that wasn't why it hurt.

"I know it's been hard, but—"

"Hard?" A short laugh, one with absolutely no humor in it. "You don't know what you're talking about. Bad enough to lose my brother, to inherit his power and this clan and everything that goes along with. But then to have to look at you, to see what you did every time I look into your eyes—"

Something was blocking my throat, making it hard to speak. A monolith of unshed tears, like a wedge between me and sound. But somehow I got the words out. "You said you understood why it had to be done."

"I thought I did understand. I thought I'd be— well, not okay with it, but accepting. Or something. But I can't." He pushed a hand through his hair. It had been cut only the day before, so it wasn't quite as unruly as it normally would have been, but he still managed to make it look more or less disheveled. "I look at you, and I see him dying. I can't get the image out of my mind. And I think the only way I might ever be able to is if I don't have to look at you."

Cold, so cold, as if every single icy day of that bitter winter had somehow commingled and invaded both my body and soul. At least I didn't have to worry about crying now, because that cold had completely frozen my tears. "Are you telling me to leave?"

"I'm—*shit*. Yes. Maybe. I need some time. I need to not be around you for a while." He wasn't quite looking at me as he said this, but I didn't know if that was simply because I reminded him of Damon's death…or because he didn't want to see my pain.

"Fine. I'll go." I couldn't meet his gaze, either, not and maintain my dignity. I walked past him and went up the stairs, taking them one at a time, slowly, deliberately, wondering whether there had always been so many of them. First to the guest room, to retrieve the duffle bag and the suitcase I'd brought with me from my brief visit to Jerome, and then over to our room—*Connor's* room—to pack my things. My gaze fell on the concho belt he'd given me for my birthday, and that lump in my throat seemed to double in size. I choked, and shoved the belt toward the back of the drawer. No way was I taking that with me, not when it would remind me of him every time I looked at it.

A side trip to the bathroom to get some toiletries and other odds and ends, and then I was packed. I heard feet out in the hallway, and saw Connor standing there.

"What?" I demanded. "I'll be out of here soon enough."

"No, it's not that—" The words stumbled and fell over themselves. I could see the guilt in his face, as if he knew he shouldn't be doing this but couldn't stop himself. "I mean, I can take you home."

Oh, no. No way. Sitting next to him for more than an hour as he drove me back to Jerome? Not going to happen...especially if he thought by doing so he could somehow assuage his guilt at abandoning me. "It's all right. I'll call someone to get me."

"But—"

"I said it was fine." I picked up the suitcase and duffle bag, and pushed past him so I could go downstairs. My purse was still sitting on the dining room table, so I slung that over my shoulder, and then pulled the green wool coat Marie had bought me out of the closet. I'd put it on later, after I was out of here. I didn't want to delay for even the minute it would take me to put down my purse so I could button up the coat.

When I shut the closet door, Connor was standing in the hall. "You should really let me take you home."

Anger flared in me then, a heat that began to melt the ice in my core. "I don't want any favors from you, Connor Wilcox."

And I marched to the door, opened it, and let myself out. When I was about halfway down the corridor that led to the street, I realized he wasn't going to come after me. Holding back tears, I went out to the street, then paused for the briefest moment, looking up at the apartment. I saw a pale, sad face at the window, and realized it was Mary Mullen, staring down at me. She lifted a hand in farewell, and disappeared.